Praise for *Music for Wartime*

**Named one of the best short story collections of 2015
by *Bookpage* and *The Kansas City Star***

"[An] excellent debut collection of stories . . . characterized by a striking blend of whimsy and poignancy, elegy, and ebullience . . . While some stories are straightforwardly realistic and others wildly fantastical, all are witty, rueful, and wise. . . . I look forward with great anticipation . . . to anything else this immensely gifted writer produces."   —Priscilla Gilman, *The Boston Globe*

"Rebecca Makkai is a rising literary star."   —*Vanity Fair*

"Ricocheting from the war-torn twentieth century to the reality-show-rich present day, the stories in this impressive collection feature characters buffeted by fate—or is it mere happenstance? . . . Our sense of history is probed, too, not without humor."
                                                                —*The New Yorker*

"Richly imagined."   —*Chicago Tribune*

"[An] impressive first volume of stories." —*O, The Oprah Magazine*

"Exceptional . . . [Makkai] writes with economic precision. . . . She designs a catalog of unique structures to convey her meanings, and she narrates with unflagging confidence, secure in her experimentations and digressions. . . . Provocative, compelling reading."
                                                         —*Cleveland Plain-Dealer*

"Engrossing."   —*Minneapolis Star-Tribune*

"The short story is the ideal venue for Makkai's considerable talent, not only for drawing nuanced characterizations, but for contriving strange and fascinating premises. . . . With *Music for Wartime*, Makkai takes her place—one she deserves—among the artists with aplomb." —*The Guardian*

"Haunting . . . Seventeen stories with the impact of a quiver of arrows aimed at the heart." —BBC.com

"'The Briefcase' . . . is a story that displays remarkable compression, force, and agility, and is also one of the very few I've read that would fit just as snugly into Kafka's oeuvre as it would into Amy Hempel's or Joy Williams's." —Kevin Brockmeier, *The Arkansas Times*

"[Makkai's] stories were anthologized in *The Best American Short Stories* for four years in a row, and *Music for Wartime* proves these honors were well deserved, highlighting her poised voice, willingness to experiment, deft hand at structure, and capacity to surprise." —*Dallas Morning News*

"Nearly perfect . . . [Makkai] has penned a collection filled with beauty and heartbreak, surprise and wonder, guilt and innocence. . . . The stories complement one another perfectly, linked not by characters or plot, but by theme and craft. . . . An exceptional book." —*The Iowa City Gazette*

"*Music for Wartime* shows off Rebecca Makkai's surprising range. . . . Yet the collection still manages to feel like a cohesive, stunning whole, tied together with the wit and heart that courses through each and every story." —Buzzfeed

"Quintessential Makkai—witty, intelligent, a little irreverent, but not afraid to venture into emotional territory." —*Bookpage*

"Haunting and enchanting, wonderfully strange, and unforgettably gorgeous."
                                                        —*Book Riot*

"These tales will delight and haunt you long after you have closed the book."
                                                        —*Woman's Day*

"Magnificent. . . . The writing is clever and rich with the perceptiveness and human insight that earned Makkai a place (or four) in the *Best American Short Stories* series."   —*Los Angeles Magazine*

"Makkai's first short story collection demonstrates why the already-acclaimed novelist is also a master of this more succinct form. Each of the stories in the collection is vividly wrought and individually compelling, and features a precision and beauty that leaves the reader full of wonder."   —*The L Magazine*

"[An] outstanding debut story collection . . . Though these stories alternate in time between WWII and the present day, they all are set . . . within 'the borders of the human heart'—a terrain that their author maps uncommonly well."
                                        —*Publishers Weekly* (starred review)

"Rife with sentences that will stop you in your tracks with their strangeness and profundity . . . Makkai is a musical writer with a strong voice."   —*Library Journal* (starred review)

"Rebecca Makkai is one of our best writers—witty and precise, brilliant and compassionate—and every one of these stories contains all the depth and heartache of a doorstop-sized novel. I've been waiting for years for this book. *Music for Wartime* isn't simply wonderful—it's essential."

—Molly Antopol, author of *The UnAmericans*

"I have been waiting for this collection since 2008, when I read 'The Worst You Ever Feel' and it basically took the top of my head off. Deeply intelligent, stylistically playful, full of razor wit and grave historical accounting, what is most enthralling about these stories is their insistence that the political and the personal are never separate categories, that art's attempt to make sense of the senseless is at least as noble as it is doomed, and that atrocities large and small begin, as love does, in the human heart."

—Pam Houston, author of *Contents May Have Shifted*

"It's not often you read a story collection with the range and depth of Rebecca Makkai's *Music for Wartime*. The stories are about war and guilt and secrets, but also about romance and art and reality TV, and they come together, as the best collections do, as an assured and satisfying whole. It's a wonderful book, haunting, funny, and wise."

—Maile Meloy, author of *Both Ways Is the Only Way I Want It*

"Rebecca Makkai's *Music for Wartime* is a collection of the first order. The stories diverge and coalesce, practically in conversation with one another, always hewing to the varied consolations of beauty in the midst of conflict. To read one is to crave the next, each story feeding a pang you didn't quite know you had. *Music for Wartime* isn't a song, it's a sublime double-LP."

—Smith Henderson, author of *Fourth of July Creek*

PENGUIN BOOKS

MUSIC FOR WARTIME

Rebecca Makkai's work has appeared in *The Best American Short Stories*, *The Best American Nonrequired Reading*, *Harper's*, *Tin House*, *McSweeny's*, and *Ploughshares*, and has been read on NPR's *Selected Shorts* and *This American Life*. She is the author of two novels: *The Borrower*, a *Booklist* Top Ten Debut, an Indie Next pick, and an *O, The Oprah Magazine* selection; and *The Hundred-Year House*, which won the Chicago Writers Association's Book of the Year Award and was named a Best Book of 2014 by *Bookpage*, PopSugar, *Chicago Reader*, and more. The recipient of a 2014 NEA Fellowship, Makkai lives in Chicago and Vermont.

Twitter: @rebeccamakkai
www.rebeccamakkai.com

REBECCA MAKKAI

MUSIC
for
WARTIME

Stories

PENGUIN BOOKS

PENGUIN BOOKS
An imprint of Penguin Random House LLC
375 Hudson Street
New York, New York 10014
penguin.com

First published in the United States of America by Viking Penguin,
an imprint of Penguin Random House LLC, 2015
Published in Penguin Books 2016

"The Worst You Ever Feel" first appeared in *Shenandoah;* "November Story" in *Crazyhorse;* "Other Brands
of Poison (First Legend)," "Acolyte (Second Legend)," and "Bird in the House (Third Legend)" in *Harper's;*
"Couple of Lovers on a Red Background" in *Brilliant Corners;* "The Briefcase" in *The New England Review;*
"Cross" in *Michigan Quarterly Review;* "Peter Torrelli, Falling Apart" in *Tin House;* "Painted Ocean, Painted
Ship" in *Ploughshares;* "The World's Last Englishman" in *The Sewanee Review;* "Everything We Know About
the Bomber" in *Pleiades;* "Suspension: April 20, 1984" (in very different form) and "The Museum of the
Dearly Departed" in *The Iowa Review.*

THE LIBRARY OF CONGRESS HAS CATALOGED THE HARDCOVER EDITION AS FOLLOWS:

Makkai, Rebecca.
[Short stories. Selections]
Music for wartime : stories / Rebecca Makkai.
pages ; cm
ISBN 9780525426691 (hc.)
ISBN 9780143109235 (pbk.)
I. Title.
PS3613.A36A6 2015
813'.6—dc23
2015010569

146122990

for Jon,
at last

Then why did you to the end,
live with the dark,
sing into your ruin?
    —Duane Niatum,
        "Consulting an Elder Poet on an Anti-War Poem"

CONTENTS

THE SINGING WOMEN

The composer, with his tape recorder, crossed the barricades at night and crawled through the hills into the land his father had fled. Between the clotheslines, three cottages were still inhabited. Three old women still tended gardens and made soup and dusted—once a month—the trinkets of those killed. Once a month, they made their way through empty houses, empty streets, empty stores, empty churches. Once a month, they spoke the names of the dead.

The composer surprised the three women by speaking their dialect, knowing their words for *spoon* and *daffodil* and *hat*. At first they feared he'd been sent by the dictator as a spy—yet who but the son of a native son would know the story of the leaf child, the rhyme about the wolf maiden?

He lived with them a week and recorded (this had been his purpose) their songs, of which they were the world's last three singers. A song of lamentation, a song of mourning, a song of protest and despair. They had forgotten the song for weddings.

Back safe across the border, the composer set scores around the songs, made records of string instruments wailing behind the women's voices. He was fulfilled: He had preserved, before its last breath, their culture.

When the dictator learned of the record, he became enraged. Not over the songs (what was a lamentation, to a dictator?) but over the evidence of life in a village he had been assured was wiped out in its entirety.

One October morning, he sent his men to finish the job.

(But I've made it sound like a fable, haven't I? I've lied and turned two women into three, because three is a fairy tale number.)

THE WORST YOU EVER FEEL

When the nine-fingered violinist finally began playing, Aaron hid high up on the wooden staircase, as far above the party as the ghosts. He was a spider reigning over the web of oriental rug, that burst of red and black and gold, and from his spider limbs stretched invisible fibers, winding light and sticky around the forty guests, around his parents, around Radelescu the violinist. There were thinner strands, too, between people who had a history together of love or hate, and all three ghosts were tied to Radelescu, to his arcing bow. But Aaron held the thickest strings, and when he thought, *breathe,* all the people breathed.

After dinner, his mother had not nodded him up to his toothpaste and away from the drunken conversations as she had when he was nine, ten, eleven, and Aaron wondered whether she'd forgotten in the wine and noise, or whether this was something new, something he could expect from now on. To be safe he'd changed to pajama pants and a white T-shirt, so he could claim he'd come down for water. He remembered to muss his hair, staticky enough on its own but now a halo of rough brown in the bedroom mirror. Through the balusters, he watched the man and his violin duck in and out of the yellow cone of light that fell from the lamp above the piano. Yesterday morning, Aaron's mother had brought Radelescu a plate of scrambled eggs with parsley and toast as he sat at the bench, slowly picking out the chords of the accompaniment and marking the score. Tonight, she played the accompaniment for him.

Aaron guessed that by moving in and out of the light, Radelescu was blinding himself to the room, to the eager faces and cradled wineglasses of the greedy listeners. Now, as the old man began to play faster, Aaron felt tired, and he needed the bathroom, but he didn't want to move himself from the wooden step and away from the music. His throat had been sore all day, glue and needles, but now he was able to forget that. He squinted to see the stump of Radelescu's chopped-off finger, to see if he held the bow differently than other people, but the arm moved too fast.

Behind Radelescu, leaning against the fireplace, Aaron's father rolled the cup of his empty wineglass back and forth between his hands, eyes closed. Aaron's father was the luckiest man in the world. Exhibit A: He'd been rescued from drowning three different times. Exhibit B: The third time was by an American pianist much younger than he was, a woman so beautiful he married her and she became Aaron's mother. Exhibit C: He left the university, and Iaşi, and Moldavia, and all of Romania on June 20, 1941, nine days before the start of the Iaşi pogrom. Exhibit D: He left because he had won a scholarship to Juilliard and it took a long time to cross the ocean in an ocean liner, especially in the uncertain time of war, and once you've gone to Juilliard you have connections, and connections are what matter in life, even more than talent.

Aaron could not hear much difference between this music and that on Radelescu's last record, the one from 1966 with no cover. The man had aged twenty-four years since then, and this perhaps accounted for the small moments of shakiness, the vibratos that warbled on the far side of control. He was old. The hair stuck out from his head in white, wavy lines. The wrinkles on his face were carved deep, and the ones across his forehead were as wavy as his hair. Radelescu spoke only a little English, and Aaron spoke no Romanian at all, so at dinner the night before, Aaron and his mother had sat quietly while the two men spoke. Occasionally, Aaron's father would translate something for them, but it was only about the concert preparations or the delicious food. Later, when Radelescu overheard Aaron talking to his mother about the book report due Monday, the old man began to laugh. Aaron's father translated that he was amused to hear a child speak English so quickly and so fluently. And so all day today, Aaron had tried to speak faster and louder and use longer words. "Pathetic," he had said at lunch, and "electrocution" and "cylinder." When Radelescu asked to borrow Aaron's rosin for his own bow, Aaron had said, "Indubitably."

In the afternoon, Aaron had gone with the two men to the Jewel-Osco. He assumed they were there to pick up some last things for the party, but then they simply went and stood in the middle of the produce section. They stood a long time by the bins of different apples, pointing at mushrooms and grapefruits and bananas and speaking Romanian. Radelescu was happy, but there was something else on his face, too, and Aaron tried to read it. Devastation, maybe. When a lady passed with her plastic basket, Aaron pretended to investigate the tomato display. Finally they got a cart and began to walk through the aisles, grabbing olive oil, seltzer, five kinds of cheese. They returned to the produce section, where Aaron's father put five bunches of green onions in the cart and handed Radelescu a bright tangerine. Radelescu said something, laughed—and then, pressing his mouth to the orange skin, kissed the fruit.

Aaron could feel now that the people in the room below were breathing less, as if afraid to propel the old man back to Romania on the wind of their exhalations.

And no, he could not actually see the three ghosts with their violins—the three students who died in 1941—but he knew where they would be and he traced their flight with his eyes, over the crowd, around the light, against the ceiling. Until he was ten, whenever Aaron was sick or bleeding, his father would say the same thing: "May this be the worst pain you ever feel." By which he meant: "This is nothing. American boys will never receive thin-papered letters by airmail that their mother, father, two sisters, one brother, grandparents, uncles and aunts, thirteen cousins, have all been killed. You do not know suffering."

But that changed two years ago, when they all went to West Germany before his father's concert in Bonn. It was the closest Aaron had ever been to Romania, though now that things were suddenly different his father promised a trip before the year was out. As they pulled their luggage through the streets of Bonn, jet-lagged, Aaron had felt a spook, a chill, something that made him want to run, and, half-asleep, almost dreaming, he dropped his backpack to break off around the corner and down an alley until he came to a kind of park. He couldn't feel his legs. He had run toward the chill, he realized, not away from it. He did not picture dead bodies, he did not see ghosts or hear voices, but he felt something terrible and haunted, the skin-crawl of being alone in a house and pressing your back to the wall so nothing can get behind you. When his father caught him hard by the arm and asked what he was doing, Aaron said, "This is where all the people died." He didn't mean it, didn't believe it, but these words were the only way he could express his strange nausea, the feeling that he was surrounded by graves. His eyes must have looked scared and honest enough, because when they finally found the hotel, his mother asked the old, long-nosed concierge the history of the square. "Yes, yes, there was a synagogue," he said. "A terrible massacre. This is 1096, almost a thousand years." And his parents looked at each other, and his father said something in German to the concierge, and his mother's face became lighter than her hair. Aaron was as shocked as his parents, and he spent the rest of the trip wondering whether this was luck, maybe inherited from his father, or a real vision he just hadn't known enough to trust fully.

He tried every day now to focus on the things he felt but couldn't see. It made him even odder to his classmates, he knew, the way he'd sometimes close his eyes in history class, concentrating. He tried to sit in the back row whenever he could. It was people's sadness, mostly, that he attempted to feel, the ghosts that surrounded them, the place where a finger used to be but no longer was. He imagined pain traveling through the air on radio waves. If he positioned himself in a room and concentrated and listened, he could catch it all.

Since then, his father had not belittled his fevers or broken bones. Aaron knew his father suspected that he was haunted, that he saw ghosts and fires and the evils of the world, past, present, future. He would ask Aaron sometimes what he was thinking, wait for the answer with squeezed eyebrows. He would sit by his bed on nights Aaron couldn't sleep.

But Aaron was half a liar. When he felt something—for instance, that a woman on the train was sick—he wouldn't say it aloud until later, when there was no way his parents could ask if she needed help. It was something his mother would probably do, go up to a stranger like that. Most times, he never found out himself whether he was right or wrong. And he didn't want to know, because if he were wrong even once or twice he'd stop trusting himself. For the same reason, when his father asked him for lottery numbers, he just shook his head. "But think!" his father would say. "With my luck and your psychic powers!" It was the only time he joked about it. When he told the story of Bonn at parties, as he had tonight, it was with reverence. He called Aaron "our little rabbi," but he wasn't poking fun.

The six best things about parties were: (1) having so many people to spy on; (2) the job of opening the door for guests and waiting
for the curbs to fill with parked cars until yours was the house everyone passed and said, "Oh, they must be having a party tonight!"
(3) pastries; (4) the old Romanian men who always brought choc-
olates, including ones filled with coconut; (5) watching people get
drunk and seeing if any ladies tripped in their high heels; and (6) the
music.

Radelescu stopped, and people clapped. Aaron decided to pay
more attention to the next piece, to follow the music itself rather
than what it made him think of. This might be impossible, he knew,
to hear only the notes and not daydream or invent pictures. Aaron
owed the habit to his first violin teacher, Mrs. Takebe, who insisted
that every piece tells a story. As he practiced, he invented quite elaborate ones: One sonata was about a Chinese spy. Another told of a
man who had lost his wife in an art gallery and spent the rest of his
life looking for her hidden in the paintings.

Aaron knew that no one in the room, least of all himself, could
listen without dwelling on Radelescu's missing finger, on how he'd
almost starved to death, on how he'd kept his arms strong in prison.
And so a minute in, he gave up focusing on the music alone. Instead
he willed himself to feel, more than anyone else in the room, the old
man's memory. *This piece will tell the story of his life*, he decided, and
he tried to understand each note as a separate moment, to hear the
thoughts Radelescu himself pulled into them.

Aaron's father had told him about the university in Iași, the oldest in Romania, where the young Radelescu had taught only two
semesters before quitting in a rage, setting up his own studio in a
decrepit two-story building behind campus. He'd brought many
students with him, including Aaron's father, who secretly left the
university grounds for lessons three times a week. Soon a piano

teacher joined him, and the place was full of music. Wherever in the thin-walled building you took your violin, you could still hear the piano. And so the two teachers began to specialize in duets, because what else could you do? Aaron imagined that the building smelled old, that mildewed rugs covered the floors, but that the piano was impeccably tuned. His father had always spoken of the two teachers in one breath: Radelescu and Morgenstern and their famous music factory. Morgenstern, he said, had fingers like tree branches and legs like a stick insect's. When he reached for notes, the piano looked as small as a child's tin keyboard. Next to Radelescu's old records on the shelves were several of Morgenstern's: 1965, 1972, 1980, 1986. Aaron liked flipping through the jackets in chronological order to watch the man's hair go from brown to gray to white and to see his jowls slowly drop.

The music factory's star violin student had been Aaron's father, and on the last day before he set off for America, they'd had a party with a small cake. They must have known there was danger around them. There had been pogroms in other Romanian towns. Aaron imagined a stack of newspapers sitting on the lid of the piano, largely ignored. They might have put the little cake right on top of the papers. They might have said, "Be careful on your journey." No one would need to say why.

The piece ended—softly—before Aaron could continue the story. No one clapped this time. They sighed and nodded and closed their eyes. Aaron hoped the next piece would be full of noise and minor keys so he could feel how Iași had turned on itself, how the Iron Guard had rampaged for nine days through the town, finding every Jew. It was worse than Nazis, because these were people they had trusted. Some of Radelescu's old students would have been among them. Aaron could not picture the Guard without imagining men in suits of armor, even though his father had corrected this notion long ago.

But the next piece was quiet and tense, and so instead Aaron imagined the inside of the music school, where, when the pogrom began, Radelescu, Morgenstern, and six students barricaded themselves. Four of the students were Jewish. Both teachers were. Around him in the room, Aaron felt the swaying of the forty-two people who were not Radelescu, and he felt them try to imagine his time in the little room. They would be wrong.

Radelescu's hair would have been wavy still, but black and thick, catching the light of the building's scattered bulbs. Aaron imagined the musicians would have chosen one single room, the one with the piano, and although the entrances to the building were locked, they would have locked this other, smaller door too, in case the Iron Guard broke through the first barrier. They would have moved the piano up against the door. In here they were safe. Since the building was stone, they might even survive a fire. And since their little school was new and unmarked, almost entirely unknown, perhaps the Guard would not think to batter down the doors and shoot through the windows and douse the porch with gas. Aaron knew from what Radelescu told his father that the eight of them survived on only the small, sour candies Radelescu kept in a bowl on his desk. Aaron did not know whether there was running water. There must have been, because humans do not survive for ten days with no water.

On the seventh day, the only female student, a young Jewish woman whom Aaron's father had once dated, collapsed from hunger and exhaustion. He used to take her for coffee across the street. He used to study his poetry and history downstairs while he waited for her lesson to finish. She had strong little fingers, perfect for the violin. She would live to stagger out of the building at the end, but she would die the day after from having eaten too much too quickly. Aaron tried to feel her hunger, but his bladder was full and his stomach pressed out into the elastic of his pajamas. He imagined instead being bloated with starvation, but this didn't fit with his picture of the small, dark woman in a flowered spring dress, lying in the corner among fallen sheaves of music.

They were sick, all of them, unable to stay awake much. If they had indeed moved the piano to block the door, they must have worried they wouldn't have the strength to move it back when the fires and gunshots ended. At some point, they had to accept that they would die in the room. Those who were married would have written farewell letters to spouses they feared already dead. Aaron tried to feel despair in the music—in the scratch, below the note, of bow against string.

The first to die, though, was Zoltán, a Hungarian student who was not Jewish but who, like the other gentile in the room, had stayed maybe out of loyalty and maybe out of a musician's fear of violence. Violinists need thin hands; they tend to be small people. As Aaron himself grew larger and broader this year, his fingers had started to overreach the strings and bump together. His teacher talked about switching him to cello. On the eighth day, when terrible smells rose from the streets, thicker and muskier than the burning before, Zoltán vanished into the supply closet for several minutes. When they heard him coughing, they called his name. He emerged, his lips and chin and hands covered in a pale yellow powder. He began to cry, and the tears made lines through the yellow. Radelescu was the first to realize Zoltán had been eating from the cake of cheap, powdery rosin. If they had water, they must have given him some, but during the night he died—whether from the rosin or starvation or fear, they didn't know. Aaron wondered what they had done with the body. His picture of a room barricaded by a piano gave them no choice but to keep it there or throw it out the window. If he could find a way, he would ask his father.

But that next day, the streets had begun to quiet down. There were no more gunshots. In the afternoon they sent out one of the students, a Jewish boy Aaron's father hadn't known—the youngest, sixteen and brave. To do this, they must have moved the piano. Aaron imagined the boy had forged some system of communication to tell the others either to stay put or to run out the door and through the streets to the house of the second gentile student, the star pianist, whose wife, Ilinca, would be waiting, hoping he was alive. They might have had a string, a long string like Theseus used in the labyrinth, which the student dragged out the door by one end. If he tugged once, it meant to stay put. Two tugs meant run. But the boy was gone only four minutes, and then they heard a gunshot.

It was possibly the last gunshot of the pogrom, but they did not know this. They stayed an extra day, a day when the collapsed girl could have found a doctor. They stayed and then using the last of their energy they stumbled through the streets and (Aaron's father perhaps having left behind some of his famous luck) found Ilinca at home.

As Aaron finished his story, the piece ended. He took this as a sign that he was right about the string and everything else. He had been tuned to the correct frequency. He tried swallowing to test his sore throat, but every swallow made it worse.

The five times Aaron knew for certain he had been right, in chronological order: (1) the synagogue in Bonn; (2) when his aunt was pregnant; (3) his teacher was getting a divorce; (4) the goldfish was going to get sick; and (5) right now.

A young couple he didn't know had sat down on the second stair from the bottom, and the woman was leaning on the man, her head on his shoulder. People whispered while Radelescu and Aaron's mother shuffled through some music, and Aaron heard the man say to the woman, "He'll never fully have it back."

"Astounding, though," the woman said.

Aaron hadn't thought there was much missing at all, besides the finger. Concentrating on the room now, he became sure that what many people were whispering was "No, he'll never have it back," and he imagined the three ghosts—the woman, the young boy, the yellow-faced Hungarian—crying silently for the way Radelescu's hands had changed. The Hungarian ghost shook his head, and invisible rosin snowed over the room.

The ghosts and Aaron's father alone would know the real difference, and so Aaron watched his father's face a long time. What he saw there, he was certain, wasn't disappointment but a host of other, terrible things: guilt, sadness, anger. Primarily guilt, which Aaron guessed was from his leaving, from his luck.

Aaron watched now as his father and Radelescu conferred. Breathe, Aaron commanded the people in the room, and he felt them all exhale.

"Mr. Radelescu has invited our young rabbi to join him," Aaron's father announced to the room, and then looked right at him, on the stairs, and so did all the guests. He didn't know how his father had seen him sitting in the darkness, but now he felt everyone's gaze surround him, tie him in a knot. He was the fly now in the web, not the spider. He shouldn't have changed his clothes.

Aaron stayed still a moment, but he knew from his father's look that he couldn't remain on the stairs. In his pajamas and bare feet, he walked down, between the parted couple, to join his father at the fireplace. He felt like the boy he'd been at five years old, when he routinely came down before bed to kiss the guests and be admired. He wanted to glare at his father, to express his embarrassment in some public way, but he knew this was the worst night for that and so he pulled himself up and held it in. Radelescu said something in Romanian, and a handful of guests understood and laughed.

"Violin part of the *Trout Quintet*," his father whispered. "Just the fourth movement. Mr. Radelescu and your mother will fill in the other parts." It was what he'd been practicing for two months now, often with his mother covering all the rest on the piano, and so he was relieved. Aaron retrieved his violin from the cabinet and quickly tuned. He guessed his father had planned this trio days ago but kept from telling Aaron so he would not get nervous. He knew how his son thought too much.

As he started to play, Aaron's throat was parched and throbbing, but he knew he could ignore it. He angled himself so he could watch Radelescu's right hand. He could see, as he'd seen last night at dinner, the stub extending just beyond the base knuckle of his ring finger, hardly a bigger bump than if the finger had simply been closed in a fist.

Once Aaron relaxed into it, the music beside him made his own playing better, and he found himself taking rubatos where he never had before, the accompaniment holding his notes suspended in the air until he felt the moment to move on. He knew his tone was not perfect, his fingering not exact, but this was what people meant when they talked about playing with passion and feeling. He hoped his father was paying attention.

Most people in the room would not be thinking about those ten days in the music school, but about the twenty years Radelescu had spent in prison, unable to play the violin. Aaron knew they all felt privileged to be here, to witness the great man's exclusive, private return. He'd been out of prison only the four months since Ceaușescu's fall—and here, in this suburban living room, he tried the steadiness of his hands.

When the Soviets came in 1944 they at least made things safe for the Jews, despite the lines for bread and the men like Ceaușescu and the posters telling you to work harder. "They rescued us from Hell to Hades," Aaron's father said. He always said "us," though he'd never been back. At the end of the war Radelescu, recovered from malnutrition, returned to his old university post. The Communists favored him, sponsored his concerts, and then suddenly put him in prison. What he had done to fall from grace Aaron did not quite understand, but then his father knew many people they had put in jail. It was what the Communists did best.

Aaron suddenly stumbled back into the consciousness of his own playing, and wished he hadn't. His instinct had been carrying him along, but now he had to stop and think where he was, second-guess, catch up, count. He felt everyone's eyes on him except Radelescu's; the old man was lost in the music. Radelescu did not close his eyes when he played, but he squeezed his face tight and gazed into the middle distance.

Everyone knew the story of Radelescu's time in jail, and so there wasn't much for Aaron to figure out. When they first took him there, they wanted to ensure that he would never play violin again. The guards observed which hand he ate with, and when they were sure it was the right, they took him to a room and chopped off the ring finger of that hand. They had been allowed one finger, and they chose the one that would allow them to take the signet ring other-wise irremovable over the man's swollen knuckle. They weren't, any of them, musicians, or they would have known that he used his right hand for bowing, his left for fingering. And they would have under-stood, furthermore, that losing a pinky would have been more crip-pling. Or, Aaron realized, maybe they *were* musicians. Maybe that was the point. All it would take was one sympathetic, music-loving guard to slyly convince the others that this was the finger to pick.

After the bandage came off, Radelescu set about building a silent violin in his jail cell. From the cuffs of his prison uniform he pulled out a great many threads and braided them together to make the strings.

He knew the thickness of each by heart. Next, from the wooden base of his bed, he took a thin board. He rubbed down the sides until it was the width of a violin neck, then took a nail from the bed and carved notches for the strings. And then with more wood and more gray linen threads, he made a bow. Every few months, the guards would find the violin hidden in his bed and take it away, but he would make a new one. All the beds were wood, so they could not stop his efforts to wrench instrument after instrument from the bones of the prison. Aaron wondered why they didn't take it all away and make him sleep on the floor, but perhaps even the Communists had rules of fair treatment. Perhaps they liked the game. With a nail, Radelescu carved onto the back of each model the name of his fellow teacher, the pianist, as if that man were the maker of the instrument: Morgenstern, it said, in place of Stradivari.

It hadn't occurred to Aaron before now that of course the piano teacher had been Radelescu's boyfriend. He didn't receive this as a vision so much as recognize the clues, now that he was old enough to know about these things. This was the reason his father had always spoken of the two men together, as one entity, but in a voice that held some unspeakable tragedy. And it was true that Radelescu was here alone. Either the pianist had died or had left him during the long prison sentence. But Morgenstern's last album, the one from 1986, showed a healthy older man, his eyes bright and his cheeks rosy. So he had left him. While Radelescu had been carving the pianist's name, that man had forged some other life that was not made only of prison and memory and loss.

Five times a day, immediately after the guards had passed, Radelescu would take his violin from its hiding place and play one of the pieces he remembered. His prison cell would be silent but for the scraping of string on string.

What Aaron tried to feel, now, was what actual music would

sound like to the old man, what that first thick scratch of real violin sounded like after twenty years' silence. As rough and raw as a dried-out throat.

Again suddenly he was back in the music, picturing the notes on the page, and he heard his part come out all wrong—not wrong just to him, but audibly wrong to everyone in the room. He waited a beat to rejoin on the right note, but found it was like a train he'd missed. Radelescu glanced at him, then seamlessly picked up the melody. He turned so Aaron could see his fingers on the strings. Aaron copied him until he got back the stream of things himself, and Radelescu returned to floating between the structural notes and motifs of the other three string parts.

Looking out at the gathered faces, Aaron saw that they were all smiling indulgently, that it was no consequence to them whether he flubbed his part or not. He realized they did not see him and Radelescu as two musicians, but saw Aaron as youth personified, a living example of what the old man had lost. They were thinking, *He has his whole life ahead of him.* They were thinking, *Oh, how he must be inspired now to work for the things Radelescu lost.* They were thinking, *Lucky American boy, he does not know suffering.*

Aaron kept playing, but not as well as before. He took no risks with the tempo now, but tried to stay steady and count.

His father had moved out to the front of the crowd, and it was easy for Aaron to read his mind: He was giving a gift. Maybe this was all a gift to Aaron, something he felt his son would understand more as he grew older and treasure as a memory—or maybe it was a gift for Radelescu, a younger version of himself returned to the master teacher. Aaron saw in his bright eyes and the clench of his jaw how his father was willing together the old and the new. The ghosts flew over his head like kites.

Aaron could not stand his father's face like that, and he looked away, but not in time. Nausea flooded him, stronger than that day in Bonn, and the flow of the music was utterly lost. He shook, and the bow flailed loose in his hand.

In an instant he realized two things, and the first of them, most starkly, most obviously, was the core of the guilt in his father's face: that his father was not simply lucky, but had *looked* to leave Romania, had left early for Juilliard on purpose, had left behind his family and girlfriend, his teacher—not in order to study, but in order to save himself. And what was wrong with that? What was wrong with getting out? It was the same thing Morgenstern must have done, moving his piano across town, never walking by the jail, and even Radelescu had saved himself in that little building, from the gunshots that killed the women, from the trains that drove the men back and forth across the country until they all died from heat. Except escaping is its own special brand of pain, and tied to you always are the strings of the souls who didn't save themselves.

But the second and more devastating thing was this: These were not divine revelations available only to Aaron. They were common sense, floating for anyone to see, more tangible and opaque than any ghost. He'd missed them simply because he lived here in America and now in the present—and the air was filled with things he would keep missing forever unless they happened to hit him, sudden and accidental as an errant knife.

It was when Radelescu stopped playing and turned with concerned eyes that Aaron began to cry like a much younger child. He was tired like he'd never been, and the wet chill of a fever washed unmistakably over him, and the room was a storm-tossed boat. When he sank to the ground he felt hot urine on his leg and ankle. He still gripped the violin in his left hand and the bow in his right, remembering somehow not to let them drop.

His father was above him, touching his hair and forehead, first saying, "No matter, no matter," then whispering words like an incantation: "May this be the worst you ever feel."

Behind him, among the drunken guests, the ones who'd heard the story of Bonn at dinner, who'd seen the quiet, pale boy grow paler and fall, rose a murmur: He has had a vision, they were saying. The young rabbi has had a vision.

THE NOVEMBER STORY

*M*arkus is a gifted crier. We just say, "Tell us how your grandfather would feel," and he gushes like Miss America. "My grandfather would be so proud of me," he says, and blows a kiss to the sky.

Or we ask if he feels that his whole life has been a struggle. He says, "I just feel like my whole life has been just this huge struggle," and then he starts snorting and choking and holds up a finger.

The producers love the criers, and they love the cocky bastards, and they love the snarky gay men. The others, we try to get drunk. If there are any straight guys, we flirt. (Ines flips her hair. I undo one more button on my blouse.) If necessary, we feed them lines.

I don't try very hard anymore to explain to Beth what I do, why my voice is never actually on the show. Really, I think she's pretending to be confused. I think she likes saying, "Okay, but why don't they just have the contestants talk to the camera on their own? Aren't they smart enough?"

She eats her unfrozen lasagna on the couch with her heavy blanket around her, even though it's the middle of June and pretty warm, and if I try to tell her about Sabrinah screaming at the judges, or Astrid getting drunk, she says, "Don't tell, you'll ruin the show for me." Even though half the time, she doesn't watch what I've worked on. And so I stop talking, because what else could I possibly talk about?

———

Hour after hour, Ines and I sit side by side in folding chairs. The contestants sit on what looks like a throne—something oak and leather the producers found in the library. Ines is great at maintaining a lethally bored expression, so that whoever we're interviewing feels compelled to say more and more interesting things—more outrageous, more emotional. More likely to make their relatives change their names and move to Arizona.

Or we say, "This isn't who we picked. We picked someone vivacious, opinionated, funny. Please remember that the producers have the final decision."

We say, "We're not getting a character arc from you. This is going to be boring TV."

We say, "Remember that this is a job, that we're paying you, and your job is to answer all the questions." Then we ask, "What do you hate about Lesley?"

"I don't hate her," they say.

"Yes, but you need to answer the question."

"Well, she's pretty sure of herself. I mean, she's *good*."

We say, "That's great, go with that. What does her confidence remind you of?"

"Umm, like a gorilla? Like, this big silverback gorilla that's bigger than you?"

"*That*'s what we're looking for. Now we need a full sentence. About how you hate it."

"Lesley's been swaggering around like some big silverback gorilla, like, beating her chest and telling everyone how great she is. It's driving me crazy."

If you've ever seen *Starving Artist*, if you've ever even heard of it, you're probably a gay man between twenty-five and forty. We gather artists from all different fields—this season a sculptor, a painter, a dancer, a poet, a singer-songwriter, a glassblower, a graphic artist, a playwright, a piano composer, and a puppeteer—and stick them in an old, defunct artists' colony in northern Pennsylvania for twenty-three days. We give them prompts: The first episode was "Nightmare." Then "Shakespeare." Then "Baseball." They work for a day and a half, creating something small and potentially beautiful and always tragically rushed, and then they're judged, eliminated, given warnings, awarded prizes, the usual deal. The poor playwright got a fifty-second performance limit on each play. It seemed like nothing, but it was an eternity on air, and we were giving him at least twice as much screen time as anyone else. He went home sobbing after the second elimination, twitching and covered in hives. The winner gets an agent and a hundred-thousand-dollar grant. The losers get publicity cut with humiliation.

I come home upset about the playwright, and I try to tell Beth. She says, "But I thought the point for these people was the exposure."

I say, "I don't think that's what he even wanted. He wasn't typical." His name was Lincoln, and he seemed so surprised by everything, so constantly startled by the number of people involved and by our lifting his shirt to retape his mike. "People are going to remember him as the twitchy hive guy, and I don't think he'll even know how to take advantage of the publicity."

"Then why did he sign up?" Beth is knitting at the speed of light with tiny wooden needles. She's the kind of person who can undo a knot in any necklace and get broken toasters to work again. That was how we met, in fact. We lived in the same building in L.A., and when she looked out her second-story window and saw me throwing a toaster in the Dumpster, she called down that she bet it was just the heating element, and she could fix the calibration with a screwdriver. And a beer.

Right now I shrug at her question. Because I don't know why Lincoln signed up for the show. Optimism, I suppose.

But I don't say that. This is the way a lot of our conversations have been ending lately: one of us asking a question, the other not answering.

My job is to pretend to be everyone's friend. Back in the day, you could have just taken a guy into a corner by Craft Services and said, "I think you're the most talented one here. It's ridiculous how Gordy's getting all these wins, when he paints like a drunken toddler. Do you know what he said about you?" But now they're savvier. They like to think they're in on the production aspect. So you say, "You're doing well, but we need to plan for your postshow marketability. We'd like to help you develop a catchphrase."

Eight days in, the producers tell us we need a romance arc. Kenneth says, "It has to be Leo and Astrid, because she's the hottest girl, and he's the only straight guy. We have to go hetero on this." And then he says to me, "No offense, Christine, it's the network, they're asses. And they don't get our demographic at all."

Ines says, "You expect us to make them fall in love?"

He slurps his coffee through the lid and then looks at the ceiling. "Yep."

The next time Astrid sits down, she's just escaped elimination—she's in that wonderful spot between ecstatic and vulnerable. She's the glassblower, and the judges are getting bored with her. I want to tell her she'll be safe if she can just pretend to love Leo, but I don't think she can act that well.

So I say, "How do you feel about Leo being the only straight guy here?"

Astrid has long blond hair with a pale blue streak. Her nose is pierced, and she's beautiful. If you saw her on the street, you'd think she was already famous. "Leo's getting along well with everyone. It's got to be hard being the only straight guy here," she says to the camera.

Ines takes over. "Can you see anything happening between the two of you?"

"I don't see anything happening between me and Leo," she says, but she's blushing, so we can use it. "He's cute, but I'm focusing on my art right now."

I would have stopped there, knowing we got "He's cute," but Ines, brilliant Ines, keeps going. "What do you think about his flirting with you? Is it distracting you from the challenges?"

Astrid tilts her head and her hair falls down in waves. "I don't think he is."

"But if he were. Would that bother you?"

"No."

"Can you say it in a full sentence?"

She rolls her eyes. "It wouldn't bother me if Leo flirted."

Bingo.

We tell Leo, "So, Astrid told us she thinks you're cute. She said she wouldn't mind if you flirted a little."

There's a sudden wash of blood under his freckled skin.

I say, "What do you like about Astrid?"

"Astrid is a talented glassblower. I think she's a real threat."

"Do you think she likes your music?"

"I hope that Astrid likes my music."

At least ninety percent of his blood is in his face now. Ines says, with a smile to let him know she's not really serious but that she still expects an answer, "A lot of viewers will be wondering if you're really gay. Are you?"

"I'm not gay. I'm attracted to women. There are a few cute girls here."

Ines looks triumphant. They'll use that last sentence over a shot of him awkwardly stepping aside to let Astrid pass him in the dining room.

Back at our little apartment in town above the old lady's garage, Beth spends hours trying to figure out what she feels. She'll start sentences this way: "It's just that sometimes I think that maybe I feel like . . ." I imagine her chasing her emotions with a straight pin, trying to jab them down in place before they get away again. They always get away again.

I tell her, "It's okay to make decisions with your brain."

She says, "I don't work that way."

Beth's hair is long and curly and always in her eyes, and I'm so used to getting people to pull their hair out of the way for interviews that I want to grab hers and tie it back.

All day long while she's supposed to be designing websites, she sits on the couch writing in her journal, trying to decide if she wants to stay with me and someday have children, or if she needs to discover more about herself by dating other people and "excavating other parts of her personality." Then when I get home she reads me her journal. I tell her she'd give great interview.

But really she wouldn't. We don't even *cast* the people who can't make up their minds. We take the ones who issue blanket statements and manifestos, the ones who live by pithy mantras. If we ask a contestant how he feels, we want him to say, "I'm on top of the world!" or "I feel like a sack of shit!" The camera doesn't have patience for someone who feels iffy, weighs the options, equivocates. And maybe that's why I want to throttle Beth when she tells me she's been making a list. "Of the pros and cons," she says. "Of our relationship."

I ignore this and tell her how Ines and I are making two people fall in love.

"That's sick," she says.

"Why?"

"I thought this one was supposed to be a serious show. Like, focused on the actual competition."

It *is* a good show. It's non-union, and it's alarmingly low-budget, but it's not like in L.A. when I worked on *The Princess and the G*— but she's been against it ever since I told her we'd have to pack up and spend the month in Pennsylvania. They'd let her stay with me if we wanted to live in the east wing of the artists' colony along with most of the crew, but she wants nothing to do with it. "It would be all inside jokes," she said before we came out here, "and you'd be talking about, I don't know, key grips and best boys. It's just that sometimes I think I feel like you have more in common with those people than with me." When I told her I'd be gone from five in the morning till one at night, that I'd rarely be awake in our apartment, she shrugged. It wasn't the point.

And now, in a different town, with a different bed, a different couch, different windows, it feels like the spell has been broken. More to the point, it feels like the set has been struck. All the things that held our two lives together have been replaced by other, different things, and our bodies seem out of place here, like awkward actors with bad scenery. I moved the mirror from the bedroom to the living room, hanging it next to the window, approximately where our mirror is in L.A. I got Beth to flip the refrigerator door so it would open from the left, like ours at home. When my cousin, as a joke, sent us a cheesy postcard of the Santa Monica beach, I hung it on the bathroom wall.

When Beth asked about it, I told her I was just nesting. "You're *producing*," she said.

———

Ines is mad that she can't flirt with Leo now. "He was the only cute guy here," she says. She means out of everyone—the crew, the producers, the cast, and the entire population of Strathersburg, Pennsylvania.

Kenneth tells us they have footage of Leo and Astrid giggling in a hallway, choosing adjacent seats at the big dinner table in the formal dining room, taking an early morning jog. "My genius Cupids!" he calls us, and we know he says this more to encourage our future work than to tell us our job is done.

By the next round of interviews, we're able to say, "So you and Astrid are spending a lot of time together. Is there anything you want to tell us?"

On nice days, Craft Services sets up picnic tables out on the grounds. Today, people keep stopping me in the buffet line. "Heard you made Kenneth very happy," they say, and "Those two gotta name their first kid after you." I smile and feel not nearly as good as I thought I would. I've done sleazier things every day for the past five years, but for some reason this one is starting to feel wrong. Beth is getting to me, maybe. Or maybe I'm growing up. Or maybe it's something about being outside L.A., here in the real world, where the normal rules of behavior should somehow apply.

Kenneth comes up and slaps me on the shoulder. "We're changing the next prompt to Love. This is great stuff, Christine."

When I get home early, a little after midnight, Beth is stirring risotto and watching *The Godfather*. I say, "What if we buy a house when we get back home?"

She says, "Do what you feel."

"No, I think we, plural, should buy a house."

She slowly pours more chicken stock into the pot and then says, "Sometimes I feel like you're crushing my head."

I decide to ignore this. I sit on the couch and spend a few min-utes watching Vito Corleone make people offers they can't refuse. I say, "What's wrong with it if we help two people find love?" She doesn't even get what I'm talking about, so I have to remind her about the whole Astrid and Leo thing. I don't know what I'm hoping for—a friendly debate, maybe. I'm hoping for us to stay up, talking and eating on the couch. My body doesn't need sleep anymore.

But she just stares at me. "Because you can't tell people how to feel," she finally says. "Those aren't their real emotions."

"Right," I say, "but we're *not* telling them what to do. We're just playing Cupid."

"You're playing God."

I do sense that she's talking about more than just the show, but I'm too tired to work it all out. When the risotto is done cooking, she puts it in the refrigerator without eating any and heads to bed.

Vito Corleone dies with an orange peel in his mouth, and I call to Beth that she's missing the best part.

Astrid sits down in the interview chair and asks if we can turn the cameras off. "Sure," we say, and give Blake, the camera guy, the signal to cover the red light but keep taping.

She leans forward and says, "I know what you guys are trying to do. With your questions about Leo. I get that you're supposed to create drama and everything, but frankly this is insulting."

I look at Ines, hoping she can lie better than I can. "All we're doing," she says, "our role, is just to speed along what would happen in the real world if we had a lot more time. Let's say in real life you know a guy, and maybe after six months, something starts to hap-pen. Okay, so here we don't have six months. We have two more weeks, and that's *if* you stay to the finale. We're not making you date him, Astrid. We're just stirring the pot."

"Well, I want you to stop."

"Okay," I say, "sure," although Ines is looking at me strangely. "Turn the camera back on, Blake. Remember present tense, full sentences. So Astrid, tell us about this week's prompt."

She straightens up in the chair, tucks her hair behind her ear, and smiles, suddenly full of energy. "This week's challenge is Love. I'm super excited to show the judges I can go beyond simple blown shapes and do something really spectacular. I'm really gonna rock this one."

Ines and I take our only half hour off in five days to head out to the one coffee shop in Strathersburg, and we must look odd perched there at the tall table with our BlackBerrys, surrounded by men with newspapers and potbellies. "Why in the hell did you say we'd leave her alone? Tell me it's part of some master plan."

I don't tell her I'm suddenly and deeply sick of messing with people. I say, "We need her on our side. She's not an NPD." The casting directors are great at spotting borderline narcissistic personality disorder, the kind that makes you just crazy enough for great TV but not crazy enough to destroy a camera with a baseball bat. The best casts are around 50 percent NPD, but no more. Astrid was picked for her charisma and talent rather than her belief that she was destined to be famous. "I see her shutting down in interview if she thinks we're manipulating her."

"I'm just saying Kenneth had *very* high hopes for the Love challenge interviews."

"You can go to town on Leo, then. Tell him she's pregnant with his child."

Ines laughs, pretends I'm not annoying her, and we finish our lattes. "I wish you were living at the colony. I'm not into hanging out with the camera guys."

I wish I were, too. The loneliest thing in the world is lying awake beside someone asleep. Beth snores quietly, like a little girl, and she turns her back and grabs all the sheets up around herself. It feels as if she's ignoring me, as if—through her closed eyelids—she should be able to see that I'm sad. She should startle awake and ask what's wrong. But she never does. She just mumbles and steals another pillow, and I'm alone in the dark for hours with my worst thoughts.

As we walk up the endless grass hill to the colony, our shoes in our hands, Ines says, "You don't seem happy." She's known me a few years, on and off, so I figure she's probably right. "Can I ask something? Why exactly are you with this person?"

I'm saved from answering by Dale running toward us, telling us Kenneth is pissing mad that we're late and asking if we brought back lattes.

"Where do you think we're hiding them?" I ask, and he swears and runs his hand through his Mohawk and races back to the house.

Ines takes off to help mike up the judges and I check in with Kenneth, and the whole time I'm tearing at my thumbnail and trying to answer her question, as if I'm a contestant and *must* answer the question, and must rephrase the question as part of the answer.

I am with Beth because:

I've been fighting against her leaving for so long that it's the only thing I know how to do. It's like that's my character arc, like some producer has said, "We need you to be the high-strung girl with the short hair who doesn't want her girlfriend to leave." And, like the best contestants, the ones chosen for their compliance, the ones who are secretly actors in their real lives as well as pianists or dancers, I go along with it. Because what other role do I have? Because who else am I?

———

Ines and I always sit in at the back of the judgment room so we don't have to get debriefed before the interviews. Kenneth is brilliant. He lines the five remaining artists up in front of the bookshelves, then tells them we won't tape for a few more minutes—when really, the cameras are already rolling. He tells them to stand still for the light guys, and then says, "We're having more digital issues. We're gonna be here pretty late tonight, folks." And the sleep-deprived artists, dehydrated and trying to hold still and awaiting judgment, give the most beautiful looks of disgust and despair. The cameras are getting it all. The editors will splice it in with shots of their work being critiqued, or a competitor winning.

Kenneth has managed to pull something like this off every episode, and they always fall for it. Once he had a camera guy give all the contestants incomprehensible instructions in a thick accent, while the other cameras captured the grimaces of confusion. At the third judgment, he directed Ines to have a loud phone argument with a boyfriend in the corner of the room. That time we had enough snickering and eye-rolling to manufacture an entire implied rivalry between Leo and Gordy. It became one of our best plotlines.

Later, Ines and I will ask the artists, one by one, to go through the whole day, speaking in the present tense and pretending they don't know what's ahead.

"I'm so nervous," they'll say, long after the judgments are over, "because I don't know if the new puppets are even going to hold together."

The glorious present tense—that blindest of tenses, ignoring all context, all past and future failures.

Even the losers, the ones who know they've just been sent home, are somehow willing to talk about their work optimistically, as if they're about to strut onto the stage of the colony's Little Theater and show their best stuff. We'll say, "Okay, it's ten minutes before the show starts, and you've just been called in. What are your hopes? What are you excited about?"

And off they go, like puppies who don't get that no matter how many times they hump their master's leg, he always swats them with the paper. "I'm so excited for the judges to see my work!" cry the artists who've just been mocked and upbraided and grilled for the two hours that will be edited down to five on-screen minutes. As if by trying hard enough, they can convince us to love them again.

They remind me of someone.

Leo should go home, it's obvious—all his compositions are the same anemic jazz in various minor keys—but our matchmaking has spared him. It's Markus, the sculptor, the great crier, that they eighty-six. His Love sculpture is incredible, really: a three-foot-tall heart made of bars, like a rounded cage. He coated each wire of the framework in lumpy clay, then painted the whole thing bright blue. Inside the heart was a live dove he had procured at a pet store in town with his fifty dollars in "funding." The problem was that the dove, stuck inside the cage for six hours waiting to be judged, had made a fairly convincing public bathroom of the heart floor. The judges used that as their excuse: "You didn't plan ahead. You didn't think about longevity. We wanted love, and you showed us a sad old dove. We wanted excitement, and you showed us excrement." Kenneth had written that one down for them on a note card.

Markus gives us a nice monologue about how they can't expect his best work when there isn't even time for the clay to dry, how he's more about emotional realism anyway, and you can't do emotional realism on a schedule. He says the colony has been good for his soul, and then he cries and tells us how famous he's going to be.

Beth has left me a note on the refrigerator door: "Don't eat risotto. It has my germs."

She hasn't told me she's sick, and there are no mountains of Kleenex lying around, but maybe it's true. I'd be the last to know. I read the note again. If this is some message about the status of our relationship, or some cryptic directive as to how I can salvage things, it's utterly lost on me. The risotto is half-gone anyway.

I write "OK!" on the bottom of the note, and I add a smiley face and a heart. Then I think better of it and rip off the bottom edge, but some of her writing rips off too, and she'll notice. I take the whole note and tear it into little shreds and drop them in the garbage.

Even after all our work, by the end of the shoot Kenneth has decided to drop the love arc. "We're way more into Leo's falling-out with Gordy, and I think we'll want to paint Astrid as kind of a loner, so that everyone roots for Sabrinah," he says. "She's going to win." They'll never use the beautiful footage of Leo blushing, just like they'll throw away 99 percent of everything that happens. Those are the last four standing: Beautiful Leo, Gordy the Mediocre Painter, Sabrinah the Shouter, and Astrid the Blonde.

We have two days left on the shoot. They'll be told that the final prompt is "November," then do their last interviews and shoot the promos for the finale. They'll go home to work on a portfolio of five pieces, preparing to come back before the judges and the almighty agent to present their work and make a case for their careers. They'll tell us all to love them, to care about their work, to see that they alone have embodied November.

Of course, it won't actually be November. It's only June now. They'll have ten weeks off and we'll shoot the finale the last week of September. But it will *air* in late November, and that's all that counts: not what time it is here, but what time it is on the other side of the TV screen.

By the end, I never see Beth awake. I don't know if we're broken up, if we're reconciled, if we're the same as we always were. All I have is her unconscious body, beside me in the dark when I get into bed and beside me in the earliest gray light when I roll out. It might be a nice way to fade out of things: a life-size Beth doll to wean me off the real thing.

On the last day of the shoot, I'm up in the house's attic, searching among piles of abandoned furniture for a rug, since one of the judges spilled coffee on the cream one. We used to have two set-dressers, but when they walked off the set, their jobs fell to everyone else. Identities are slippery here, with no union to delineate things, no laws of normalcy. No mirrors in the bathroom, lest the camera reflect itself. Days go by when I forget what I look like, when I startle at the sound of my own name, when I couldn't tell you what the hell business I have in this place. I look out the window, down to the grounds, and there, back near the woods, with no one else around, Leo and Astrid are kissing. Passionately, but slowly, like they've done it before, his hands in her hair, her hands in his back pockets. A giddy flood of adrenaline sends me halfway down the stairs on my way to tell Kenneth, before I stop and think. Kenneth would love me for it forever. I could maybe get someone to lug a camera up the narrow stairs and shoot them before they walk away. I wonder for a long time afterward why I don't. It might be because I hate my job, or it might be because I still believe in love.

Instead I walk back up the stairs, as quietly as I can, as if they could hear me way out there on the grounds. I lean against the window frame and watch them. It's a movie, and I'm the only one in the world with a ticket.

And then there's this: Did we make them fall in love, or were they already on their way? And if it's all our fault, then are they really even in love?

—————

Ines carries my weight for the last interviews. "Tell us why you're going to win," she says. "Tell us why Leo deserves to lose."

Afterward, she asks me what's wrong. "I'm just not sure what I'm going home to," I say. "Back in L.A."

She thinks I'm talking about jobs, and she tells me she'll be working on the new one about anorexics gaining weight back. She thinks she can hook me up.

We shoot the artists packing and leaving, we shoot them looking out the backseat window of a moving car, and then suddenly we're done. Instead of going home to Beth, I stay for the party. The camera guys do actual keg stands on the lawn. Ines says, "They're living out their fraternity fantasies." We're standing on the porch watching, and she's well on her way to drunk. She says, "I'm going to sleep with Blake tonight." Blake is the hairiest one.

"Go for it," I say, and attempt to get drunk myself. I won't miss the place at all.

In September, Astrid, I think, will bring back delicate glass leaves and gray bubbles. Gordy will paint empty city streets. Sabrinah will dance like an empty tree. Leo will play sad, beautiful, modern things on the piano that only I will know are for Astrid. And I'm certain I'll be coming back here alone.

Before the shoot starts, Ines and I and everyone lower on the totem pole will run around making the place look like November: desolate and cold and fading. We'll stand on ladders to pull leaves off the trees. I've done it before. I've done stranger things, too. We'll spray some of the remaining leaves yellow, some red. We'll make everyone wear a coat. We'll kill the grass with herbicide.

It's sick and it's soulless, but it's one of the addictive things about my job: Here, you can force the world to be something it's not.

We'll take the four contestants one by one into the foyer and put them on that ridiculous chair, and ask them, Why do you deserve to win? How passionate do you feel? What do you love about your work? How much do you love your work? What *is* this sucker punch, love, that ruins us so completely?

And can you say it in a full sentence?

THE MIRACLE YEARS OF
LITTLE FORK

*I*n the fourth week of drought, at the third and final performance of the Roundabout Traveling Circus, the elephant keeled over dead. Instead of stepping on the tasseled stool, she gave a thick, descending trumpet, lowered one knee, and fell sideways. The girl in the white spangled leotard screamed and backed away. The trainer dropped his stick and dashed forward with a sound to match the elephant's. The show could not continue.

The young Reverend Hewlett was the first to stand, the first to signal toward the exits. As if he'd just sung the benediction, parents ushered their children out into the park. The Reverend stayed behind, thinking he'd be more useful here, in the thick of the panic and despair, than out at the duck pond with the dispersing families.

The trainer lifted his head from the elephant's haunch to stare at the Reverend. He said, "Your town has no water. That's why this happened."

The elephant was a small one, an Asiatic one, but still the largest animal the Reverend had ever seen this close. Her skin seemed to move, and her leg, but the Reverend had watched enough deaths to know these were the shudders of a soulless body. The clowns and acrobats and musicians had circled around, but only Reverend Hewlett and the trainer were near enough to touch the leathery epidermis, the short, sharp hairs—which the Reverend did now, steadying one thin hand long enough to run it down the knobs of the creature's spine.

The Reverend said, "There's no water in the whole state." He wondered at his own defensiveness, until he saw the trainer's blue eyes, accusatory slits. He said, "I'm not in charge of the weather."

The trainer nodded and returned his cheek to the elephant's deflated leg. "But aren't you in charge of the praying?"

At home in the small study, surrounded by the books the previous Reverend had left behind two years prior, Hewlett began writing out the sermon. *Here we are,* he planned to say, *praying every week for the drought to end. And yet who among us brought an umbrella today?* He would let them absorb the silence. He'd say, *Who wore a raincoat?*

But no, that was too sharp, too much. He began again.

The Roundabout was meant to move on to Shearerville, but now there was the matter of elephant disposal. The trainer refused to leave town till she'd been buried, which was immaterial since the rings and tent couldn't be properly disassembled around the elephant—and even if they could, their removal would leave her exposed to the scorching sun, the birds, the coyotes and raccoons. The obvious solution was to dig a hole, a very large hole, quickly. A farmer offered his lettuce field, barren anyway. But the ground was baked hard by a month of ceaseless sun, horses couldn't pull the diggers without water, and although the men made a start with pickaxes and shovels, they calculated that at the rate they were digging, it would take five full weeks to get an elephant-sized grave. These were the men who weren't away at war, the lame or too-old, the too-young or asthmatic.

The elephant was six days dead. Reverend Hewlett called a meeting in the sanctuary after Sunday services, which a few of the circus folk had attended—the bearded lady, the illustrated man, the trainer himself—and now more filed in, joining the congregation. A group of dwarfs who might have been a family, some lithe women who looked like acrobats. Reverend Hewlett removed his robe and stood at the pulpit to address the crowd. He was only thirty years old, still in love with the girl he'd left in Chicago, still anxious to toss a ball on Saturdays with whoever was willing.

He looked at them, his flock. Mayor Blunt sat in the second row—the farthest forward anyone sat, except, once a year, those taking first Communion—with his wife on one side, his daughter, Stella, on the other. The mayor had decided that the burial of the dead was more a religious matter than a governmental one, and had asked Reverend Hewlett to work things out.

The Reverend said, "I've been charged with funeral arrangements for the elephant. For—I understand her name was Belle. We ask today for ideas and able hands. And we extend our warmest welcome to the members of the Roundabout." In the days since the disaster, his parishioners had already opened their homes, providing food and beds. (The circus trailers were too hot, too waterless, too close to the dead elephant. And the people of Little Fork had big hearts.) The performers, in turn, had started helping in the gas station and the library and the dried-out gardens, even doing tricks for the children on the brown grass of the park. They were drinking a fair amount of alcohol, was the rumor by way of the ladies at the general store, more in this past week than the whole town of Little Fork consumed in a month.

Adolph Pitt, of Pitt's Funeral Home, stood. "I called on my fellow at the crematorium, and he says it's nothing doing. Not even piecemeal, even if the beast were—forgive me—even if it were dismembered."

"*She,*" the elephant trainer said from the back. "Not *it.*" The trainer still carried with him, at all times, the thin stick he'd used to guide the elephant, nudging it under her trunk, gently turning her head in the right direction. No one had yet seen him without it. Reverend Hewlett imagined he slept with it under his arm. The man slept alone in his scorching trailer, having refused all offers for a couch and plumbing. Hewlett was an expert now in grief—they hadn't told him, at seminary, the ways his life would be soaked in grief—and it wasn't the first time he'd seen a man cling to an object. Usually he could talk to the bereaved about heaven, about the warm breast of God, about the promise of reunion. But what could he say about an elephant? The Lord loveth the beasts of the field? His eye is on the sparrow? Surely the burial would help.

Reverend Hewlett saw it as his duty to raise an unpopular option the men had been mulling over the past few days. The mayor couldn't bring it up, because he had an election to win in the fall. But Reverend Hewlett was not elected. And so he said it: "The swimming pool was never filled this summer. It's sitting empty."

Some of the men and women nodded, and a few of the children, catching his meaning, made sharp little noises and looked at their parents. The circus folks didn't much respond.

"It's an old pool," the Reverend said, "and we can't dig a hole this summer. We can dig a hole *next* summer, and that can be the new pool. This one's too small, I've heard everyone say since the day I got here."

"There's no dirt to bury him with!" Mrs. Pipsky called.

"Maybe a tarp," someone said.

"Or cement. Pour cement in there."

"Cement's half water."

The mayor stood. "This town needs that pool," he said. The youngest Garrett boy clapped. "We'll find another solution."

And before the meeting could devolve into argument, Reverend Hewlett offered up a prayer for the elephant (the Lord loveth the beasts of the field), and a prayer that a solution could be found. He invited everyone to the narthex, where the women of the Welcoming Committee had laid out a sheet cake.

The Reverend made a point of greeting each visitor in turn, asking how they were enjoying their stay in Little Fork. "Not much," the illustrated man said.

The Reverend thought, with awe, how God had a plan for everyone. Some of these people were deformed—a man with ears like saucers, a boy with lobster-claw hands—and yet God had led them to the circus, to the place where they could find friendship and money and even love. And now He had led these people to Hewlett's flock, and there must be a purpose for this, too.

In the corner, the fire eater chatted with the mayor's daughter. Stella Blunt was sixteen and lovely, hair in brown waves, and he was not much older, with a small, dark beard that Hewlett figured was a liability for a fire eater. Stella leaned toward him, fascinated.

The following Sunday, most of them returned. They sang along with the hymns and closed their eyes to pray, and one of them put poker chips in the communion plate. The fire eater sat in the rear next to Stella. They looked down at something below the pew back, giggling, passing whatever it was back and forth.

Over the past week, the smell of the elephant had crept from the tent and over the center of town. It was a strangely sweet smell, at least at first, more like rotting strawberries than rotting meat.

Reverend Hewlett had planned a sermon on the beatitudes, but when the time came for prayer requests, Larry Beedleman asked everyone to pray for enough food to last his guests (all five trapeze artists were living in the Beedlemans' attic), and Mrs. Thoms asked them to pray for the Lord to take away the stench of the elephant. Gwendolyn Lake wanted them all to beg forgiveness for the sins that had brought this trial upon them. So Reverend Hewlett preached instead about patience and forbearance.

After the service, he caught Mayor Blunt's arm. He said, "Isn't it time we used the pool?"

Blunt was a large man who tucked his chin into his neck when he spoke. He said, "I'll lose the vote of every child's mother."

"Have you seen," Hewlett said slowly, "the way your daughter looks at that boy?"

"We've taken him into our home," the mayor said. As if that were definitive and precluded the possibility of teenage love.

"Joe," the Reverend said. "You'll lose more votes to scandal than to a hole in the ground."

And so on Tuesday fifty men and women dragged the elephant to the town pool on waxed tarps and lowered her until she rolled in with a thud and a sudden release of the smell they'd all been gagging against to begin with. They covered her with cartloads of hay—everyone had a lot of hay that summer whether they wanted it or not—and they covered the hay with the gravel Tom Garrett had donated, and they covered that all with fresh tarps, held down by bricks.

Reverend Hewlett gave the funeral service right there, with the locals and circus folk in a ring around the pool. The elephant trainer sobbed into his small, calloused hands. He did not have the stick with him, for once.

Afterward, when the other circus workers went to take apart the tent, to fold up the benches and load things into their trailers, the elephant trainer stayed behind. He put his hand on Reverend Hewlett's arm, then drew it back. And, as if it choked him, he said, "I can't leave her here."

"Will you pray with me?"

"I'm saying I don't think I can leave this town."

"My son, I won't let anything happen to the grave."

"I'm saying that my parents were drifters, and I'm a drifter, and I've never had a part of myself in the soil of a place before. And now I do, and I think I ought to stay here for the rest of my life."

Hewlett marveled at the ways he'd misread this man. Perhaps it hadn't been grief he'd seen in the man's face, but thirst.

He said, "Then it must be God's will."

The tarp stayed put through the dry fall and the dry winter, and the smell subsided.

Before Christmas, Stella Blunt came to Reverend Hewlett for help. The fire eater was long gone, but her stomach had begun swelling and she was panicked.

The Reverend arranged, to her parents' naive delight, for Stella to spend the spring semester doing work at the VA hospital downstate. Only she didn't really go there; he set her up in the vestry with a bed and a little library. She wrote her parents postcards, which Reverend Hewlett would mail in an envelope to Reverend Adams down in Landry, just so Adams could drop them in the postbox and send them back to Little Fork.

Hewlett visited her three times a day, and Sheila Pipsky, who used to be a nurse and could keep a secret like a statue, stopped by twice a week. The Reverend would sit on the floor while Stella sat on the bed, legs folded. If he had time, he ate with her. They spoke French together, so she wouldn't grow rusty. When the church was locked up for the night, he'd turn out the lights and let her know she was safe—and she'd walk around and around the pews, up to the little choir loft, down the hall to the Sunday school classrooms. As she grew bigger, less steady on her feet, he'd hold her arm so she wouldn't trip in the dark. If he closed his eyes—which he let himself do only for a second at a time—he could believe he was walking down a Chicago street with Annette, the breeze on their chests, her hair in a clip.

"It's funny," Stella said to him once. They were standing in the nursery, the rocking horses and dollhouse lit with moonlight. "I thought I loved him. But if I loved him, I'd remember him better. Wouldn't I?"

Hewlett had the utterly inappropriate urge to touch Stella's cheek, the top of her white ear. He slowed his breath.

Stella giggled.

"What is it?" he said.

"Your shoes. They're untied, like a little kid's."

In May, the doctor came in the middle of the night and delivered a healthy baby girl, and Reverend Hewlett called the Millers, who had come to him praying for a child that fall, and they were given the baby and told she came from Shearerville. They named her Eloise. Hewlett had looked away when Stella said good-bye to the baby. He muttered a prayer, but it was a pretense—he couldn't absorb her pain just then. He chose, instead, to think of the Millers. He chose to thank the Lord. Stella stayed two more weeks in the vestry, and then she went home. Hewlett continued his nighttime circuits of the church, though. They'd become habit.

The elephant trainer worked on one of the farms, tending the cows and horses, until he decided to open a restaurant in the space left empty when Herman Burns had gone to war. He used to cook for the circus folk, after all, and he missed it. He served sandwiches and soup and meatloaf. Soon they were calling him by his name, Stanley Tack, and by June he had fallen in love with the Beedleman girl, and she with him.

It made Reverend Hewlett think, briefly, of writing home to Chicago, to Annette. He worried she was waiting for him, the way her girlfriends were waiting for their boys to return, battle-scarred and strong and ready to settle down. But the war abroad would eventually end; Hewlett's war never would. And Annette would not join him on this particular battlefield. She'd made that clear. She would stay in Chicago, in her brownstone, and type for a firm, until he came to his senses and moved home to teach history. That she never doubted this would happen broke his heart doubly: once for himself, and once for her. She hadn't written in three months. And he did not write to her. To do so would be to punch a hole in his own armor.

As soon as summer hit, there was torrential rain—as if all the town's prayers from last year got to heaven at once, far too late. The bridge flooded out, and Stanley Tack's restaurant flooded, and nearly everyone you passed, if you asked how things were, would respond, "I'm building an ark!"

There were drowned sheep and missing fences at one farm, where the river now came to the barn door. An oak toppled in the park, roots exposed, like a loosened weed. Stella Blunt, lining up with the choir and looking through the stained glass, said, "It's like someone's trying to tear apart the world."

They sang "our shelter from the stormy blast" as thunder shook the roof. They sang "There Shall be Showers of Blessings," and some of them laughed.

Stanley Tack had come every Sunday that whole year, but always sat quizzical and silent through the prayers, the hymns. He never carried the stick anymore. He was always alone; the Beedleman girl worked the Sunday shift at the hospital. He never put anything in the offertory and he never took Communion. Reverend Hewlett started to see this as a personal challenge: Someday, he would give the sermon that would bring Stanley to his feet, that would open his blue eyes to the light shining through above the altar, that would make him pause on his way out of church and say, "Do you have a minute to talk?"

They planned, as soon as the rain let up, to pour cement into the old pool and dig the hole for the new one. But the rain never let up. On the fortieth day of rain, folks stopped Reverend Hewlett at the pharmacy and the gas pump to joke: "Tomorrow we're due our rainbow, right? Tomorrow we get our dove?" At least no one much minded not having a pool that summer.

The Millers brought little Eloise to church, and she was baptized as Stella Blunt looked on from the choir. Reverend Hewlett poured water on the baby's head and marveled at her angry little eyes. The daughter of a fire eater, born into a land of water.

Despite the tarp, the pool had filled around the elephant and the hay and the gravel, and if you walked by and peered through the chainlink fence, you'd see how the tarp was now sort of floating on top, how the whole pool deck was covered in an inch of water that connected with the water in the pool. The children dared each other to reach through the fence and touch the dirty elephant juice. Mrs. Thoms wondered aloud if the elephant water would go through the pool drains and into the town supply.

One day, Reverend Hewlett braved the rain to visit Stanley Tack's restaurant. After the downstairs had flooded, Stanley had taken over the vacant apartment upstairs, cooking out of its small kitchen and serving food in what used to be the living room. On an average Saturday you'd find three or four families huddled around the tables, eating soup and listening to the rain hit the windows, but today the Reverend was the only one in the place. It seemed people were leaving their houses less. The spokes of their umbrellas were broken, and their rain boots were moldy, and they realized there wasn't much they truly needed from out in the world. A lot of sweaters were knit that summer, a lot of books read.

The Reverend sat, and when Stanley brought his cheese sandwich and potato soup, he sat across from him. He said, "I believe this is my fault."

The only "this" anyone in town was talking about was the rain.

Reverend Hewlett said, "My child. This weather is the will of God."

"You preached—you gave a sermon, right after I chose to stay. And I couldn't help thinking it was intended for me. The story of Jonah trying to sail away from Nineveh. Of God sending the storm and the whale."

The Reverend tried his potato soup, and nodded at Stanley. The soup was good, as always. Never great, but always good. He said, "I was thinking of many things, but yes, one of them was you. The way the Lord sends us where we need to be, regardless of our plans. I was reflecting on my own life, as well. I ended up in Little Fork by chance, and in my first year, when I felt doubt, I'd think of Jonah in the belly of that fish. It was preaching, you know, that he was meant to do in Nineveh. That's what he was running from."

"Yes. But"—Stanley looked out the window, where the rain was slicing sideways—"what if this isn't my Nineveh? What if this is the place I've run away *to*, and all this, all the rain, is God trying to wash me out and send me on my way? Just as he sent that storm for Jonah."

This troubled the Reverend. He bought some time by biting into his sandwich, but then it troubled him even more. Stanley had reminded him of Annette, on the day he left Chicago, fixing him with dry eyes: "I don't see how you're so *sure*," she'd said. And he'd said, "There's no other way to be." And whether or not he was truly sure back then, he'd grown sure these past three years. Or at least he'd been too busy counseling others to foster his own concerns. He'd broken down in doubt a few times—not in God so much as in his plan—when he'd had to bury a child or when soldiers came home in boxes, but he'd always returned to a place of faith. Look at little Eloise, for instance, growing plump at the Millers' house. Exactly as it was meant to be. But somehow the elephant trainer's question had hit a sore spot in his own soul, a bruise he hadn't known was there.

He said, "All we can do is pray, and ask that God make clear the path."

"And how, exactly, would He make it clear?"

"If you listen, God will speak."

Most always, when he said something like this, his parishioners smiled as if assured they'd hear the voice of God that very night. Sometimes he even had to clarify: "This is not the age of miracles, you realize. His voice won't boom from the clouds. You'll have to listen. You'll have to look." And they'd leave to await the message.

What Stanley said was, "God doesn't talk." It wasn't something Reverend Hewlett was used to hearing in this town. And then, in all seriousness, he said, "I think I've broken the universe."

Reverend Hewlett looked at his own hands, the veins and creases. He imagined they might crack open like the parched earth had last summer. Or at least, he felt a small crack somewhere inside, one that didn't hurt but was letting in a bit of air. All he could think to say was, "It's raining in the next town over, too. And in the next town beyond that."

Reverend Hewlett's name was Jack. This was increasingly easy for him to forget. He'd become John, and then—in the bulletins and on the sign outside the church—Rev. J. Hewlett, and since there was no one in Little Fork who didn't know him as the Reverend, since even the few Catholics who drove to services in Shearerville greeted him as "Rev" or sometimes, slipping, as "Father," he hadn't heard his own name in three years. Annette no longer wrote to him at all, no longer extended the tail of the J down like the first letter of a chapter.

And why had he left her? And why had he come here? Because he was needed. Because his mentor at seminary had said, "God is calling you there. God is calling me to send you there."

And that man, with his great beard, his walls of books, his faith in the hand of God, could not have been wrong.

That night there was a dance at the Garden Club, on the east end of town. It was Little Fork's version of a debutante ball, the same youngsters debuting themselves each year, in the same white dresses, until they were too old for these things, or married. Only tonight they were soaked through. Reverend Hewlett stood against the wall watching—his mere presence, everyone agreed, was salubrious—and observed the boys in their sopping bowties, hair plastered to their heads, and the girls wrapped against their will in their mothers' shawls. No boy would see through a wet dress tonight. Heaps of galoshes and umbrellas by the door.

They coupled and uncoupled in patterns that seemed casual, chaotic, but of course were not. Every move, every flick of the eyes, was finely orchestrated. There were hearts being broken tonight. You just couldn't tell whose.

Gordon Pipsky sidled up and offered a sip from his flask. Gordon's son was out there dancing, a girl on each arm. When Hewlett accepted, Gordon winked and grinned. "I'll never tell," he said. Even though he saw the Reverend take the Eucharist every Sunday. Perhaps what he meant was, "I'll never tell that you're just a man like me."

Was it a secret, really? He'd never been anything else.

He had felt like an impostor when he first put on his robe—but then everyone felt like an impostor, he'd learned in seminary. And now, after all this time, he rarely considered himself a fraud. But nothing had changed, really. Except that he had grown used to that robe, that second skin, just as he'd grown used to God's silent ways.

There was Stella Blunt, dancing in white. A debutante still.

The next morning, the rain stopped. Not the kind of pause that makes you worry the sky is just gathering more water, but a true, clear stop, the air bright and clean and dry.

And then the wind started.

For the first few hours, it just shook the windows and door hinges and made people sneeze—all that new mold now flying through the air—but by nightfall, it was bringing down tree branches and shingles. By morning, it had knocked down phone lines and garden fences and was tearing at the awnings on Center Street.

And worse: By late afternoon, with most of the surface water gone (blown to Shearerville, everyone said), the tarp blew off the old pool. No one was outside to see that part, but a fair number were witness to it flying smack up against the library, five blocks south, before continuing on its way. It took folks a while to realize what it was—and by that point, there was gravel skittering down the streets nearest the pool. There was moldy hay in everyone's yard.

Gwendolyn Lake came banging on the parsonage door to tell Reverend Hewlett. His first thought was to run and see if the elephant was uncovered, but his second thought was of Stanley, who should be kept from the pool. Stanley, who would want to run there but would regret it later. Who might take it all as some sort of sign.

Hewlett told Gwendolyn to get her brothers. "Use sheets," he said, "and bricks." He himself ran in the opposite direction, toward

Center Street. The wind wasn't constant but came in great lumps: Every three or four seconds, a pocket of air would hit him, would lift him from beneath. If he'd had an open umbrella, he'd have left the ground. Trees were down, garbage blew through the streets, the bench in front of the barbershop was overturned.

Sally Thoms ran crying down the other side of the road, blond hair sucked straight up like a sail. "My cat blew away!" she cried. "He was in a tree and he just blew away!"

"I'll pray for you!" the Reverend called, but the wind ate his words.

He pulled with his full weight on the door beside the one that read STANLEY'S DINER, the door that everyone knew led up to the real place. Stanley stood in the kitchen, peeling carrots.

He said, "You're early for lunch, Rev."

For some reason—even later he couldn't figure out what had possessed him—the Reverend said, "I'd be happy if you called me Jack."

"Sure," Stanley said, and laughed. "Jack. You want to peel me some carrots, Jack?"

They stood side by side at the counter, working.

"What do you make of this apocalypse, Jack?"

He began to answer as he always did of late—something about God wanting to test us now and then, maybe something about Job—but instead he found himself telling a joke. "You hear about the man who couldn't see what the weather was like, because it was too foggy?"

"Ha!" He wasn't sure he'd ever heard Stanley laugh before. It was more a word than a laugh. Stanley said, "I know an old circus one. Why'd the sword swallower swallow an umbrella?"

"I—I don't know."

"Wanted to put something away for a rainy day."

It was a terrible joke, but Hewlett started laughing and couldn't stop—perhaps because he was picturing Stella Blunt's bearded fire eater, an umbrella blossoming in his throat just as the baby had stretched Stella's figure. This wasn't funny either, but the laughter came anyway.

He went to the sink for a glass of water, to cure his laugh and the cough that followed it. As he drank, he looked out the back window, over the yards behind Fifth Street and the abutting yards behind Sixth Street. Down below, on the other side of the block-long stock-ade fence, the Miller family had ventured out into the yard with baby Eloise. In the time between gusts, they were examining the damage to the old well, the top of which had tumbled into a pile of stones. A summer of baking and a summer of rain must have loos-ened everything, and all it took was a day of wind to knock things about. There was Ed Miller, peering down the hole, and there was Alice Miller, holding the baby, when a blast of wind—up here Jack Hewlett could see and hear but not feel it—tore limbs from trees and tore shutters from houses and tore Eloise from her mother's arms and into the air and across the yard. He must have made a noise, because Stanley rushed to peer over his shoulder just in time to see the baby, her pink face and her white dress, go flying over the garden and over the next yard and finally into the Blunts' yard, where, just as she arced down, there he was, Mayor Blunt, running toward the child. He caught her in his arms.

Hewlett heard Stanley inhale sharply. Neither man moved.

The mayor had been outside alone—presumably inspecting the maple that had fallen across his yard, the one that, were it still standing, the baby would have blown straight into—but now his wife ran out, and his son, and Stella. The two men watched from above as Stella leaned over the baby, covering her own mouth. Her mother's hand was on her back, and Hewlett wondered if she was crying, and—if she was—how she'd explain it. Well, who wouldn't cry at a baby landing in their yard?

The wind took a break, and Mayor Blunt handed the baby to Stella and wrapped his coat around her front, covering them both. Hewlett imagined what the man would have said: something about "You know I can never hold a baby right." Or "This should be good practice for you!" And the mayor led a procession around the front of the house and down the street to the Millers'. Hewlett hadn't thought to look back to the Millers for a while—they weren't in their yard. Ed Miller had scaled the fence to the lawn between his and the Blunts' and was running through the bushes, around the trees, behind the shed. Alice Miller stood out front, hands to her head, shouting for help. She ran toward the Blunts when she saw them, but she couldn't have known what was under Stella's coat until the mayor pulled it back, chest puffed out, proud of his miracle. He handed the baby back himself. Alice Miller covered the infant with kisses and raced her into the house, Mayor and Mrs. Blunt following. Stella stayed out on the walk a minute, looking at the sky. What she was thinking, Hewlett couldn't even guess.

"Well," Stanley said. "Pardon the expression, but Jesus Christ." The carrot and peeler, still in his hands, were shaking.

Hewlett wanted to run down, to see if Stella was all right, to make sure the baby wasn't hurt. But he wasn't a doctor. And he couldn't leave Stanley alone, couldn't let him think of checking on the pool. So he just said, "I think we've seen the hand of God." He wasn't at all sure this was true. Part of him wondered if he hadn't seen a miracle at all but its precise and brutal opposite—a failure of some kind, or the evidence of chaos. Whatever he'd just seen, it troubled him deeply. Was God in the wind, blowing that baby back to Stella where she belonged? Or was God in the catch, in the impossible coincidence of the mayor being in the right spot, in the return of the child to the Millers? Or—and this was the thing about a crack in faith, he knew, the way one small fissure could spread and crumble the whole thing into a pile of rocks—was God in neither place?

Stanley put his carrot down and turned. His face was soft and astonished, blue eyes open wider than Hewlett had ever seen them. He looked like a man who'd just survived an auto crash, a man who'd taken part in something bizarre and terrifying, not just witnessed it from above. "It's not true, is it?" Stanley spoke slowly, working something out. "What I said before, about Nineveh. We're—we're all where we're supposed to be. I was supposed to wind up here." He braced himself on the counter, as if he expected God to blow him across town next. "A beast brought Jonah to Nineveh, and a beast brought me here."

Hewlett said what he'd said so many times before. "The thing is to be listening when God speaks."

By the time Reverend Hewlett walked home that night by way of the old pool, Davis Thoms and Bernie Lake were down there mixing batch after batch of cement and pouring it into the hole. For the first time in more than a year, there was both enough water to mix the stuff, and not so much water falling from the sky that it would turn to soup.

He continued toward the parsonage. The wind was done. It had simply left town.

It was so strange to be outside without the roar of wind or rain, without the feel of air or water ripping at his skin, that Reverend Hewlett stood awhile on his own porch feeling that he was floating in the midst of vast and empty space. Everywhere he turned, there was nothing. No baking sun, no drenching storm, no raging wind. There were people coming out of houses, and people going into houses, and people walking from one store to the next. And people picking up branches, and people sweeping up glass. As if they'd been directed to do these things.

All this happened a very long time ago. And it's hard now to argue that what happened so far back *wasn't* inevitable. If the elephant hadn't died, there wouldn't be, on top of the old swimming pool, the playground that originally had some other name but quickly became known as Elephant Park; and the Little Fork High School football team would not be the Mammoths; and Stanley Tack wouldn't have stayed in town, and the son he had with the Beedleman girl (she was expecting already that day of the windstorm, she just hadn't told him yet) wouldn't have married Eloise Miller, and today the town of Little Fork wouldn't be half-full of Tacks of various generations, all descended (though they none of them know it) from a fire eater.

Jack Hewlett might not have given up the cloth and returned home to be with his girl, with Annette, who'd waited for him even after her letters stopped—only to be drafted two months later, no longer clergy, no longer exempt from war. He might not have died in France, a bullet through his lung. But who's to say that the outcome of that battle—even of the entire war—hadn't hinged, in one way or another, on the bravery of one man? He was, after all, an exceptional soldier. He took orders well.

Or at least it can be said: This world is the one made by the death of that elephant.

The Sunday following the storm, Reverend Hewlett looked out from the pulpit at his battered congregation. There were black eyes and broken arms from the wind, and the women with husbands stationed overseas were exhausted from cleaning up their own yards and their elderly neighbors' besides. It was a good town that way. These people believed in things. Eloise Miller, unhurt and pink, slept in her mother's arms through the service. A green bonnet framed her face.

Hewlett, under his robe, was thin. He'd lost five pounds that week. His stomach felt empty even when it was full, so why bother to fill it?

Stanley Tack held hands with the Beedleman girl. For the first time, he joined the hymns. He opened the book of prayer.

Stella Blunt looked pale and tired. Hewlett tried to catch her eye. He felt he owed her at least a look, one she'd be able to interpret later, tomorrow morning, or whenever it was that the citizens of Little Fork would find the parsonage deserted.

If he owed anything to Stanley Tack, he'd already given it. Hadn't he handed the man his own faith? It was in safer hands now than his own.

He said, "Let us read from Paul's letter to the Romans: *Whom he did predestinate, them he also called: and whom he called, them he also justified: and whom he justified, them he also glorified.*"

He said, "Let us lift up our hearts."

OTHER BRANDS OF POISON
(FIRST LEGEND)

$\mathcal{W}$hether or not there were, at that moment, Jews hiding in the house at the lake, no one can now remember. The point is that there had been, and there would be again; and even if there was not now a human ballast holding that house to the shore, surely there were other things as incriminating. Likewise, it is unclear from this far in the future if the soldiers were even German, or if they were the Russian liberators who so soon became the Russian occupiers. That summer, in that part of Hungary, both were equally likely.

The soldiers pounded at the door looking for whatever it is nineteen-year-old boys in uniform are always looking for: food, lodging, sex, warmth, inebriation, water. In other words: the closest subconscious approximation of their mothers.

They found at this particular house an eight-year-old boy, and a woman too formidable to rape. They found kohlrabi soup and ate it, and they found the boy's swing set, a four-legged frame standing right in the water, with a swing to jump from and a slide that ended beneath the surface. They left their clothes on the shore and swung from the top bar and broke the whole thing. If no one has exhumed its bones, it is still at the bottom of Lake Balaton. When night fell and there was insufficient firewood, they tore books apart and threw those on the fire. They demanded socks. The woman said, "Would you prefer a lady's size or a small boy's?"

That boy stood half-inside a kitchen cabinet, his fingers curled around the handle, his heel kicking the canned fruit he hoped they wouldn't take. If the story is hazy, seventy years later, that is because it is his. If the details are strangely specific—the dialogue, the type of soup—that is because they are mine.

By the time their flasks ran out, the soldiers were drunk enough to insist on more alcohol, but the woman told them she herself was out and her son did not drink. They began a Russian drinking song, or perhaps a German one, depending on your version of the story.

One undisputed fact: They saw on the kitchen table the large bottle of black ink that had been the boy's birthday present—a rare gift, dearly bought—and the drunkest soldier announced he had found the alcohol.

The woman told the truth. "That is ink," she said, "you idiots." But the soldier opened the top, got an astringent whiff, and declared her a liar and a slut. With his friends pounding the table, he guzzled the entire bottle, and then—friends laughing, pointing, demanding a camera—sputtered black and coughed black and wiped black ink down his arms.

The woman said, "I am a writer. I have plenty more such drinks for you upstairs. Perhaps you'd like a typewriter ribbon."

The soldier cursed her with black teeth and tongue and lips, his face an abyss. He was already ashen as he stumbled to the door.

My grandmother claimed for the rest of her life that she once killed a soldier with a bottle of ink. Is it possible he did more than empty his stomach in the bushes? I could ask a doctor the effects of eight ounces of cheap ink on top of alcohol and months of hard living.

But if this were your family legacy—this ridiculous assertion of the might and violence of ink, this blatant and beautiful falsehood—could you change it? Would you dare?

THE BRIEFCASE

$\mathcal{H}$e thought how strange that a political prisoner, marched through town in a line, chained to the man behind and chained to the man ahead, should take comfort in the fact that all this had happened before. He thought of other chains of men on other islands of the earth, and he thought how since there have been men, there have been prisoners. He thought of mankind as a line of miserable monkeys chained at the wrist, dragging each other back into the ground.

In the early morning of December 1 the sun was finally warming them all, enough that they could walk faster. With his left hand, he adjusted the loop of steel that cuffed his right hand to the line of doomed men. He was starved, his wrist was thin, his body was cold: The cuff slipped off. In one breath he looked back to the man behind him and forward to the man limping ahead, and knew that neither saw his naked, red wrist; each saw only his own mother weeping in a kitchen, his own love on a bed in white sheets and sunlight.

He walked in step to the end of the block.

Before the war this man had been a chef, and his one crime was feeding the people who sat at his tables in clouds of smoke and talked politics. He served them the wine that fueled their underground newspaper, their aborted revolution. And after the night his restaurant disappeared in fire, he had run and hidden and gone

without food—he who had roasted ducks until the meat jumped
from the bone, he who had evaporated three bottles of wine into
one pot of cream soup, he who had peeled the skin from small
pumpkins with a twist of his hand.

And here was his hand, twisted free of the chain, and here he
was running and crawling, until he was through a doorway. It was
a building of empty classrooms—part of the university he never
attended. He watched out the bottom corner of a second-story window as the young soldiers stopped the line, counted ninety-nine
men, shouted to each other, shouted at the prisoners in the panicked voices of children who barely filled the shoulders of their uniforms. One soldier, a bigger one, a louder one, stopped a man
walking by, a man in a suit, with a briefcase, a beard. Some sort of
professor. The soldiers stripped him of his coat, his shirt, his leather
case, cuffed him to the chain. They marched again. And as soon as
they had passed—no, not that soon; many minutes later, when he
had the stomach—the chef ran down to the street and collected the
man's briefcase, coat, and shirt.

In the alley, the chef crouched and buttoned the professor's shirt
over his own ribs. When he opened the briefcase, papers flew out, a
thousand doves flailing against the walls of the alley. The chef ran
after them, stopped them with his feet and arms, herded them back
into the case—pages of numbers, of arrows and notes and hand-
drawn star maps. Here were business cards: a professor of physics.
Envelopes showed his name and address—information that might
have been useful in some other lifetime, one in which the chef could
ring the bell of this man's house and explain to his wife about empty
chains, empty wrists, empty classrooms. And here was a note from
that wife about the sandwich she had packed him. There was no
sandwich left. Here were graded papers, a fall syllabus, the typed

draft of an exam. The extra question at the end, a strange one: "Using modern astronomical data, construct, to the best of your ability, a proof that the sun actually revolves around the earth."

The chef knew nothing of physics. He understood chemistry only insofar as it related to the baking times of bread at various elevations. His knowledge of biology was limited to the deboning of chickens and the behavior of yeast. What did he know of moving bodies and gravity? He knew this: He had moved from his line of men, creating a vacuum—one that had sucked the professor in.

The chef sat on his bed in the widow K———'s basement and felt, in the cool leather of the briefcase, a second vacuum: Here was a vacated life. Here were salary receipts, travel records, train tickets, a small address book. And these belonged to a man whose name was not blackened like his own, a man who was not hunted. If he wanted to live through the next year, the chef would have to learn this life and fill it—and oddly, this felt not like a robbery but like an apology, a way to put the world back in balance. The professor would not die, because he himself would become the professor, and he would live.

Surely he could not teach at the university; surely he could not slip into the man's bed unnoticed. But what was in this leather case, it seemed, had been left for him to use. These addresses of friends, this card of identification, this riddle about the inversion of the universe.

Five cities east, he gave his name as the professor's, and grew out his beard so it would match the photograph on the card he now carried in his pocket. The two men no longer looked entirely dissimilar. To the first name in the address book, the chef had addressed a typed letter: "Am in trouble and have fled the city. Tell my dear wife I am unharmed, but for her safety do not tell her where I am. If you are able to help a poor old man, send money to the following postbox.... I hope to remain your friend, Professor T————."

He'd had to write this about the wife—how could he ask these men for money if she held a funeral? And what of it, if she kept her happiness another few months, another year?

The next twenty-six letters were similar in nature, and money arrived now in brown envelopes and white ones. The bills came wrapped in notes (Was his life in danger? Did he have his health?), and with the money he paid another widow for another basement, and he bought weak cigarettes. He sat on café chairs and drew diagrams of the universe, showed stars and planets looping each other in light. He felt that if he used the other papers in the briefcase, he must also make use of the question. Or perhaps he felt that if he could answer it, he could put the universe back together. And, too, it was something to fill his empty days.

He wrote in his small notebook: "The light of my cigarette is a fire like the sun. From where I sit, all the universe is equidistant from my cigarette. Ergo, my cigarette is the center of the universe. My cigarette is on earth. Ergo, the earth is the center of the universe. If all heavenly bodies move, they must therefore move in relation to the earth, and in relation to my cigarette."

His hand ached. These words were the most he had written since school, which had ended for him at age sixteen. He had been a smart boy, even talented in languages and mathematics, but his mother had needed him to make a living. He was not blessed, like the professor, with years of scholarship and quiet offices and leather books. He was blessed instead with chicken stocks and herbs and sherry. Thirty years had passed since his last day of school, and his hand was accustomed now to wooden spoon, mandoline, paring knife, rolling pin.

Today his hands smelled of ink, when for thirty years they had smelled of leeks. They were the hands of the professor; ergo, he was the professor.

He had written to friends A through L, and now he saved the rest and wrote instead to students. Here in the briefcase's outermost pocket were class rosters from the past two years, and letters addressed to those young men care of the university were bound to reach them. The amounts they sent were smaller, the notes that accompanied them more inquisitive: What, exactly, had transpired? Could they come to meet him?

The postbox was in a different city than the one where he stayed. He arrived at the post office just before closing, and came only every two or three weeks. He always looked through the window first to check that the lobby was empty. If it was not, he would leave and return another day. Surely one of these days, a friend of the professor would be waiting there for him. He prepared a story, that he was the honored professor's assistant, that he could not reveal the man's location but would certainly pass on your kindest regards, sir.

If the earth moved, all it would take for a man to travel its circumference would be a strong balloon. Rise twenty feet above, and wait for the earth to turn under you; you would be home again in a day. But this was not true, and a man could not escape his spot on the earth but to run along the surface. Ergo, the earth was still. Ergo, the sun was the moving body of the two.

No, he did not believe it. He wanted only to know who this professor was, this man who would teach his students the laws of the universe, then ask them to prove as true what was false.

On the wall of the café: plate-sized canvas, delicate oils of an apple, half-peeled. Signed, below, by a girl he had known in school.

The price was more than a month of groceries, and so he did not buy it, but for weeks he read his news under the apple and drank his coffee. Staining his fingers in cheap black ink were the signal fires of the world, the distress sirens, the dispatches from the trenches and hospitals and abattoirs of the war—but here, on the wall, a sign from another world. He had known this girl as well as any other: had spoken with her every day, but had not made love to her; had gone to her vacation home one winter holiday, but knew nothing of her life since then. And now, a clue, perfect and round and unfathomable. After all this time: apple.

Once he finished the news, he worked at the professor's proof and saw in the coil of green-edged apple skin some model of spiraling, of expansion. The stars were at one time part of the earth, until the hand of God peeled them away, leaving us in the dark. They do not revolve around us: They escape in widening circles. The Milky Way is the edge of this peel.

Outside the café window, a beggar screeched his bow against a defeated violin. A different kind of leather case lay open on the ground, this one collecting the pennies of the more compassionate passers-by. The café owner shooed him away, and the chef sighed in guilty relief that he would not have to pass, on the way out, his double.

After eight months in the new city, the chef stopped buying his newspapers on the street by the café and began instead to read the year-old news the widow gave him for his fires. Here, fourteen months ago: Minister P——— of the Interior predicts war. One day he found that in a box near the widow's furnace were papers three, four, five years old. Pages were missing, edges eaten. He took his fragments of yellowed paper to the café and read the beginnings and ends of opinions and letters. He read reports from what used to be his country's borders.

When he had finished the last of the box, he began to read the widow's history books. The Americas, before Columbus; the oceans, before the British; Rome, before its fall.

History was safer than the news, because there was no question of how it would end.

He took a lover in the city and told her he was a professor of physics. He showed her the stars in the sky and explained that they circled the earth, along with the sun.

That's not true at all, she said. You think I'm just a silly girl.

No, he said and touched her neck, You are the only one who might understand. The universe has been folded inside out.

A full year had passed, and he paid the widow in coins. He wrote to friends M through Z. I have been in hiding for a year, he wrote. Tell my dear wife I have my health. May time and history forgive us all.

A year had passed, but so had many years passed for many men. And after all what was a year, if the earth did not circle the sun?

The earth does not circle the sun, he wrote. Ergo: The years do not pass. The earth, being stationary, does not erase the past nor escape toward the future. Rather, the years pile on like blankets, existing at once. The year is 1848; the year is 1789; the year is 1956.

If the earth hangs still in space, does it spin? If the earth spins, the space I occupy I will therefore vacate in an instant. This city will leave its spot, and the city to the west will usurp its place. Ergo, this city is all cities. This is Kabul; this is Dresden; this is Johannesburg.

I run by standing still.

At the post office, he collects his envelopes of money. He has learned from the notes of concerned colleagues and students and friends that the professor suffered from infections of the inner ear that often threw off his balance. He has learned of the professor's wife, A———, whose father died the year they married. He has learned that he has a young son. Rather, the professor has a son.

At each visit to the post office, he fears he will forget the combination. It is an old lock, and complicated: F1, clockwise to B3, back to A6, forward again to J3. He must shake the latch before it opens. More than forgetting, perhaps what he fears is that he will be denied access—that the little box will one day recognize him behind his thick and convincing beard, will decide he has no right of entry.

One night, asleep with his head on his lover's leg, he dreams that a letter has arrived from the professor himself. They freed me at the end of the march, it says, and I crawled my way home. My hands are bloody and my knees are worn through, and I want my briefcase.

In his dream, the chef takes the case and runs west—because if the professor takes it back, there will be no name left for the chef, no place on the earth. The moment his fingers leave the leather loop of the handle, he will fall off the planet.

He sits in a wooden chair on the lawn behind the widow's house. Inside, he hears her washing dishes. In exchange for the room, he cooks all her meals. It is April, and the cold makes the hairs rise from his arms, but the sun warms the arm beneath them. He thinks, The tragedy of a moving sun is that it leaves us each day. Hence the desperate Aztec sacrifices, the ancient rites of the eclipse. If the sun so willingly leaves us, each morning it returns is a stay of execution, an undeserved gift.

Whereas: If it is we who turn, how can we so flagrantly leave behind that which has warmed us and given us light? If we are moving, then each turn is a turn away. Each revolution a revolt.

———

The money arrives less often, and even old friends who used to write monthly now send only rare, apologetic notes, a few small bills. Things are more difficult now, their letters say. No one understood when he first ran away, but now it is clear: After they finished with the artists, the journalists, the fighters, they came for the professors. How wise he was, to leave when he did. Some letters return unopened, with a black stamp.

Life is harder here, too. Half the shops are closed. His lover has left him. The little café is filled with soldiers. The beggar with the violin has disappeared, and the chef fears him dead.

One afternoon, he enters the post office two minutes before closing. The lobby is empty but for the postman and his broom.

The mailbox is empty as well, and he turns to leave but hears the voice of the postman behind him. You are the good Professor T———, no? I have something for you in the back.

Yes, he says, I am the professor. And it feels as if this is true, and he will have no guilt over the professor's signature when the box is brought out. He is even wearing the professor's shirt, as loose again over his hungry ribs as it was the day he slipped it on in the alley.

From behind the counter, the postman brings no box, but a woman in a long gray dress, a white handkerchief in her fingers.

She moves toward him, looks at his hands and his shoes and his face. Forgive me for coming, she says, and the postman pulls the cover down over his window and vanishes. She says, No one would tell me anything, only that my husband had his health. And then a student gave me the number of the box and the name of the city.

He begins to say, You are the widow. But why would he say this? What proof is there that the professor is dead? Only that it must be, that it follows logically.

She says, I don't understand what has happened.

He begins to say, I am the good professor's assistant, madam—but then what next? She will ask questions he has no way to answer.

I don't understand, she says again.

All he can say is, This is his shirt. He holds out an arm so she can see the gaping sleeve.

She says, What have you done with him? She has a calm voice and wet brown eyes. He feels he has seen her before, in the streets of the old city. Perhaps he served her a meal, a bottle of wine. Perhaps, in another lifetime, she was the center of his universe.

This is his beard, he says.

She begins to cry into the handkerchief. She says, Then he is dead. He sees now from the quiet of her voice that she must have known this long ago. She has come here only to confirm.

He feels the floor of the post office move beneath him, and he tries to turn his eyes from her, to ground his gaze in something solid: postbox, ceiling tile, door. He finds he cannot look away. She is a force of gravity in her long gray dress.

No, he says. No, no, no, no, no, I am right here.

Of course he does not believe it, but he knows that if he had time, he could prove it. And he must, because he is the only piece of the professor left alive. The woman does not see how she is murdering her husband, right here in the post office lobby. He whispers to her: Let me go home with you. I'll be a father to your son, and I'll warm your bed, and I'll keep you safe.

He wraps his hands around her small, cold wrists, but she pulls loose. She might be the most beautiful woman he has ever seen.

As if from miles away, he hears her call to the postmaster to send for the police.

His head is light, and he thinks he might float away from the post office forever. It is an act of will not to fly off, but to hold tight to the earth and wait. If the police aren't too busy to come, he feels confident he can prove to them that he is the professor. He has the papers, after all—and in the havoc of war, what else will they have time to look for?

She is backing away from him on steady feet, and he feels it like a peeling off of skin.

If not the police, perhaps he'll convince a city judge. The witnesses who would denounce him are mostly gone or killed, and the others would fear to come before the law.

If the city judge will not listen, he can prove it to the high court. One day he might convince the professor's own child. He feels certain that somewhere down the line, someone will believe him.

PETER TORRELLI, FALLING APART

When Carlos asked why I would risk my whole career for Peter Torrelli, I told him he had to understand that in those last three years of high school, Peter and I were the only two gay boys in Chicago. Because I really believed it, back then, and twenty-five years of experience proving otherwise was nothing in the face of that original muscle memory: me and Peter side by side on the hard pew during chapel, not listening, washed blind by the sun from the high windows, breathing in sync. It didn't matter that we weren't close anymore, I told Carlos. The point was, he'd been my first love. I'd never actually loved him, but still, listen, believe me, there's another kind of first love.

It was during one of those long lectures or concerts or assemblies that Peter and I had discovered our common neurosis: the fear of magically switching bodies with the speaker or singer or priest and then having to improvise an exit. I would slide toward Peter on the pew, open a hymnal, and above "A Mighty Fortress Is Our God" scribble in pencil: "Tuba player?" Peter would look up to the stage to watch the fat sophomore from Winnetka puff his cheeks like a blowfish and write back: "Stop playing—no one misses a tuba." "1st Violin?" I wrote. "Feign a swoon," he'd write back. And then he'd mouth it to me, relishing the "oooo" of "swoon." We joked about this fear, but really I think it bothered us both—this idea that we might suddenly be thrust in front of our peers and examined. It doesn't take a psychotherapist to figure out why. Peter later claimed the whole reason he became an actor was that the only way he could enjoy a show was from the inside.

Everyone else knew it was his looks. I hadn't understood until we were sixteen what it meant to turn heads. I'd considered it a figurative expression. But when we stood in line for pizza slices, or walked down Dearborn toward the bus, he was a human magnet. He was the North Pole. The girls at school would feel his sweater and tug his necktie. He said he had a girlfriend back east, that she was Miss Teenage Delaware, and everyone believed it. How could he *not* be onstage with that dark, sad face, that ocean of black hair, those sarcastic eyes? By the time we graduated, he'd done two seasons of professional summer stock. I was the varsity soccer goalie, and he was a movie star walking among us. When we sat together in chapel we looked like the kings of the school, and nobody knew any different.

And then the next day we were thirty-six years old, and Peter fell to pieces. During a matinee of *Richard III*, right in the middle, my friend abruptly and forever lost the ability to act. He said later it was something about the phrase "jolly thriving wooer," the strangeness of those words as they left his mouth, the pause a second too long before Ratcliffe entered. Since Peter told me all this, I've read the page ten times in my Signet Classic—which is how I know that Peter's next line, as Richard, was "Good or bad news, that thou com'st in so bluntly?" It was a line he'd have made lewd jokes about backstage. "And I said it," he told me. "But it came out in this *voice*, like all the costumes had fallen away, like I was some kid in eighth-grade English and I had to read my poem out loud. It was just *me*, and there was no character, no play, just these words I had to say. You know our whole thing about leapfrogging into someone else's body? It was like that, but like I suddenly leapfrogged into myself." He said he could see each face in the audience, every one of them at once, smell what they ate for lunch. He could feel every pore of his own skin, and the ridiculous hump strapped to his back. Backstage, they knew something was wrong even before he started to shake. By the end of the next scene, the understudy was dressing.

Peter told me this the next week over lunch. Actually, he told me many times, over many lunches in the following year, as if through the retelling he could undo something. We met every other Thursday at the Berghoff, where he'd have root beer and I'd have two pale ales and we'd both eat enormous plates of bratwurst and chicken schnitzel and noodles with butter sauce. We had set these lunches up two years earlier, quite formally. We'd been in and out of touch for ages when we found ourselves alone on the living room futon of a boring party in Hyde Park, drunk, wondering aloud if knowing each other when we had acne was the reason we'd never dated as adults. We had kissed just once, sophomore year, after a SADD meeting when we stayed behind to pick up the leftover fliers. I didn't know he was gay. I hardly knew *I* was. He came over with the green fliers in a stack as if to hand them to me, but when I took hold of the papers he pulled them back and me with them. The only person I'd ever kissed before was a girl named Julie Gleason. Afterward he said, "You're pretty dense, aren't you?" That was it. We didn't talk for two weeks, and then we were best friends again, before the paper cuts on my palm had even fully healed.

I had looked at him that night at the party—beautiful and grown-up, a beer bottle sweating against the leg of his jeans—and said, "I never see you anymore."

"Yes, I'm slowly becoming invisible." Peter was the kind of guy who would try for any joke, any chance to flash his perfect teeth. Even when it wasn't funny, you had to appreciate the showmanship. And then he looked at me seriously, which was rare at the time. "We *should* get together and talk. I mean regularly, because I miss you. It would be like therapy." I should have known I would always be the therapist. I told him once that he was the Gatsby to my Nick Carraway. He said, "Yes, but I throw *much* wilder parties."

And like stupid little Nick, I ended up trying to fix things. If I hadn't spent American Lit distracted by Zach Moretti and his amazing forearms, I might have registered that these stories never end well.

Let me say, Peter had been brilliant. Chicago breeds its own stage stars, who stay local even if they're good enough to go to New York, and he was one of them. When I saw his Hamlet at Chicago Shakespeare, all memories of Mel and Lord Larry vanished in a celluloid fog. He was the right age, the right build, and those eyes could turn like lighting from irony to terror. I wonder how that colored our friendship, that I saw him simultaneously as both Peter and Hamlet. If nothing else, it made me more tolerant of his ramblings.

After the day he froze ("The Day of Which We Shall Not Speak," he called it whenever he spoke of it, which was constantly), he took sick leave for a week, then tried again. If anything, he was worse. He quit before they could fire him, and spent the next two months looking for work. He walked into each audition knowing everyone in the room had heard about his big dry-up. His agent dropped him, and so did his boyfriend.

A few months later, Peter moved near Milwaukee and took a job doing dinner theater, and our lunches became less frequent. In late November 2005, almost a year after The Day of Which We Tended to Speak Obsessively, we sat by a window in the Berghoff and watched the year's first snow collect in the street. He told me about his new role as Bob Cratchit in something called *Let's Sing a Christmas Carol!* The director wanted British accents from everyone. Peter could do a perfect one, of course, but not without sinking further into the hollow cadences, the glazed eyes, the strangling sense of the ridiculous.

"Most of them sound southern, it's terrible," he said. He was on caffeine today or something worse. He was literally bouncing on the springy seat of the booth. "The eleven o'clock number is, I shit you not, called 'God Bless Us Every One.' Jesus Christ, you should hear it, it sounds like Scrooge drops by Tara for pecan pie." Every time I saw him he talked faster, as if he were running out of time. He still flashed the smile, but perfunctorily, as if displaying his incisors for the dentist.

When our food came, he finally asked me a question so he could stop talking and eat his schnitzel. "How's life in phone-a-thon land? Are you giving away thousands of tote bags?"

I was the special events coordinator for Chicago Public Radio, and for several years before we officially reconnected, Peter and I would run into each other in the restaurants of the monstrous tourist trap on Navy Pier where Chicago Shakespeare and WBEZ both live. Once, after we'd drifted apart for a few months, our lunch parties at Riva joined together, and when someone introduced us and said we might hit it off, we started laughing so hard Peter dropped his wineglass.

"We're doing better than last year," I answered.

"I've been telling everyone in the Land of Moo about the Republicans trying to shut you down. I'm going to assemble an army of cheeseheads for your defense."

"Thanks, Peter. That's thoughtful."

He started mixing all the food on his plate: schnitzel, potato, creamed spinach, kraut.

"So, what about trying my shrink?" I said. "She's good. I wouldn't lie to you."

The old Peter would have cued up his German psychiatrist impersonation, drawing the attention of everyone around, but the new Peter just stared at his mixed-up food. "She might be good, but how far is she from Kenosha, Wisconsin, the epicenter of the theatrical world?"

"She's here in the Loop, and that would be good for you."

He agreed to call her and then told me about his great-uncle, who, after undergoing electroshock, became obsessed with licking copper objects. I wanted him to ask about me, to ask about Carlos, who was moving out of my apartment in gradual increments and breaking my heart in painful slow motion, leaving me for the jazz singer we used to go see every few weekends at the Back Room until I finally realized the guy's bedroom eyes were directed not at the whole room but at the seat next to mine in particular. I'd have to find someone else to complain to.

"Listen, though," said Peter, "I'm on the mend. If I had more serious roles again, that might do it. I mean, I was never a comedian, and that's what they're asking me to do."

As much as I didn't believe his optimism, I was glad he wasn't giving up. I constantly pictured him hanging himself from the closet rod of his cold little apartment, or drinking something medieval and poisonous. Maybe I'd just watched his Romeo too many times.

"I've got an offer for you," I said. I'd thought about it in the car on the way there, and decided I couldn't ask him. I decided it several times, in fact, but now here it was, coming out of my mouth. "I want you to do some work for me." He nodded, eyes wide, as he mashed his food and listened to me explain the project: In cooperation with the Art Institute, we'd commissioned twenty local poets and authors to write short works relating to the museum's crown jewels— a mystery writer casting Van Gogh's *Bedroom at Arles* as a crime scene, a Pulitzer-winning poet extolling Picasso's man with the blue guitar in sonnet. Richmond Barthé's sculpture *The Boxer* got a prose poem that shattered my heart, one I wanted to frame and wear around my neck. The writing would hang beside the art, and my job was to find actors to read a few of the pieces aloud at the gala opening and then record them all for NPR and for the museum audio tour that people could rent with headphones. My brilliant idea had launched a yearlong nightmare of collaboration with a hateful little man I'd come to call Institute Steve, the only unlovely person on the entire museum staff. "It's December thirtieth, if your show is done. The thing is," I said, grabbing for the only available out, "the other actors might be people you knew."

"People I *know*, Drew." His face stilled itself long enough to shoot me one of his complicated, devastating looks: part annoyance, part sarcasm, part glee that he'd caught me saying what I really thought. "I'll do it, if you don't think I'd embarrass you."

And so the die was cast.

He walked out with Dr. Zeller's business card in his pocket and both of our leftovers in Styrofoam boxes. He was eating plenty despite his meager paycheck because he got free food at the dinner theater, but every night he had to choose between chicken à la king and Lake Superior whitefish.

I stayed behind to pay the bill, and as I waited for the busboy to come back I pressed my cheek to the dirty, cold glass of the window beside me. I felt like I needed to wake myself up. I had just risked my career on his ability to be Peter again, to jump back into himself, and I strongly doubted he could do it.

The next time we met for dinner was before the Art Institute event. I had more important things to do, but I'd been in earlier to see that my interns were on task, and I wanted to make sure Peter was ready and calm. The Berghoff was right around the corner, and I knew neither of us would get a chance to eat the shrimp and strawberries at the reception. He'd been down two weeks earlier to record at the studio, and I'd been relieved how good he was, at least without an audience. I'd invited him over then for dinner with Carlos, who was still hanging around to see what further damage he could inflict on my psyche, but Peter had an audition in Milwaukee with the Kinnikinnick Players for *Night of January 16th*. He hadn't gotten the part.

Tonight Peter looked skinnier and pale and had a soft stubble he might have been growing for insulation, the way he sat there in his coat and hat, his jaw shaking against the cold. To put it delicately, he looked like a few friends I had in the early 1990s who are not with us anymore. I got the waitress to bring us some tea as soon as we sat down. He held the cup, letting it warm his hands, but didn't drink any. It was all over the news that the Berghoff would be closing in a couple of months. We'd stood outside in the cold for forty minutes just to get a table. People around us were taking pictures, touching the menus as if they were the faces of dying lovers.

"I went to your shrink," he said. "Twice. You didn't tell me she was beautiful. Like Juliette Binoche. And we're *very* hopeful." He was warming up enough to lay his woolly hat on the table.

"Great," I said. I couldn't keep from staring at his brow and cheekbones, which stuck out sharply from his face, his skin stretched over them, shiny and translucent. He went on and on about the therapy, about opening himself up to pain, about locating his core. I barely listened.

There's one thing I still remember him saying, though. At one point he put down his fork and he leaned across to me, as if I had all the answers. "I mean, why do I even feel this need to *act*? It's weird, right? We're living in this terrible world with wars and broken hearts and starvation, but some of us are compelled to make art, like that's supposed to help anything. It's a disease, Drew. Don't you remember how it felt, when we were sitting there obsessed with finding ourselves in the orchestra? It was awful. Only you grew out of it, and I didn't. Or maybe I just finally did, last year. Like I was cured and cursed all in one moment. I mean, what if the universe decided it was done using me?"

I shook my head. "I can't imagine you as anything other than an actor."

"Right. Right. I know. But how can it be who I am if it's not what I do?"

We left it rhetorical and continued eating.

"So, how's Carlos?" he asked once we'd ordered dessert.

It was too late in the meal, and he was too far behind on the story. "Not great, but you know," I said, confident he didn't care enough to press further. "He's gotten into jazz lately." To be safe, though, I changed the subject. "So, I had a dream about the Berghoff last night. I was running around downtown, trying to give everyone vitamin shots because of this disease I'd exposed them to. For some reason it was a battle zone, with tanks in the streets, and wild animals. And if people didn't get these shots they were going to die. I had to find everyone I ever slept with and get them to come to the Berghoff to get this shot. So I'm knocking on doors, but people have moved, and by the time I find Carlos he tells me he won't take the shot, he'd rather die. He's lying there in the snow, dying, and he goes, 'You can't save them all, Drew.' And I woke up screaming. I mean, what the hell *is* that?"

"Dreams don't mean anything," he said. "I used to believe they did, but they really don't. Random synapses." As I signed the bill, he dug into his apple tart like someone just rescued from the wilderness, his eyes wide with the wonder of sugar and crust. He chewed so fast it looked like his teeth were chattering. He gestured behind me with a jerk of his eyes, and I turned to look at the next table, pretending to get something out of my jacket pocket. I assumed he meant the teenage girl with a roll of fat hanging over the back of her low jeans. She was with her parents. "What would you do?" he said. His mouth was full of tart.

Sometime after high school, the game had evolved away from musicians and actors, and we (or at least Peter) had begun obsessing about leaping into regular people's lives, about how to fool their families. I was tired of it after twenty years, but this wasn't the day to put him in a bad mood. "Okay. Pretend to get sick so I don't have to go to school, and spend the whole time doing aerobics. I could get fifteen pounds off, at least. Do I get to be myself again after?"

"Presumably."

"Then I finish reading Proust."

Peter took a sip from his root beer bottle, and I noticed his hand shaking. I wondered briefly if it was Parkinson's, if the whole personality shift was that easy to explain—but Peter was such a hypochondriac, he'd have thought of it already. "You're so fucking boring," he said. "I'd run that ass into the street right now and see if I could stop traffic. I'd see how many laws I could break."

"You could do it anyway," I said. "You could run out there and just ruin your life. Nothing stopping you."

He put his napkin on his plate and stood up. "I thought that's what the museum was for."

As we headed through the front doors of the Art Institute, the last regular museum visitors of the night were bundling past the stone lions and out into the cold. "Did you ever read that book when you were a kid?" Peter said as we walked through the emptying halls. "The one where the kids run away and live in the Met?"

"And they bathe in the fountain," I said.

"That's my new plan. I want to camp out under some dinosaur bones and just . . ." He let his sentence trail off, as if the suits of armor we were passing would explain the rest. I imagined them as a hundred failed geniuses, hiding behind the glass, starved down to thin, steel exoskeletons. They knew what he meant.

We stopped at the Chagall windows, stood for a minute in the warmth of their thick blue light, then headed into the special exhibit hall. I left Peter staring at a messy Klee while I talked to Lauren, my boss, who'd hated the idea of this event from the time I brought it up two years before and was waiting for everything to fall apart. Her over-plucked little eyebrows arched up her forehead as she asked me why half the writers weren't there yet. I went to check on the champagne, and once the evening started moving I lost track of Peter among the tablecloths and microphones and whining interns, and finally among the rush of people and coats. Half were Art Institute supporters with vintage bracelets or Frank Lloyd Wright neckties, and half were NPR junkies with professor haircuts. Some might have been both, bless them.

I knew I should have introduced Peter to the other actors, told him where to be, but leaving him alone was my small way of shaking him by the shoulders, of telling him to grow up. When I saw him again, he was talking to one of the actresses he knew from Chicago Shakespeare, a woman who'd just returned from off-Broadway and chopped her hair short. She was laughing at something he'd said, and he was teetering back and forth as if he might at any second lose a lifelong battle with gravity. He was laughing, too, but the way his skin stretched across his jaws, he looked deathly.

I took the microphone and welcomed everyone. My voice could never command a room; people milled and talked and jostled for position. I introduced the five actors, and it wasn't until they came and stood beside me that I noticed Peter still had his puffy green coat on, his hands shoved down in its pockets. I wondered if he was punishing me for leaving him alone, or if he was so thin under there that he didn't want to frighten people. In high school, he would take his shirt off at every opportunity, claiming it was hot out at sixty degrees. I'd assumed back then that his dark skin was from Italian genes, but now I saw it must have been the sun.

The two other men were dressed in sleek sweaters, and the two women wore silk blouses and pants. Audition outfits, like Peter used to have dozens of. He looked now as if we'd grabbed him off the street.

We started with the first painting, Caillebotte's *Paris Street; Rainy Day*, and the short-haired actress read a brief Stuart Dybek story called "Rainy Day Chicago." When she finished, the crowd moved across the gallery to a tiny Picasso, where one of the men read a poem called "Triangle Woman." We'd pulled a miracle, getting the Art Institute to move so many of its own crowd-pleasers into one exhibit. Even so, there were certain works they wouldn't let us use. We'd asked the writers to e-mail us their wish lists, and *Nighthawks* topped almost every one. It must have been something about the loneliness, the coffee, the silence—everyone wanted to lay private claim to that one desolate corner of the universe. In the end, no one got it because it was on loan in New York. How could this one object embody loneliness, I wondered, when people crowded shoulder-to-shoulder around it, shared it, traded it, paraded it? If Hopper's little coffee counter was lonely, it was in the way a prostitute was lonely. Or an actor.

I had a hard time paying attention, and I stood there thinking how flat the readers all were, how little grace they showed compared to Peter in his prime. He played Edgar in *Lear* one summer up in Evanston, in the park by the beach. He was beautiful in a red shirt, and his voice made every line sound like something you'd been on the verge of remembering, if you'd only had time.

Peter's first reading was for my least favorite story, as well as my least favorite painting in the entire museum. A very young, way-too-hip fiction writer from Bucktown named Sam Demarr had e-mailed us that the only painting he felt like writing on was "the one with the giant gum." I'd actually loved it as a child—that enormous pack of gum floating over the city skyline. Now I hated how the gum hovered there, out of proportion. It had nothing to do with the city below it, no shared color palette, the garish green wrapper rendering the brown skyline drab and uniform. On one of our first dates, Carlos and I had stood there joking that it was based on a true story, the Giant Gum Crash of '72. Since then, I'd always thought of the gum as about to land, to flatten the unsuspecting workers below, so I'd found it particularly funny that the story Sam Demarr had submitted was called "The Gum Flew Away." Demarr himself was standing at the side of the room in dirty khakis, smirking into his wineglass.

Peter pulled a tube of papers from his coat pocket and unrolled it so he could read the top one. The other actors held theirs in the black folders we'd sent them in. "First, all the gum flew off," he read, "leaving Chicago in its spearmint dust. Then the department stores floated away." Aside from the fact that his papers were visibly shaking, Peter sounded like himself, strong-voiced and in full command of the English language. This story suited his flat, ironic delivery. I'd chosen it for him specifically because it was monochromatic and free of dialogue. "The hot dog stands were next," I heard him say. For all my daydreaming about finding myself stranded onstage, this was the closest I'd come to feeling as if it were my own energy propelling an actor, as if when I stopped focusing, the whole thing would fall apart. Peter was gesturing around now, with the still-

shaking papers, backing toward the wall and away from the old ladies in the front row. Even his legs were bouncing, and it finally
occurred to me that maybe it was drugs making his limbs and voice
and eyes jump around like that. It didn't seem like something he'd
do, but who was I, anymore, to say what Peter would do?

And then, as he read the line about the mayor launching himself
off the Hancock tower, Peter actually put the back of his hand
against the painting and swept it up the canvas. The gasp from the
crowd was so loud and so high that I couldn't tell where it stopped
and the alarm started. A security guard I'd barely noticed trotted
from the room, and another stepped forward, speaking into a radio.
Peter froze, and I could feel his stomach flip. I could feel the sweat
sticking the papers to his hand. The alarm turned off, and people
started talking quietly.

"And this is why we didn't broadcast live," Lauren whispered
beside me. She was glaring like I'd done it myself. The Institute co-
ordinators talked in a cluster while two more guards and a woman
in a suit rushed in, asking Peter to step aside so they could inspect
the painting for damage.

The crowd just looked embarrassed, touching their faces and
chatting a bit but waiting politely for the reading to resume. Sam
Demarr seemed to find the whole thing hilarious. Peter had stepped
aside, but he was still up there in front of everyone, the only movement coming from his eyes, which jumped around liquidly, looking
for their chance to leap free from his face once and for all. One of
the guards talked with him in what should have been a whisper, but
everyone could hear. He asked for his name, his driver's license,
copied everything down on a big clipboard.

And I thought, maybe that's what I would have done, if I'd leapfrogged up there into Peter's body, if I needed to get away before
anyone realized I was a fraud: I'd hit the painting and make the

show stop. But I didn't think he'd done it on purpose. Or at least not consciously.

It was a good five minutes before the woman in the suit stepped away from the painting and signaled that we could continue. She stayed there, though, in the corner of the room, frowning. I assumed she'd have a long night of paperwork now. I felt bad for her.

I took the mike again and said, with a big fund-raising grin, "Now you've seen what fine security your contributions support!" Lauren was at the front of the crowd, shaking her head to show how disappointed she was, as if I hadn't gotten the message yet. "We're going to try that one again." I waited for a meek laugh from the audience and then turned to the actors. Peter looked at me with those blank, jumpy eyes like he didn't even recognize me, like I was just another blurred member of his audience, watching and breathing and waiting for him to fail. I'm still not sure what I felt, standing there. Maybe I felt my heart break, or maybe I felt Peter's heart break. When you've known someone that long, when you formed yourself around his personality back when you were just a fourteen-year-old lump of clay, isn't it really the same thing? Aren't his heart and your own somehow conjoined? Perhaps that's what I could never explain to Carlos: Ours was a kind of first love that wasn't aimed at each other, but somehow out at the world. We We were forever side by side on the chapel bench, watching the show.

Peter whispered something to the short-haired actress and handed her his papers. He held up his open hands to the audience in apology, ten pale, bony fingers, then walked around the people and out of the exhibit.

"The Gum Flew Away," the woman read, the clarity of her voice a reassurance, a wiping clean. "By Sam Demarr. First, all the gum

flew off, leaving Chicago in its spearmint dust. Then the department stores floated away."

I thought of following Peter out. I'd done it so many times before, chasing him down as he stormed from a party, calling his
name five times until he finally turned to look at me, tear-streaked
or red-faced on the wet sidewalk. "He didn't mean it," I'd usually
say, or "You're just drunk," or "We all love you." I never said that *I*
did. Just all of us, meaning everyone at the party, everyone he'd ever
met, everyone who'd ever seen him from across the street. It wasn't
true anymore; the world didn't love him, just I did, and I had the
feeling that even if I could say that, it wouldn't be enough. And if it
were, then what? What would I do with that responsibility? And
now Lauren, who was still my boss if I was lucky, was finally shooting me a look of conspiratorial relief. "*Actors*," said her face. "I
know," said mine.

It hit me like cold water that I wouldn't see Peter again, that he'd
avoid my calls until he drifted to another city to try again and fail.
Someone would hire him at a third-tier regional theater on the basis
of his résumé, and he'd last one show, if that. He probably wouldn't
know how to give up.

After the readings, I propped myself up at the microphone and
said my bit about membership and shortening the pledge drive with
early donations, and Institute Steve said something I couldn't follow in his nasal little whine, and I got a drink in my hand. It was cold
enough outside that I wanted to drink just so I wouldn't feel the
bone chill on the way home. I chatted up as many people as I could
stomach over the wine and shrimp. People didn't want to talk to me,
though. What they wanted was to meet the actors. "I saw you in
Phèdre at the Court," a woman said to one of the actresses, who
smiled graciously. "It was just gorgeous. You wore that red dress.
Tell me your name again."

Another woman asked the actor who'd read the Stuart Dybek piece to sign her program. She didn't seem to notice Dybek himself standing a few feet away, laughing with a friend and wiping his glasses on his tie. If the actor found the request strange he didn't show it, signing his name on the margin of the paper. Peter would have written something like "Peter Torrelli is *fabulous*. Love and kisses, Pablo P." Or the old Peter would have, the one who knew magic.

I felt the wine go to my head, and I felt relief that the whole thing was over. I drank more to shut out the suspicion that I was glad Peter had left. I got through the next hour and walked out into the cold, relieved to be drunk and half-expecting to find Peter there on the sidewalk, eighteen years old and scribbling in ballpoint pen on the knee of his khakis. He was gone, and there were just people waiting for buses and people waiting for taxis, everybody waiting to leave.

It was like that after our kiss sophomore year, the way I'd stood frozen thirty seconds and then ran after him into the cold night, one of my duck boots untied, my left palm bleeding in parallel paper-cut stripes. He was gone, and I stayed under the school's archway entrance looking for his breath in the air, thinking it would tell me which way he'd gone. I thought, If he ran back inside I'll follow him, and I'll kiss him again. If he got a cab, there's nothing I can do.

He *had* found a cab that night, as he probably had now. Or maybe he'd slouched all the way down Adams, his parka blurring him into the frozen crowd, the crowd sweeping him onto the train, the train shooting him up north and off the face of my earth.

This is the way it happens: First, my friend floats away, leaving Chicago in his dust. Then he leaves me—no breath above the concrete, no voice in the air to catch and hold. Then the Berghoff closes, and the radio stations all shut down. The school chapel folds its benches and windows and flies away. The frozen sidewalks peel up like strips of gum. The skyscrapers drift like icebergs into the lake, up the Saint Lawrence and out to sea. The citizens grab for things to rescue, but everything's too cold to touch. Mayor Daley holds a press conference. "We can't save it all," he says.

In a month, they've all forgotten. Standing in the empty streets of their empty city, the people look up and say to no one in particular, "Something used to be here, something beautiful and towering that overshadowed us all, and it seemed so important at the time. And now look: I can't even remember its name."

COUPLE OF LOVERS ON
A RED BACKGROUND

I've been calling him Bach so far, at least in my head, but now that he's started wearing my ex-husband's clothes and learned to work the coffeemaker, I feel it's time to call him Johann. I said it out loud once, when I needed to get him off the couch before the super came up, but I'm not sure I pronounced it right, *Germanic* enough, because he didn't respond—though I'm not sure I'd recognize *my* name, either, in the midst of someone screaming a foreign language. He got off the couch and went to the vacuum closet only because I practically carried him. No easy task, pushing someone so big and sweaty, even with the weight he's lost since he got here. I'd take him out for some real German food, but if there's one thing I've learned from the movies about caring for transplanted historical people, it's never to take them out in public among the taxis and police and department store mannequins.

I've kept the curtains closed and the TV unplugged, but I did introduce him to the stereo so he'd have something to do every day while I'm gone. I'm proud of how carefully I did it: First, I dug my angel music box out of the Christmas decorations and played it for him. He seemed familiar with the concept, so I pointed back and forth between the angel box and the CD player, then put on some Handel. He was pleased, not at all scared, and now he's pushing buttons and changing discs like he was raised on Sony. At first I only let him have Baroque, but recently we've been moving up in history. He's fond of Mozart, unsurprisingly, but for some reason

Tchaikovsky makes him giggle. When I played him "Dance of the Sugar Plum Fairy," I thought he was going to wet the couch. Five minutes later he went to the piano and played the main part from memory, busted out laughing at certain phrases. If such a thing is possible, he played it *sarcastically*. He has a laugh, incidentally, like you'd expect from a pot-smoking thirteen-year-old, whispered and high-pitched. At first, when I thought I was making this all up, I wondered if I'd borrowed that bit from Tom Hulce in *Amadeus*. But on the phone the other day, my mother said, "Who's that laughing over there?" At least she thinks I'm dating again.

He doesn't seem to remember living in the piano. He never lifts the lid to look inside, which I would certainly do if I'd lived there ten days. The morning he came, I was in my sweats playing his Minuet in G—the one you know if you ever took lessons, the first "real" piece you learned by a serious composer: DA-da-da-da-da-DA-da-da. I was remembering that the day I learned to play it was the same day my father, the journalist who wished he were an opera baritone, first took interest in my lessons. I was seven. He would stand behind me and beat time on his palm. He even made up a little song for it, when I wasn't getting the rhythm right: "THIS is the way that BACH wrote it, THIS is the way that BACH wrote it, THIS is the merry, THIS is the merry, THIS is the merry tune!" I'd keep playing even though it panicked me, and I'd think of the picture from my cartoon book about Beethoven, the one where his father stood behind the piano with dollar signs in his eyes. I wasn't gifted enough that my father was thinking of money. Maybe he wanted me to entertain at his dinner parties, or just to be better than he was. Treble clefs in his eyes.

I was remembering all this, playing the Minuet in G pretty damn well despite a few glasses of wine, when I started to feel like something was stuck in my throat. Since my hands were busy playing, I didn't cover my mouth—just turned my head to the side and coughed something up. I think I passed out then, although I don't remember waking. There's a bit of time I can't account for. I remember being in the kitchen later. I remember making tea.

The next day I heard scratching inside the piano and figured I had mice again. I didn't want to open the lid and poke them out with the end of a mop. I didn't want them running panicked across the carpet, their terror feeding mine.

The piano's an old upright, a cheap Yamaha that Larry, my ex, bought used right out of college, before he even bought a couch. Well, not my ex yet—my almost-ex. My ex-in-progress. I thought, If mice eat out the insides, it's not the worst thing. An excuse to get something nicer.

The scratching kept on for almost a week, and every time I hit a note something would scurry around, hit against the strings. I stopped playing the piano. One morning I was sitting at my little glass table eating breakfast, getting my papers ready for the condo I was going to show, and the lid of the piano lifted up. I'm not a big screamer. In fight-or-flight situations, I tend to pick option C: freeze. I just sat there paralyzed, and out climbed what I can only describe as a small troll. It was about a foot tall, and it moved so fast I didn't even notice its clothes or hair. It ran smack into the side of the couch, then out to the middle of the floor, where it scampered in smaller and smaller circles. I held my papers in front of my legs like a shield, chased it into the vacuum closet, and shut the door. Assuming it was a hallucination—what else would I think?—I tried to put it out of my mind because I had twenty minutes to find a cab, get across the city, and tell the Lindquists why they should invest their eight hundred thousand in a walkup with non-perpendicular hallways. I told myself I *had* to go because I was about two failures away from fired. It's possible that I also wanted an excuse to get the hell out of there.

"It's a beauty," I told the Lindquists. "Very raw. And so close to street level! It's almost earthy!" But Mrs. Lindquist tapped her pink nails on the mantel and said that it didn't feel like home. I was sure everything would be better when I got back and saw the empty vacuum closet. I reminded myself I'd been dehydrated, that I should drink more than just alcohol and coffee. But when I got home I found my guest fully grown, just a little shorter than I am. He'd let himself out of the closet and was sleeping on the couch.

I had no idea who he was at first. His clothes looked ancient, but I'm not good at fashion history. All I could tell was old, grimy, European, too much lace at the cuffs for my taste. He doesn't have a wig as in his pictures, just messy, reddish, greasy hair. But after I stared at him for half an hour, he woke up and walked to the piano and started to play. Just scales at first, like he was getting used to it—and then he launched into a couple of those Inventions that drove me crazy in high school. So I looked up Bach online, and it's definitely him, the exact same fleshy cheeks, the same dark eyes pinched small between thick brows and heavy, sleepless bags.

I decided I should look respectable in the presence of a genius, so I started freshening my face every day in the cab on the way home, not just on the way out. I bought a whole pack of razors at Duane Reade and began shaving my legs again. I tidied the apartment, too. I cleaned out the freezer, all those Ziplocs of Larry's chili, and I finally filled in the missing lightbulbs above the bathroom sink. It was startling to see my face so clearly there—loose skin on my eyelids that caught the green eye shadow in clumps, and my roots growing in gray. I'm only thirty-eight. Johann is supposed to be the one with white hair. I made an appointment for the spa.

I introduced Johann to soap and deodorant, and the other day while I was gone he finally changed his clothes. Now he's wearing Larry's gray flannel shirt and old corduroys. He looks so normal, sometimes I glance up from my magazine and forget it's not just Larry sitting there, drinking his beer.

When I was ten years old, my father started the game You Can't Get Out of the Car Till You've Named This Composer. He'd have hidden the cassette case throughout the drive, and he'd only pose the question as he pulled up to the curb where he was dropping me. I would ignore his conversation for blocks, knowing what was coming and concentrating on my guess. My older brother had a practiced method of shouting the name of every major composer in a rapid, memorized succession, a litany that started with "RavelRachmaninovSaint-SaënsBeethoven" and ended with "BuxtehudeChopinSchoenbergBernstein." I took the more methodical approach, at least establishing a general period before naming my probable suspects. Once, when the answer was Smetana, I sat there until I was half an hour late for swim team. I suppose he'd have been proud of me, identifying Bach so quickly.

Johann, no surprise, is remarkable at naming composers. Every time we put in a new disc, I'll say the name, loud and clear— "*Schu-bert*"—and he'll repeat it. I'm not sure if he can read the CD covers, or if he's used to a more gothic script.

He's been learning English. I suppose this shouldn't surprise me, when I consider that he *is* a great genius, and he has a good ear and so forth. I came home from an open house the other day and he started pointing around the room, doing nouns. "Table," he said. "CD Player." He must get this all from me. I've been talking constantly, the way you would with a baby or a dog, things like, "Now I'm putting the milk in your coffee, mmm, that will taste delicious."

On my way out of the elevator the next morning, my super stopped me, bobbing her head and smiling. "Such piano you play! You are like concert!"

"Practice, practice, practice," I said. And what propelled me out the door and down the street was a mixture of relief that I'm not crazy and panic that there's a real human being up there who's not just going to vaporize. So calling a shrink is out, but calling anyone else is out, too, because they'll *think* I'm crazy. I find myself wishing the Ghostbusters were real.

That night, I started telling Johann about my life. I figured, if I can't take this to a shrink, maybe *he* can be my shrink. All they do anyway is sit and listen. So I made us a nice meal, chicken with cream sauce and rosemary, and opened some Riesling. "Johann," I said, "I understand you had something like twenty children. Babies." I rocked my arms back and forth, and he smiled. "Not to bring up a touchy subject, because I know half of them died, right? Dead?" He looked confused, but just as well. "Back then people dealt with things and moved on. It wasn't some life-halting devastation because it was the *norm*. No one went around wailing, 'Oh, why me, why does God hate me?' And that's how I've always looked at things. So last year our city was attacked. Let's just say they knocked down some castles." I pantomimed it, idiotically, with my arms. "And we're all terrified, and no one can eat, and no one can sleep. Granted. But to Larry, who didn't even lose anyone he knew, it threatens his whole worldview, makes him question his religion. I say, 'So your whole vague, lapsed-Episcopal belief in God was based on those buildings being there? On nothing bad ever happening?' It was like he'd never previously registered that there was evil in the world. This is the man whose clothes you're wearing. *Clothes.* And then Larry says I was more upset when we miscarried last year than when the towers got hit. True, true, but really that was the hormones. Johann, you would not believe how the chemicals can wash over you. Your wives never even had to deal with postpartum, did they? Just got pregnant again and squeezed the next one out."

He nodded, used his bread to sop up sauce, yawned. I don't know if nodding is something he learned from me or if they did that in old Germany. He was looking very American right then, with the haircut I gave him. And his breath has been so much better since he learned to use the electric toothbrush. I assigned him the removable brush head with the blue edging. I have the pink. And he's not that old, really, maybe forty. I looked him up again online to make sure I hadn't altered history, stealing him away like that in the middle of his life, but he still seems to have died at sixty-five. I didn't learn much else new, except that he never liked pianos. Didn't think they'd last.

Which is all to say, he's not bad-looking. It makes you think. Technically he's a married man, but even more technically, his second wife died three hundred years ago. And it's not as if I can go out on dates now and leave him alone, and I can't bring anyone back *here*. Then there's this: He's clearly very fertile, and any child of his would be a musical genius. His sons certainly were, and his daughters might have been, given the chance. Could that be the reason this happened, so I can have his daughter and give her a decent shot at life?

The question, then, is how to seduce an eighteenth-century German. If I just show up in a nightgown, he'll think I'm some kind of harlot.

I did it by introducing jazz. We went chronologically, from my *African Rhythms* CD through Dixieland, and by the time we got through two bottles of wine and up to Coleman Hawkins, he was leaning close, murmuring things in German. I wasn't expecting much. Every month in *Cosmo* they keep announcing some new sex position, as if for years people reproduced like Puritans and we're only now figuring out the pleasure aspect. But Johann, he knows exactly what he's doing.

I try not to talk on the phone in front of him, since he can't understand I'm not talking to *him*. He'll laugh when I laugh, try to stand in front of me, nod when he thinks I'm asking a question.

When I got in the cab the morning after our first night together, I turned on my cell for the first time in two days and found a message from Larry. "It's me," he said. I could picture him standing with the phone, his back to the smudgy window of his efficiency. "Wondering if my shoe polish is still there. In the hall closet. Call me." I haven't known Larry to polish his shoes in the past ten years, so this meant he had a date. Or wanted me to think so.

I called his land line, since he'd be at work. I talked to his voicemail. "Me," I said. "Wednesday morning. If you left any polish, it's probably gone. My friend moved some things in, so I had to make space. My friend John. Nothing too serious, but he's staying awhile."

When I finished, a prerecorded woman asked if I'd like to review my message. I did. Then I taped over it. "Me. Sorry I took so long. Can't find the polish. It was old anyway, wasn't it? You should just buy some new. So. Good luck with whatever the shiny shoes are for."

The cabbie smiled in the rearview. If he understood my English, he probably approved of my benevolence.

Johann is obsessed now with jazz, especially blues. Funny, I'd have pegged him for a Charlie Parker fan, something more complex. He still speaks only a few words of English—*coffee, eat, pajamas, no*—but he's memorized a number of blues lyrics. Across the table most nights, between dinner and ice cream, he'll start into something like "What Did I Do to Be So Black and Blue?" and he even does that low, gravelly Satchmo voice.

> *"No joys for me*
> *no company*
> *even ze mouse*
> *ren from my house*
> *all my life srough*
> *I've been soooooo*
> *bleck and blue."*

Only he's grinning when he sings it. I think he's proud of himself.

When he plays from the Chopin book I got him, it sounds different than it should—sharper, less Romantic, I suppose—but then there's something wonderful about the way he plays fantastical music in this normal, rhythmic way as if it weren't Chopin at all, just Hanon warm-up exercises. It reminds me of a Chagall painting: Here are some people, floating above a town. Here is a cow on the roof. Here is the blanket sky, poked through with blinding stars. But this is just the way my town looks at night! I took my easel into the street to paint my flying neighbors, to get the purple starlight right. Normal, normal. Nothing Romantic going on *here*.

I gave him some staff paper the other day, thinking maybe he'd write something while he's here, but he just looked at it, said, "Nein, nein," shook his head sadly. Maybe it's against the rules to compose here, to leave parts of his genius as evidence. Maybe he can leave his sperm, but not his handwriting.

My father used to make me and my brother try to compose. He'd sit us down, have us close our eyes, tell us if we cleared our minds of every noise and picture, something would come. It never did. I feared it was because of my cheating, my inability to filter out random images. I'd almost be clear, and then: Gorilla! Airplane! Christmas! I want to ask Johann how he does it, how he can sit and just concentrate. How he can keep out everything that isn't sound— the fifty thousand colors of the world, the smell of something burning four stories below.

The longer he's here, the more I think I should learn German. We could piece together a conversation then, between us.

My Brahms-bearded art professor, the one who introduced me to Chagall in the first place, would use a piano during lectures. The class met in the small recital theater at the back of the fine arts building, and there was a Steinway on the stage, and somehow he'd gotten a key to the lid. He loved to run from his projection screen to that piano, talking about "Colors are like notes; together they make chords." He probably thought he was being quirky.

"This is blue and green," he said, playing C and D together. "Analogous. So similar they create tension. Now blue and yellow." A third. "Now blue and orange." A fourth.

Another time, he ran to the piano to explain a terrible Rococo painting, something with clouds and bosoms. "The whites in the Fragonard are like *this*," he said, and trilled high up, delicate and saccharine.

But I was never sure he knew what he was talking about. He lost my faith when we studied *Guernica* and he said there would never be a war on American soil in our lifetime. (No canvas of mangled, color-void bodies. No slaughtered bull, no spears, no pale-eyed crucifixion.) It struck me as shockingly naive for a smart man, very bag-over-the-head.

And he was wrong about colors, too. "They have no innate *meaning," he said the second week of class, "but they have *connotations* we all share, as a society and as humans, yes? Green tunes us in to nature, life, so we feel soothed. Blue is sky, so we think dreamy, ethereal, and the same with white. Black is fear. For three million years we lived without electricity, no? There are good reasons we're afraid of the dark. Red, we see blood. So violence, drama, excitement, passion." That's where I took exception, where I still do. For men, yes, maybe. But for any woman since the dawn of time, red means no baby this month. It means, for better or worse, the staining and unignorable absence of a baby.

I lied before. The sex isn't that good. I had low expectations, so I was thrilled he knew *anything*. But actually he's pretty stiff, noncreative. I've tried things a couple of times, normal things for our society, and he's pulled away from me, started talking fast in German, turned bright pink.

The last time he did it, I put my clothes back on and decided to ignore him for the rest of the day. I went to the window and opened the curtains. I wasn't thinking about it, but maybe on some level I did it to scare him. He stood staring down at the cars, saw all the buildings, saw for the first time how high we were. He didn't cry, but he looked like he wanted to. He stayed there a long time, shaking and mumbling. Then he closed the curtains and ran to the couch, ran bent over at the waist as if he were scared of falling. I'm surprised he never opened the curtains himself while I was at work. You'd think a genius would be more curious than that.

To calm him down, I got my big music encyclopedia off the shelf and showed him all the pictures in the Bach section. The house where he was born, the church in Leipzig, a portrait of his oldest son. He pointed at each and said things I couldn't understand, but they seemed to make him happy. He flipped back a page to the Vivaldi section and made some kind of joke. He giggled and giggled, so I just laughed along with him.

"Yep, that Vivaldi," I said. "One funny guy."

After I put the encyclopedia back on the shelf, I got out the little Chagall book I'd bought at MOMA.

"Here," I said, and I opened it to *The Fiddler*. "This is what I think of when you play Chopin. See how he's making music, floating there above the town? That's what you sound like, like there's nothing under your feet but you don't even notice."

Bach squinted at the picture, pointed at the fiddler's face. "Grün," he said.

"Yes, it's green. I wouldn't make fun. You looked strange enough yourself when you were twelve inches tall."

I flipped to the one called *Birthday*, the one where a man floats above the red carpet, floats above a woman to kiss her. A city window and a little purse. The man has no arms. The next page was *Couple of Lovers on a Red Background*, where they're lying in the red, and they're red themselves, drowning in it, only they're not drowning, because up above is a huge blue pool where the real water is, where the blue man throws flowers and the fish-bird jumps down.

"These are pictures of love," I said. "*Love.*" He put his hand on his heart. I'd taught him that one the week before. "Everyone in these pictures can float, because they're in love, or they're the fiddler on the roof, or just happy." I pointed out the window. "That's why we can stay up here so high. It doesn't seem possible, but it is. Twenty-seven stories up!" I flashed my fingers in two tens and a seven. "Because we're playing music and we're happy."

He crawled back to the window, his nails digging into the carpet, then reached up and lifted just the corner of the curtain. Together we watched the bus shed passengers twenty-seven stories down. Then he looked at me and pointed at the wristwatch I'd given him, the one Larry left behind because it wasn't digital.

"You want to know how long the building can hold up against gravity?" Although maybe it was something else. How long must he stay here, how many lifetimes have passed since his own, what time is it in Germany?

"Tock, tock, tock," he said.

I chose to answer the gravity question, because it was the only one I could. "A long time. *Long time.* It won't fall down while you're here, at least."

Since that afternoon, when he sings the blues, it sounds like the *blues.*

> "*I'm so forlorn,*" he sings,
> "*life's just a sorn*
> *my heart is torn*
> *vhy vas I born*
> *Vhat did I dooooo*
> *to be so bleck . . . and blue?*"

He won't look out the window anymore, but it doesn't matter. He knows. Every siren he hears now, he looks at that curtain. I've never been in the blissful ignorance camp, but in this case maybe it was too much for one man to handle. Sometime last October, Larry made us stop watching TV so we wouldn't see bad news. I couldn't understand how it worked for him, because for me it was worse. If we don't watch the news, I said, how do we know the city's not on fire? How do we know we're not the last ones alive? Since Johann's been here I've kept the TV off, but I'll turn on my radio when he's in the bathroom—if only to hear some stupid ad, because then at least I know we're all okay. Those shrill furniture store jingles are the sound of safety. There's still money to be made, they say. There's still something left to buy.

He's been turning pale, and if I'm not mistaken he's getting smaller. You can see it around the eyes, the way they're sinking back into his face. The skin feels loose on his arms. He hardly leaves the couch anymore, and when he does—when he finally gets his courage and dashes to the bathroom—it's with shaking legs and outstretched arms, like he's worried the floor will give way any moment. He's scratched the arms of the sofa to shreds.

Yesterday I played the piano to see if he would follow suit. I brought out my big blue Gershwin book and got through "A Foggy Day" with only three or four mistakes. I'm good, if a little rusty. At the end of high school I was even applying to conservatories, making tapes and getting ready to go on auditions, when I realized that although I could play almost anything you put before me, and skillfully—I'd won competitions, even—I'd never gotten through a major piece without one error. I could play the whole *Pathétique* flawlessly, then a measure from the end I'd breathe a sigh of relief and wreck the last chord. And so I majored in finance.

"Maybe that's what you are," I told Johann after I'd flubbed the last two measures. "Maybe you're my repressed ambition." Not likely, the way he sits with his mouth caving in, his glare darting between me and the window.

He sighed. "I'm vhite . . . in-side," he sang.

"You're white all over, Johann," I said. Though truth be told, lately he's a little gray.

———

I get the feeling his tock, tock, tock is running out. But if my test sticks are accurate I started ovulating yesterday, so I only need him to hold out a little longer. We made love twice this morning. I'll buy him a fattening dinner tonight.

I had to leave him on the couch at noon, lock the door, ride down in my loud, slow elevator to show the Lindquists their fifteenth (and God, let's hope, final) apartment. Johann didn't look good at all when I left him there, so small and pale, curled in the cushions. I wonder if I'd be as terrified by his eighteenth-century Leipzig, or if there's something intrinsically horrifying about our modern world, about this new century, something we can handle only because we've been so slowly inured to it. At other moments today I've wondered, too, if Johann shriveling in on himself is in fact a sign that part of me is coming back to life. Or that another life is ready to start inside me.

"I have to make money," I told him as I left. "Deutschmarks, right? You'd understand. I'm sure you wouldn't have slaved your Sundays away on half the organs in Germany if you didn't have twenty mouths to feed. I'll need to buy things. Piano lessons. For the baby."

And so I left him, and even if he's still there when I get back, I won't be surprised if he doesn't last the night, if he evaporates by morning. But I never planned on his being in the picture long-term. I don't actually want him to *raise* the baby. It'll be easy enough to explain why he's not around. "Well, the baby's father is quite a famous man," I'll say, "and this would simply ruin his reputation. Believe me. *Very. Famous.*"

Waiting for the elevator, though, I did something I didn't know I was going to do. I took out my phone and called Larry. When he answered, I said, "Don't talk." I said, "It's good that not everyone is like me, born expecting the world to come unpasted." I said, "I see it now. You were up there playing a fiddle with no roof to stand on, and one day you just looked down and lost your grip on the air and fell. And I'm sorry."

Larry was quiet, and then he said, "Okay." And then he said, "I'll call you after work."

It occurred to me—of course it did—that if I got back with Larry next week, or the week after that, he'd never know the baby wasn't his. And who's to say it wouldn't be? Am I the expert on reality these days?

On the long ride to the ground floor I slid on my stilettos, growing three inches even as I sank three hundred feet. I put on lipstick and prepared to sell the Lindquists a place to live, a nice plot of air so high above the city the Indians didn't even think to charge beads for it. I practiced saying: Look how convenient. And how stable. It'll last a thousand years, if nothing knocks it down. I know you're going to love it.

ACOLYTE
(SECOND LEGEND)

*I*n the bedroom of her Budapest apartment, using the stage makeup left from her acting career, my grandmother painted young women's faces old. Greasepaint doesn't go stale, and when properly applied— when a skilled hand traces lines that are not yet lines but the faintest shadows on taut faces—it can achieve the most astonishing prophecies of the body's eventual self-betrayal. My father, still very young, stood far from the blackout curtains with a candle, and in thanks for this illumination my grandmother called him her little acolyte. She handed out canes and shawls, taught the girls to walk with the weight of eighty years—and thus superannuated they shuffled through the streets at night, without fear of predatory soldiers. And if they chose to carry things other than yarn in their knitting baskets, so be it. Who would suspect?

Another impossibility, yet by most accounts true: More than once she voluntarily strapped a yellow Star of David on her arm before walking into the ghettos to visit old theater friends, her papers in her pocket to prove, later, her right to leave. How this could ever have worked is unclear, but then the ghettos were slippery, temporary things, their borders well guarded but shifting, the soldiers bribable and perhaps susceptible to charm and beauty. There are stranger things true. There are simpler things not.

Impossible as well: When my mother was engaged to my father in 1964, she traveled alone into Communist Hungary, which her fiancé was not allowed to reenter and her future mother-in-law was not allowed to leave. She spent three days there, and at the end of that time my grandmother asked her to smuggle out of the country the particularly incriminating anti-Communist novel she'd completed a decade prior. My mother rode the train to Austria with three hundred onion-skin pages tucked in her girdle. A *vádlott* was published in 1999, twenty years after my grandmother's death. It's the only book I've read, in rough translation, of her forty. But her longest novel, I've just learned (reeling with the glee and fear of things I don't even believe in), involves a man from the Romanian region of Moldavia shot to death by the fearsome Iron Guard. Ten years ago, I wrote a short story about an American boy learning of someone shot to death by the Iron Guard in Moldavia, in the city of Iaşi. I'd chosen the region at random, then was drawn in—drowned—by its history.

I'd love to take this confluence as an indicator of inherited memory, as evidence of further connections, further legacies—of empathy, artistry, guts. But to claim one ancestor would be to claim them all, even those on the wrong sides of humanity's decisive moral battles. The slave owners, the anti-Semites, the Huns, the cowards. And furthermore: Wasn't the presumption of a genetic morality the error at the very core of Nazi ideology?

I've written the story of the painted faces twenty times, from every perspective, at every degree of remove from reality, but my descriptions of candles and shadows have never come close to resurrecting the commingled scents of greasepaint and melting wax and fear. Certain images I've copied over so many times they've come to feel like truth. (My grandmother drawing the bristles of the brush through her lips to flatten them, naming the creases of the face as she etches each girl's future there—the lines called think-too-much, the lines called worry-too-much, and smoke-too-much, and know-too-much. The way she flips her tarot cards on the small table after the transformations are complete, telling one girl to beware tall men, another she's surrounded by protectors.)

When I tell it from my father's point of view, it is always a story of innocence. In the girls' narration, it becomes gossipy: This writer, this former actress, painting their faces in the closet, was surviving the war by pawning the family silver one spoon at a time. She had enough spoons to last five more years. She was psychic, even beyond her tarot skill. Strangest of all: Despite her liberal views, her Bohemian friends, she'd been married to the member of Parliament who had written the Second Jewish Law in 1939. (The new quotas put tens of thousands out of work, restricted Jews from the press, took their land, defined Jewishness as a race rather than a religion. Even the theater was affected. If no more than 6 percent of any cast could be Jewish, then in a play with fifteen characters, one actor was too many. No Jew could direct a play or own a theater. Of course, the girls don't really whisper this litany. But I need to. I need to remind myself of these details in draft after draft, as if the writing might wear the words thin, until their meanings won't stick.) The same year the law passed, Rózsa Ignácz divorced János Makkai. They were first cousins, the women whisper. And this boy with the candle, he is their son. As my grandmother seals their wrinkles with powder, they wonder about cause and effect. Did the political differences destroy the marriage? Or were theaters included in the law as revenge against the woman who was already leaving him? Perhaps she'd had an affair with a Jewish director. Their questions are my own.

One of these times, if I get the words in the correct order, if I retrace more precisely the lines of history, I am convinced I will learn something I need to know. If not about my grandparents' strange marriage or its dissolution, if not about bloodlines, then at least about courage in its quietest manifestations.

In any event, the faces were finished, the walking sticks distributed. The girls laughed at themselves in the mirror and headed into the night. What acts of sabotage or simple self-preservation they accomplished on the streets are not a matter of record.

EVERYTHING WE KNOW
ABOUT THE BOMBER

The briefcase he used was not the black one shown in phone footage. The black case belonged to Marion Cates, deceased, and contained two egg salad sandwiches. That the black case appeared so persistently on the news and on social media, despite being of no interest to investigators, delayed the apprehension of the bomber by as much as two days.

We're told that in third grade, his English was lacking. We're told that he refused to smile for class pictures, but he was a happy child, he *was*. We are told he loved painting. We're told that Miss Mullens is too overwhelmed at this time to answer more questions.

He was on the FBI's radar, and then he was not. He was someone's son, and then he was not. He had a girlfriend, and then he did not. He had a beard, and then he did not. His sister understood him, and then she did not.

There is no question that he acted alone.

He suffered from plantar fasciitis, cluster headaches, a borderline attention disorder, and repeated sinus infections. His heart was broken five distinct times. This much is clear from the autopsy.

———

He studied botany, specifically the sticky and miraculous unfurling of single grains of pollen into long strings that drilled down the length of the pistil and into the ovary. His graduate work addressed the lipids involved in this reaction. His research was nearly complete.

His finances were in order. He paid bills the day before the bombing, which leads us to wonder if he thought he'd get away with it, go home and need electricity, water, credit cards; or if some ingrained societal obedience overrode all he knew of the future.

His one indulgence was scarves. He spent more income, proportionally, on scarves than on entertainment. In eleven of the sixteen photographs available to the public, he wears a silk scarf of one pale color or another, tucked expertly into the collar of his leather jacket. Affected, perhaps, but not for a European, which he was, after all, even if he was also American, even if he was also a thousand other things, not the least of which was vain.

We agree, collectively, that the amount of time we have devoted to studying his skull shape, lineage, caffeine intake, and psychiatric history is neither helpful nor tasteful.

On his bookshelf: Rimbaud, Dostoevsky, Updike, Conrad, Nabokov, Murakami, Dickens, Proust, Mann. Much is made of the depth and diversity of his reading, but then much is also made of the absence of women from the shelves. The Stanford professor who has arranged access to the bomber's copious marginal notes plans, separate from his assistance in interpreting these notes for the interested government agencies, to release his own analysis of the man's liter-

ary thinking. How long he will have to wait for clearance is, naturally, the issue.

When the bomber was eleven, he took a Hershey's bar from the
pharmacy shelf and snuck it into the public restroom, where he consumed it in three bites. Terrified of the incriminating wrapper, he
folded it in half, fourths, eighths, sixteenths, but decided against the
toilet, which might clog. He put the wrapper in his mouth and
chewed it like gum, and when it was soft enough, he swallowed.
Much is still uncertain, but on this one fact we are clear.

According to his mother, he was framed. According to his mother,
the laws of the universe are incompatible with her son, her son, her
son doing this. We wonder, collectively, why it's so important to us
that she understand what we understand—that yes, he did this, that
he bought the ticket, that he wrote that letter, that the basement was
full of chemicals—despite our wish to spare her. Wouldn't it be better if she thinks it's the rest of us who've gone mad? We ask if she
hasn't been through enough. But we need her to understand.

The briefcase he used was a gift from his sister. Something to replace
the canvas bag he'd carried through his academic life. She was the
one who identified a scrap of it, charred leather and a bit of buckle.

There are things we can assume: that he was terrified, that he almost wet his pants, that he rehearsed, that he ordered a good meal
that morning but wasn't able to eat it, that he prayed, that he didn't
look at faces in the crowd. That his own name, when he checked
into the hospital, sounded to him like a death sentence. That he'd
pictured some glorious future, some altered universe, in which history would be written by the victors, among whom he'd be chief.

That he couldn't sleep the night before. But maybe those are facts about us, about the way we'd be.

The bomber's ex-girlfriend is not ready to talk, but her roommate has given certain details: the fight about the keys, the time he broke the girlfriend's wrist, the addiction to Indian food. The roommate starts most sentences with "If I'd known." We are happy to allow her this.

He liked to solve puzzles. He liked to fix machines. When his third-grade teacher, Miss Mullens, told him there was not enough time to talk about sharks, he slowed the mechanism of the classroom clock. "Look," he said. "I made the day longer."

If he hadn't felt the need to watch the explosion, he'd never have fallen from the roof of the bank, and would not have snapped his leg. Three days later he wouldn't have stumbled, dazed and infected, to the hospital. He would not, when he saw the nurses' eyes, when he realized the police were on their way, have barricaded himself, wouldn't have taken the hostage, wouldn't have demanded the suicidal drugs, wouldn't have shot himself when they were denied. Or so we assume.

The country where he was born is on the map, but only a detailed map. It has a flag, but not a flag we've seen. His country is smaller than Luxembourg, larger than Lichtenstein, with a surprising number of sheep. To be honest, we'd forgotten about his country. We aren't at all sure what he wanted.

The night before his twenty-third birthday, he sat in a mostly empty movie theater and watched Audrey Tautou run through the streets of Paris, suitcase in hand. As a botanist, he hated that the wrong things were blooming on-screen: This was meant to be August, but here were tulips in the park. Each flower, to him, had a taste. He'd rarely tasted nectar, just a few curious times—the viscosity, if not the flavor, reminding him of his girlfriend, of afternoons on her small white bed—but he knew each flower's smell so intimately, so clinically, that when these tulips appeared he felt it on the back of his tongue. He admired the director's brazenness (he assumed it wasn't ignorance) in deciding what flowers bloomed when. He admired men who molded the universe like plastic. After this thought, his popcorn lost its flavor. We've gleaned all this from the video surveillance.

His mother stands on the porch and again and again says *why*, till it doesn't sound like a word at all. It's a different *why* from ours. We are ready to accept this.

He had a tooth pulled in the spring of 2012. He was allergic to strawberries. He excelled at tennis. There was no food in his refrigerator. He was dead before they could interrogate him. His blog has been erased.

We plan to learn more. We plan to keep updated. We plan to look for patterns. We've obtained a new map, with slightly different colors.

We will repeat these facts till they sound like history. We'll repeat them till they sound like fate.

PAINTED OCEAN, PAINTED SHIP

*T*o Alex's personal horror and professional embarrassment, the Cyril College alumni magazine ran an obnoxiously chipper blurb that September, in a special, blue-tinted box. She read it aloud to Malcolm on the phone:

FOWL PLAY

Assistant Professor Alex Moore has taught Samuel Taylor Coleridge's "Rime of the Ancient Mariner" many times since joining the English Department in 2008, but she developed an unexpected intimacy with the poem when, duck-hunting in South Australia this June, she accidentally shot and killed an actual albatross.

Moore, whose doctoral dissertation at Tufts focused on D. G. Rossetti and his muse Jane Burden Morris, took aim at what she thought was a goose.

"My students are never going to let me hear the end of this," she says.

Because the birds are protected

under Australian and international
laws, Moore incurred a hefty fine—
hopefully the extent of that legend-
ary bad luck! She has no plans to
hang the bird around her neck. "The
wingspan was over two yards," says
the 5-foot-2 Moore. "*That* would be
asking for it!"

Those exclamation points killed her, the way they tacked the
whole episode down as farce. And the cheery italics. None of Alex's
tired sarcasm had come through. She vowed in the future only to
give quotes via e-mail, so she could control the punctuation.
("You're my favorite control freak," Malcolm said.) Plus there was
that photo to the side, her book-jacket photo with the half smile,
perfect for suggesting Pre-Raphaelite intrigue and scandal, but here
verging on the smug. A month stuck dealing with the South Australian police and Parks Department; half her grant spent on the fine;
her research summer wasted; and all of it snipped down by a freelance writer named Betsy into photo, irony, pretty blue box.

And as for the bad luck, it was just starting, waiting for her back
home like her postal bin of unopened mail. Not the "hefty fine"
kind of bad luck, but the "Your career is over" kind, the "Why aren't
you wearing your engagement ring?" kind.

"Didn't take you for a hunter," she heard about twenty times that
first department party back in the States.

"I'm not," she'd say, or "You don't know who you're dealing with
here," or "I'm really more of a gatherer."

She ended up telling the full story, and as she talked the whole
party squeezed around where she sat on the arm of the couch—

even Malcolm, her fiancé, who'd seen it happen. He was sweet to listen again, and sweeter still not to chime in with his own version. Her colleagues sat on the coffee table, the bar, the floor, and sipped white wine. She told them how her half brother Piet had invited her and Malcolm to his place outside Tumby Bay for June. "He's not Australian," she said. "He just thinks he is." And then once they got there, Piet, in that way of his—just masculine enough to intimidate Malcolm, just Australian enough that everything sounded like a fine, foolish adventure—convinced them to come shooting at his lake, so he wouldn't miss the last day of duck hunting season.

"Australia is the new America," announced Leonard, her department head. Or rather, he slurred it through his beard. The new hire nodded. Everyone else ignored him.

After Piet brought down three ducks and his dog had dragged them in, he wrapped Alex's hands around the gun and showed her the sight line.

"What kind of gun?" someone asked.

"I don't know. A rifle. It was wooden."

She'd seen something barely rise above the stand of trees on the small island in the lake, and shot. If she thought anything, she thought it was a white goose. It crashed down through the trees, and Piet sent Gonzo swimming out to it. Gonzo disappeared on the island, yapping and howling and finally reappearing, sans goose, to whimper at the water's edge.

"Christ," Piet said, and took off his clothes—all of them—to swim out. He emerged from the trees after a long minute, full frontal glory shining wet in the sun. Malcolm slapped his entire arm across his eyes. "She's a monster!" Piet shouted. "You've slain a beast!"

Thirty minutes later, Piet, half-drunk, was on the phone to his friend Reynie at the Parks Department, asking him to come out and tell them if that wasn't the biggest fucking bird he'd ever seen. They took two double kayaks out—Piet and Reynie, then Malcolm and Alex, who still hadn't seen her victim. It lay there, enormous, wings out, half on a bush, a red spot fading out to pink on the white feathers of the neck. Its whole body glared white, except the wings, tipped in glossy black. "It was beautiful," she told her colleagues. "I can't even describe it—it had to do with the light, but it was just *beautiful*."

"You shouldn't have brought me out here, Piet, Christ," Reynie had said. He put his hand on the bird's back, and Alex walked around to get a better look at the face, at the rounded, almost cartoonish beak. "I'll have to write you up, and you'll lose your license and pay a fortune. It's a wandering bloody albatross. They're *vulnerable*."

"Vulnerable to what?" Piet was using his phone to shoot photos, moving the bush branches for a better shot.

"Extinction. Jesus Christ. Vulnerable's a step from endangered. Piet, I don't want to write you up, but you shouldn't have called."

Piet snapped a picture. "Didn't shoot it," he said. "*She* did. Not even *from* here, never shot a gun. Girl's excelled at everything she ever tried in her whole damn life."

"Which is how I spent the next three weeks camped in Adelaide," she told her colleagues. The ones who were out of wine took this as a cue to stretch and reload at Leonard's bar.

"Hey, great story!" Bill Tossman clapped her on the shoulder, used that loud, cheesy voice more suited to an executive schmoozing on the squash court than a professor of modern poetry. "Wish I could stay to hear the end, but my two friends and I here are late for a wedding!"

They laughed, then all started in: *You must be parched! Can I get you some water? Hey, take a load off!*

"You're going to do that all year," Alex said. "Aren't you."

And yes, they did, until the real bad luck became public in November and they suddenly didn't know what to say to her at all.

She actually taught the Coleridge that fall, and passed around a copy of the photo Piet had e-mailed her. It was an unfortunately dull section of 222, half frat boys who only took classes as a pack (one, confused by her story, later indicated in his paper that the mariner killed the albatross because he thought it was a goose), a bunch of foreign students, mostly Korean, who never spoke, and a freshman English major named Kirstin who made every effort to turn the class into a private tutorial. They passed the photo listlessly, one of the boys raised his hand to ask how much the bird weighed, and Alex made a mighty effort to turn her answer into a discussion of the weight of sin and Coleridge's ideas of atonement.

Kirstin compared the poem to *The Scarlet Letter* and one of the boys groaned, apparently traumatized by some high school English teacher. Alex wished someone else would talk. Poor Eden Su, for instance, in the front row, was one of those Korean students. She wrote astounding papers, better by a mile than Kirstin's, and yet she never spoke in class unless Alex addressed her directly, and even then, she whispered and pulled her hair across her mouth. Alex had asked her to stop by her office later, and now Eden was slowly picking apart a cheap ballpoint pen.

By one o'clock she was in her office on the phone to Malcolm, the red leaves on the maple hitting the bottom of her window again and again. He was in Chicago, meeting with his thesis adviser. He'd be back the next night, and was asking if she wanted to grab dinner.

"I'll take you someplace nice," she said. "You'll need champagne." These meetings were probably his last before he defended his dissertation, and they were going well.

"Sure," he said. "It's up to you. I just won't feel like dressing up."

"Right." She found herself saying it flatly and quickly, but he didn't seem to notice. So she went on. "Sometimes girls like getting dressed up."

He laughed. "Okay. Boys like to wear jeans."

"My student is here." She wasn't. "We'll talk later." She hung up.

The problem, the source of all her snippiness, her cattiness, her being such a *girl* about everything, was that since they'd gotten engaged nine months ago he had not once, not a single time except during sex, which absolutely didn't count, called her beautiful. In sharp contrast to the courtship phase, when he'd say it several times a week, one way or another. She'd known the staring-into-her-eyes thing wasn't going to last forever, and it had been a crazy year, with the Australia trip and his dissertation, but nine months and *nothing*. Not that she was counting, but she was. She'd have settled for a peck on the head and "Hey, gorgeous." A whistle when she stepped out of the shower.

She'd been so caught up in being engaged and close to tenure and publishing her articles and generally getting everything she wanted that it wasn't until those weeks in the Adelaide hotel, alone with Australian TV and her own thoughts, that she started wondering if she could live with Malcolm the rest of her life, never seeing beauty reflected back at her. And she wondered, if she felt like this now, how she'd feel at nine months pregnant. Or fifty years old. Or terminally ill.

It was regressive and petty and uneducated to care about beauty, but she did. God help her, it was closely tied to her self-esteem and probably had been since about fourth grade.

Here was Eden, arriving like a prophecy, knocking with one knuckle on the open office door. Alex motioned her in. Eden's eyes had that jet-lagged glaze common to all the foreign students. Every year Alex assumed it would wear off by October, but it never did. She'd mentioned it once to Leonard, and of course he'd had a theory. "You know why, right? They stay up all night texting their friends back home. Refuse to adjust to American time."

Eden sat on the edge of the chair, red backpack on her lap. It almost reached her chin—a canvas shield. "Eden, I just want to touch base with you." No response. "You've been getting solid A's on your papers, but I need you to understand that twenty percent of your final grade is class participation."

"Okay." She said it through her hair, barely audible. If it hadn't been a cultural issue, Alex would have worried about depression.

"Do you feel you are participating?"

She shrugged.

"Hello? Do you?" Which was harsh. She was mad at Malcolm, not this poor girl.

Eden shrugged again. "What else could I do?" It was the most words Alex had ever heard her string together, and she was pleased to note that the English was okay. When she'd been a TA, another TA actually told her to compare foreign students' spoken English with their written English, to make sure they weren't plagiarizing. The implication being that they were more likely than native speakers to do so. Alex had never seen this borne out.

"There's nothing else you can do," she said to Eden. "You need to talk."

"Okay."

"Look, I understand that back in Korea you weren't supposed to talk in class, but you're at an American university now, and part of an American education is the exchange of ideas. Not just writing about literature, but *engaging*. Out loud." She always had trouble ending conversations with students, especially ones who wouldn't look her in the eye. "Is that something you think you can do?"

Eden shrugged and nodded, but she seemed upset, staring at the bookshelf behind Alex. She looked, for once, like she wanted to say something. But she didn't; she just stood up and left.

Alex did take Malcolm someplace nice: Silver Plum, a twenty-minute drive from home. She overdressed, in a sheer green blouse and a silk skirt, knowing he wouldn't say anything about it at all. It was like she was daring him not to.

He was exhausted. He wore khakis and a wrinkled blue polo shirt, and he was overdue for a haircut, curls everywhere. He ordered a scotch and gulped it down. He didn't want to talk about his dissertation, or Chicago, or work. She didn't even try to bring up the plans for the wedding in May, which he'd probably have talked about, but the thought was starting to make her sick. Specifically: the fact that either, after months of preparations, he'd see her in her dress and say nothing at all, or he'd say something nice and she'd suspect it was out of duty.

"I finally met Jansen's wife," he said. Jansen was his adviser, and apparently something of a god in the world of sociolinguistics.

"Yeah? What's she like?"

"Beautiful. She's just this gorgeous, sixty-whatever woman with enormous black eyes."

"Huh."

"I mean, they're like *pools* of blackness."

"Huh."

"Not what I expected, you know? I thought she'd be some little mousy person. And she's just this amazing, exuberant, stunning woman."

Winded from the effort of that much conversation, he returned to his lasagna.

Alex caught her reflection in the window to the street, and for the love of God she looked like a circus clown, all frizz and eyes and jawbone. It was a wonder he could look at her at all. But people had found her beautiful, they really had, and one of the reasons she'd even landed on her specialty (vain creature that she was) was that Donna Edwards, her college professor for Nineteenth Century British Poetry, saw her that first day of the term and said, "You—you're a ringer for Jane Morris!" The next day, she brought in a book with Rossetti's *Proserpine* and proved it to everyone.

She wanted to grab Malcolm by the collar with one hand and say, "People would have *painted* me. If I'd lived in the right century, they would have paid me just to sit there!" But with the other hand she wanted to scratch out her face with a marker or a knife, obliterate every trace of ugliness, of gawky eighth grader, of hope.

Some feminist.

That Friday it wasn't even Leonard who called her in, but Miriam Kohn, the dean of faculty. Alex was offered a glass of water, asked to take a seat on the soft leather couch. She wanted to compare the experience to being called to the principal's office, but that had never happened to her.

"So we received a letter from a student named Eden Su," Miriam said. She had nothing on her desk, nothing at all except her picture frames and her closed computer, and she rested her hands in her lap. "It was a request to drop your class."

"I think I know what this is about," Alex said. It had been one of about ten scenarios she'd rehearsed since receiving Miriam's e-mail, and she felt her best strategy was to turn this into a friendly debate about how hard to push foreign students, and whether the class participation component was out of order.

"I'm not sure you do. Tell me what you know about Miss Su."

"She *does* seem borderline depressed to me, although I question whether that's cultural, just a matter of reserve. She's not an English major." Miriam was staring at her, so she kept talking. "I believe she's a sophomore. Very good writer."

"Yes, her writing is excellent. Tell me something: You mentioned a cultural issue. What did you mean by that?"

"Oh, I wouldn't call it an *issue*. She's just very quiet, and I'm sure that's what the letter is about, that I asked her to speak more in class. I *did* acknowledge that in her previous schooling she likely hadn't been asked to speak much. I hope that didn't upset her."

Miriam opened a desk drawer and pulled out a paper. It wasn't folded—so it was a Xerox of the letter, and who knew how many copies were out there, and why. Miriam glanced through it. "In this exchange, did you refer to her schooling in Korea?"

"Right." And then her stomach turned to a wave of acid. Miriam had asked it so casually, but no, this was the whole point. "Oh God, is she not—"

"No, she's not. She's from Minnesota, fifth-generation American. And her ethnic background is Chinese."

Alex stared stupidly forward. Could she really have mistaken a whispered Minnesotan accent for a Korean one? She started to explain that Eden never spoke, that she looked so jet-lagged, but she stopped herself. It might only make things worse. She put her hand to her mouth to show that she was properly horrified, that she felt terrible on behalf of the girl. When really all she felt was horrified for herself.

Miriam looked at the letter again. "The issue, you understand, is the presumption that a student who looks Asian must be foreign-born. She's quite angry, and it seems she's involved the Minority Student Council. She says her father is upset, but we haven't heard from him yet."

"Can I ask why Leonard isn't handling this, on a departmental level?"

"He felt uncomfortable with the situation." He probably didn't even understand what the issue was. She'd heard the man use the word *oriental* on multiple occasions.

"May I please see the letter?" Alex held out her hand.

"Not at the moment, no, I'm afraid not." Miriam slid it back in the desk drawer. "But you'll see it soon. And I want you to know that I do understand how we make assumptions about *all* our students—background, socioeconomic status. If it were up to me, it would end with this conversation."

Alex didn't know what to do, and she realized some principal's office experience would have come in handy. Did one grovel now? Burst into tears? Make a joke? It was hot, so she rolled up her sleeves. In the office of the South Australian Parks Department, she'd just told her story again and again while they plied her with tea and cookies and tried to ensure she maintained a pleasant impression of Australia despite the legal trouble. A cookie might have been nice right now.

"What's going to happen next is that the dean of students will recommend Miss Su take this to the Grievance Committee, and you'll just have to do a written statement. I predict that they'll discuss this briefly and dismiss it. And if there's no disciplinary action, it won't come up in your tenure review. That's my very strong prediction."

On the way to her car, she called Malcolm and canceled dinner, saying she had a monstrous headache and ten calls to make. She'd just have seethed silently, and she couldn't bear his asking what was wrong, trying to guess if it was something he'd said or done.

Usually, it was.

That night she drank an entire bottle of red wine, played *A Night at the Opera* with the sound too low to hear, and attempted to catalog any potentially racist thoughts she'd ever entertained. When she was five, walking in Boston, she'd grabbed her mother's hand because there was a black man coming toward them on the sidewalk. But she was so young, and she'd grown up in New Hampshire, for Christ's sake.

More recently, she hated the way any NPR reporter using Spanish words would roll out the thickest accent possible, just to prove to his boss and the listening public that ten years of Spanish classes had paid off and he was down with the people. "It's going to be a big issue with Ell-a-*diiii*-no voters," for instance. In a way he'd never refer to "the *Français* community" or "*Deutsch* immigrants."

And there was a journalism professor, Mary Gardner, whose creamy brown skin Alex once stared at in a faculty forum, becoming (profoundly, inexcusably) hungry for chocolate.

But that was it. Honest to God, that was it. A resentment of overzealous reporters, a perverse admiration of Mary Gardner's complexion, a small child's ignorance.

She hadn't even been *around* much overt racism. Once, in college, a girl on her freshman hall had said, "If everyone in Asia is, like, lactose intolerant, then how do they feed their babies? Is that why they're all so skinny?"

It occurred to Alex, lying drunk on the couch, that if all she could summon up was one incident of someone else's racism, while she could pin three on herself—no, four, let's not forget the big one—that made her the most racist person she knew. By 300 percent.

Malcolm called at nine to see how she was, but she was too drunk to pick up. He called on Saturday morning, when she was too hung-over, and again on Sunday night, when she was once again too drunk. He didn't seem terribly concerned about her absence, not even in the Sunday message. "Just checking in," he said. "Call me later."

She passed herself in the mirror late that night, and the gin and the bathroom lighting made her look somehow speckled, like a grainy photograph. She gripped the sink edge and squinted, to see how she'd look to a stranger. Interesting, maybe. Striking. From a certain angle, ugly, and from a certain angle, not.

Sometime after midnight, she called Malcolm's cell phone, knowing it would be turned off. She said, slowly, trying to enunci-ate, *"Just checking in.* I want you to know, Malcolm, that I cannot live the rest of my life being ugly. You need to know that. That is all."

She drank three glasses of water and passed out.

On Monday, Eden wasn't in class. Why this should have been a surprise, Alex had no idea. Was she expecting her to show up obe-diently until the registrar came through with official permission for the late drop? Did she, on some level, think this because she ex-pected Asians to be more mindful of authority? No, no, no, she was just hungover still, from the whole long, miserable weekend, and the coffee had only made things worse. Let's be honest: She was still drunk. She thought she might be missing a couple of other Asian students, too, and the fact that she wasn't sure was a very bad sign.

" 'Tintern Abbey,' " she said, and found she had nothing else to add. "Let's read it aloud."

She ended class fifteen minutes early, threw up in the bathroom on the second floor, bought a cheeseburger from the co-op to ab-sorb some of the alcohol, and went back up to put her head on her desk until her afternoon class.

She woke to the ring of her office phone reverberating through the desk, a hundred times louder than it should have been. It was Malcolm.

"Your cell's off," he said. Really, she had no idea where it was. "So you were pretty drunk last night." He was laughing. "What were you drinking?"

"All of it."

"Everything okay?"

"You mean this morning? Yeah." She turned down openings like this all the time. Because what could she possibly say? Asking if he still found her attractive was desperate and unattractive. Telling him he needed to compliment her was worse. In either case, she'd never believe anything nice he said, ever again. She realized that what she was supposed to be upset about was Eden Su. That should have been what she was working up the nerve to tell him. But it had come down to this: After twenty-two years of schooling and eight years of slogging away at her CV, she somehow cared more about her appearance than her career.

"So what's new?" he said.

And she said, "I don't think I can marry you."

Bill Tossman found her on a bench outside the library, trying not to vomit again. She was sitting very, very still, hands clasped around a paper cup of coffee she didn't think it wise to drink. "There she sits," he said, "'as idle as a painted ship upon a painted ocean.'" She tried to laugh or smile, but it must have come out a grimace.

"I have something for you." He sat beside her, shaking the bench just enough to make her head throb and stomach slosh. He was a big man. Long limbs and a smooth, bright face, a soft gut that aged him. He had a crush on her. Or at least he'd always been sweet to her. She wasn't sure she could trust her judgment anymore. Tossman was a poet, the one department member with a Pulitzer instead of a PhD. It made his loud voice all the more surreal.

He slipped his hand into his briefcase pocket, pulled out a rubber-banded pack of playing cards, and shuffled them on his knee. "Cut," he said, and she managed to. He took four cards off the top and laid them facedown on the bench. "Okay," he said, "flip them up."

Seven of diamonds. Seven of hearts. Seven of clubs. Seven of spades.

"See? Your luck is turning!" He laughed, proud of himself.

"Where'd you learn that?"

"Where'd I learn *what*?"

He was making her feel like his niece, and although it was sweet, she didn't appreciate it. On a professional level. She gathered the cards and held them out to him, but he shook his head. "Why don't you hang onto those? And hey, I'm sorry about the whole letter thing. That shouldn't have happened. It wasn't necessary."

She stared, trying to comprehend. He wasn't on the Grievance Committee.

"In the paper."

"The paper?"

"Oh. Christ. You've seen it, yes? In the *Campus Telegraph*. I should—there's a stack in the library, if you want to—okay. Hey, I'm going to run before I make more of a jackass. Look, come by if you need to talk." He literally backed away from her—went backward a good ten steps, then stopped. "It's not like I don't know about messing up, right?" He laughed at himself and walked on, hitting his briefcase against his leg. He must have meant his marriage ending last year, and then the time he broke down sobbing in front of his Frost seminar when they discussed images of adultery in "The Silken Tent."

Alex held her head a few more seconds, then pushed herself up.

————

The "open letter" in the *Telegraph* wasn't from Eden herself, but from the entire Minority Student Council. It named Alex, described her conversation with Eden pretty accurately, and went on to include "ten stereotypes about Asian-American students"— number eight was "Asian-American students are more likely to cheat to attain high grades"—and a quote from Leonard, stating that "the English Department works hard to include everyone."

She put a nearby *Newsweek* on the stack of *Telegraphs*, picked the whole thing up, and dropped it in the big blue recycling bin behind the elevator. There were plenty more papers all over campus, but it felt good to get rid of these fifty or so.

Out on the sidewalk, two girls from her Pre-Raph seminar were waving energetically.

"Professor Moore! We waited for you for, like, twenty minutes!"

She checked her watch. She wasn't even wearing a watch. They stood in front of her, smiling, expecting an explanation, or at least further instructions.

She threw up on their shoes.

Her phone was ringing, but she didn't even know where it was, so she put pillows around her ears. She'd taken two of the Vicodin left from her knee surgery, and now everything was padded with cotton. She had told those girls she had a stomach flu and offered to buy them new shoes, but then they were gone and she was back in the English building, slumped in the door of her office, and then Leonard was asking Tossman to call her a cab, and now she was in bed in her clothes. Something sharp was jutting into her hip, but it didn't hurt. She dug around. Seven of hearts, seven of diamonds, seven of spades, seven of clubs.

In her office, on the phone, Malcolm had actually laughed at first, unable to take her seriously. She held her silence until he got it. "What the hell do you mean?"

She said, "There are people who actually find me attractive."

"I don't?" His voice was an octave above normal. It bothered her now, thinking back, that she had no idea where he'd been. She didn't know whether to picture him in front of his refrigerator, out on the deck, driving downtown, sitting on the toilet.

She'd said—perhaps too cryptically, in retrospect—"It's like some horrible inversion of 'The Frog Prince,' like the frog convinces the princess to kiss him, but then she finds herself transformed into a toad. And the frog goes, 'Hey, I'm as good as you can do now, baby.'"

There was a pause that hurt her throat. He said, "I'm supposed to be the frog?"

"No. You're supposed to *get it*." She'd hung up then, but he'd probably hung up too.

She ran a hand through her hair and realized she hadn't even showered since Saturday. Her bed swayed, and the room turned to water.

Every time she taught the Pre-Raph seminar, she waited till near the end of the semester to bring out the actual photographs of Jane Morris. They'd have seen her in Rossetti's and William Morris's paintings, they'd seen her needlework, they'd studied the decoration of Red House. And this in addition to the lectures from an art professor about the Arts and Crafts movement, the three days spent discussing Rossetti's poem "The Portrait," a major focus of Alex's own thesis:

> *This is her picture as she was:*
> *It seems a thing to wonder on,*

> As though mine image in the glass
> Should tarry when myself am gone . . .

Jane Morris was as much the linchpin of the course as she'd been the goddess of the Brotherhood—that daughter of a stableman, who posed and flirted and married and adulterated her way to the top of English society, outsmarting and outcharming the snobs. And so each year when Alex showed the photographs, the students—for some reason particularly the girls—were devastated. She wasn't half as beautiful as Rossetti and Morris had painted her. Rossetti had given gloss to her hair and depth to her eyes, added a good three inches to her neck, lengthened her fingers, straightened her nose.

It was only then that the students started to see how all Rossetti's women—Jane, Christina, Elizabeth—shared some indefinable look that wasn't their own but something Rossetti had done to them, a classical wash he'd painted over them. This was where the feminists in the class started to have fun, and someone inevitably compared the paintbrush to the penis. At which point Alex could lean on her desk and take a breather as they screamed at each other.

She wondered now, lying in bed ignoring the phone, not about Rossetti's fetishes or the invention of the classical but about how Jane Morris felt, to look at a finished painting and see a woman more beautiful than the one she saw in the mirror. Was this the reason she started her affair with Rossetti—knowing she could only be that beautiful when she was with him—or did it feel more like a misinterpretation, an abduction?

And she thought about Rossetti himself, how she'd never considered before that he might really have *seen* Jane Morris that way, not just wished he had. The way she herself had taken an albatross for a goose, an American for a Korean. *How easy is a bush supposed to be a bear.*

She finally answered the phone around eleven that night, and didn't realize until she heard Leonard's voice how strongly she'd believed it to be Malcolm.

"Thank God," he said. "You're okay, then."

"How long have you been calling?"

"All day. We were starting to think—What can I do to help?"

She knew he wanted some concrete plan to fix everything.

"Because I gotta be honest," he went on, "this doesn't look good for the whole department. As a whole."

She wasn't sure if he meant the grievance or the letter or her absence. Or the vomiting.

"Oh, come on, Leonard. It doesn't look *that* bad. Not as bad as half the stuff I've heard you say. For Christ's sake, you use the word *coed*, Leonard."

"I'm confused." He sounded tired.

"Of course you are."

And why not hang up on him, too, while she was at it?

From seventh grade (after she got over mono) through grad school, Alex had not missed a single class. Freshman year of college, her roommate had practically tackled her to keep her from leaving the dorm with a 104 fever, but Alex just kept walking, stopped to sit on the sidewalk halfway to biochem, got up again and staggered the rest of the way. It wasn't a matter of maintaining her record, but of principle. Unlike Piet, who'd once shown up at home in the middle of the semester for "National Piet Week," which he celebrated by watching television and getting his mother, Alex's stepmother, to do all his laundry.

But the next day, she stayed home. Oddly, her phone did not ring. Maybe she'd scared Leonard off. Or maybe her students hadn't said anything, grateful for the free time. After that one missed day, she couldn't imagine going back the next, because she didn't know what to expect. She pictured walking into her 222 to find someone subbing for her. Or only three students who'd bothered showing up, the rest assuming class had been canceled for the term. Or everyone asking if she was all right, and her not being able to lie. She wondered if her lifelong punctiliousness had just been a fear of losing her grip. She wondered if she'd known all along that one little thing gone wrong in her world could unravel absolutely everything else.

Oddly, she found herself taking heart in the fact that Coleridge's mariner had made it safely home. He'd done his penance, and continued to do his penance in telling the tale, and Alex wished for something heavy to hang around her neck, something horrendously painful. She considered her ring, which she still hadn't removed, but hanging it on a necklace chain would only call people's attention to its absence from her finger. Instead, she took it off and put it in a Tupperware and put the Tupperware in her freezer, which she'd once heard was a good place to store jewelry.

She felt lighter, not heavier. But it was a start. She made herself go for a walk around her neighborhood, staring at people's driveways and the falling leaves and chained-up dogs and unclaimed newspapers. When she came back, there were two messages on her phone. One was from Piet. The other was from the bridal boutique, confirming her dress fitting.

Piet was in town the next day to catch up with friends and to see a woman he'd found on the Internet.

"That's a pretty expensive date, isn't it?"

They met up in the morning, Piet usurping the entire red velour couch in the back of Starbucks. "Look at it this way," he said. "I get here, which is a nice vacay for me anyhow. She feeds me, if she likes me she puts me up, and maybe in the end I come out ahead." He was getting an Australian accent, and it suited him. The sun had aged his face fifteen years in the seven he'd been there, and that suited him, too. "Listen, Al. Where the hell's your ring?"

She managed to get the story out, or at least the parts about Eden Su and going AWOL at work and calling off the engagement. Not the girl part, the part about wanting to be beautiful. "I don't know what I'm doing," she said.

He laughed. "When have you ever not known what you're doing?" He was shredding the wooden stick he'd used to stir his coffee. "What I don't get," he said, "is what's this Asian chick got to do with Malcolm?"

"It's hard to explain."

"I got all day."

"It just set me off. Or maybe it was—maybe the idea that someone could look at you and just not see you at all. See something totally different that isn't even you."

"Right, but this is different. Malcolm knows you better than anyone, right?"

"Theoretically." This was the place where she might cry, if she were the kind of person who cried. "I need you to do something with me. You're not meeting this cyberwhore till tomorrow, right?"

"Sure."

"Okay. We're going to go visit my dress."

She figured if she already owned the dress, it might as well fit her. And a lot could happen between November and May. By May, she could be marrying someone else entirely. But really, she'd gotten this stupid idea in her head that if she tried it on, something would change. She'd been hoping for something big and white and horrible to hang around her neck, hadn't she?

It really did hang, too, from its halter strap—crisp and shiny and gaping way too big. A little Russian woman flitted around her with pins. Maybe not Russian, she reminded herself. Maybe Lithuanian. Maybe Ukrainian. Maybe Minnesotan. Piet sat on a pink-cushioned bench and watched. "Looks great," he said. "Look even better with a ring on."

She stared in the mirror, not at the dress but at her horrible face. Her skin was dry and her eyes were puffy, her hair a dark mess. She wanted a necklace with a big red stone, to match that brilliant red on the albatross's neck. What she hadn't been able to describe to anyone about that day in Tumby Bay was the sublimity, the blinding beauty of that bird as it flew, and as it lay where it fell. She could bring back in an instant that moment of white light rising beyond the leaves, her hand shaking against the gun. The echo of the shot seeming to come first because her ears went dead, then the load roar as they woke again. The flapping and cracking as something fell through the trees, branch by snapping branch. She wanted black arms on her gown, to match the dead bird's wings. She wanted to take it all back, to return to that moment at the lake's edge and take back that one moment of horrible misprision. And if she'd seen that bird wrong, and seen Eden Su wrong, who was to say she hadn't seen Malcolm wrong, too? She'd been walking around blind ever since that day.

"You look miserable," Piet said. "I'm calling him right now." He pulled out his phone.

"No! Please don't."

"I already dialed." He held the phone out of her reach, like he'd done with stuffed animals when they were kids. She couldn't move away from the Russian woman's pins.

"Malcolm, listen. It's Piet. Yeah, my sister's been an idiot, she's sorry, and she's standing here in her wedding dress looking gorgeous. You'd be a fool not to take her back. What do you say?" He listened for a minute, and she could hear the rumble of Malcolm's voice, but not his words. "Sure, sure. Good man." He clicked his phone shut. "He says call him tonight and you can talk."

"I'm going to kill you."

"No, you're not."

They walked out into the street, her dress left behind in a bag like something hung up to bleed. "See, things are looking brighter," Piet said. "As soon as I show up."

"All that's happened is you've meddled."

There was a park up ahead, so they sat on a bench. Geese flew above, real ones, with brown bodies and black faces and white chin-straps.

"So really you've got four options. You go back to Malcolm and back to work; you forget about Malcolm and focus on the job, or vice versa; or you leave it all behind and go live someplace you've always wanted to go. I mean, your problem is it's undecided. And you've never been a girl to leave things to chance, just sit there and let things happen to you. So, you take action and you select an option. One, two, three, or four."

Piet had that way of talking that you'd agree to anything he said. And if she no longer believed she could see clearly enough to find her way, at least she was starting to believe in luck. She reached into her pocket. She said, "Go ahead, pick a card."

The next morning, Eden Su was walking down the big sidewalk that cut diagonally across the campus green, hunched under a car-apace of red backpack. She wore a silky blue sweater over black leggings. Alex raced behind the music building so she could meet her face-to-face, rather than sneak up from behind. She had just dropped off her statement for the Grievance Committee, and it was a good one. Whatever Eden had to say, stellar writer that she was, it wouldn't hold up against Alex reasoning with the committee on an adult level.

When she was about ten feet away, Eden spotted her, and there was a slight trip to her step. She put her head down again, as if she planned to walk past and say nothing—which made Alex angry, rather than just desperate to end things. This girl had taken it upon herself to ruin an adult's professional reputation and tenure prospects, but now she was acting as if they were eighth-grade enemies with crushes on the same boy. And Alex wouldn't accept that. It gave her the courage to approach Eden as an adult talking to a child, rather than as a desperate woman begging a twenty-year-old for mercy.

She stopped walking right in front of her and said, "Eden." And smiled patiently.

Eden tried to look surprised. "Oh. Hi." She glanced around— not, Alex realized, out of embarrassment, but to see if any friends were around to witness the strange professor accosting her like this. "Professor Moore. I'm glad you're feeling better." Instead of pulling her hair across her face, she tucked it behind her ear.

Alex had planned on asking her to explain, from her point of view, the problem. This would lead to a rational discussion in which Alex would not apologize—doing so might give Eden more ammunition for her Grievance Committee statement—but they would eventually see eye-to-eye, and Eden would admit what a silly misunderstanding it had been. But now the girl was staring her down, and Alex didn't want to lose the little edge she had left. So she said, "Have you resolved the issue of those missed credits? You can't be picking up a new course now. Will you need to overload in the spring?"

"Yeah, I—it's okay." Eden was starting to look uncomfortable. "Actually, what I'm doing is switching to an independent study with Professor Leonard. It's the same reading, just one-on-one." Her voice was still quiet, but determined, and even—something Alex would never have guessed—a little supercilious. "He offered."

"Right. Well, I hope you're thanking him for his time. That's a lot to ask of someone already teaching two courses and acting as department head."

Eden adjusted her backpack. "Okay, sure. So I'll see you later."

"Hold on." She could absolutely not let Eden be the one to end the conversation. She put a thin layer of concern in her voice. "You know, Eden, part of me wonders if the real reason you dropped this class is because you weren't getting a strong grade."

Eden just stared ahead blankly, the way she always used to.

"Maybe you haven't really been challenged like that before, and it seems I was wrong about where you're from, but talking in class is still a part of a liberal arts education. And I can see from your recent actions that you have no problem speaking up for yourself."

Eden looked around again for those invisible, incredulous friends.

"Look at it this way, Eden. How much do you know about me? Do you know my first name? Do you know where I did my graduate work? Do you know my genetic background?"

Eden was gawking at her like she was insane and drooling. Alex found it infuriating, even with the Vicodin still in her system.

"I'm going to take your silence for a no. You've probably made assumptions about me, and I'm sure most of them aren't true. For instance, I'm not American." It was a lie, from lord knows where. "I was born in Australia. I lived there till I was eighteen. If you referred to me, say, in an article for the *Telegraph*, as an American, you'd be wrong. And one thing I could say, if I were being unreasonable, is that you were intentionally denying my Australian identity. My point is, Eden, that we can't see *anyone*, really."

The girl shifted her backpack and smiled. She didn't look uncomfortable at all anymore, just quietly, enragingly smug.

"For instance," Alex said, "I thought you were an intelligent student. And I appear to have been mistaken." She turned away before Eden could say anything, then looked back over her shoulder. "Have a super term with Leonard! I'm sure he'll enjoy your stony silence!" She managed a ridiculous grin and walked away, pleased to note in her peripheral vision that Eden stayed planted several seconds before pulling out her phone and continuing down the walk.

She showed up outside her 222 five minutes late, just to see what was going on. The door was closed, and there were voices inside. She checked the hall: only a couple of chatting students she didn't recognize, so she put her ear to the door. It was Tossman in there, talking about "The Daffodils." She went to the co-op to bide her time with greasy food.

When she walked into Tossman's office later, he actually looked frightened for a moment. Then he lit his face up and in that huge voice he said, "There she is in the flesh! The sadder but wiser girl for me!"

It took her a second. "Tossman, did you just pull a Coleridge reference by way of *The Music Man*?"

"Why, yes I did." He was quite pleased with himself. He leaned back in his desk chair and bellowed out the chorus of the song, banging his ballpoint pen on a stack of student papers to keep the rhythm: "*The sadder but wiser girl for me!*"

She sat on the chair reserved for nervous students. "I just flipped out at Eden Su. I was trying to patch things up, but apparently I'm not very good at it." She knocked her foot against a stack of literary magazines on the floor, sending them flying. She started to pick them up, but he stopped her. "So you're covering my 222?"

"They're good kids. Sandy took the Pre-Raph." He searched the jungle of his desk till he found his coffee mug. "And look, Alex, I hope you don't mind, I told Leonard you were having health issues, dating from your time in Australia. You can tell him I was wrong, but maybe you want to use that to explain what's been happening. I didn't say specifically what the problem was, so you could make up whatever you wanted. If you need to take time off, you know Leonard would agree. He just doesn't want a scene. And he'd recommend you anywhere, as would I. But it would be nice if you stayed." He smiled at her. He was a good man.

She let out a breath. "Tossman ex machina. You and my brother both, trying to save me from myself."

He said, "You'd do the same for me. Take a couple more days before you decide anything. Rest."

Two days later, there was an e-mail from Miriam Kohn: They needed Alex to appear in front of the Grievance Committee after all. "This is in light of an additional encounter between you and Miss Su," she wrote. "It's fair to advise you that Miss Su has produced a witness to the conversation." A witness? The only other students had been passing at least twenty feet away. Well, if Eden could lie, she could, too. Except it was two against one, and Alex could never convince another professor or even a grade-hungry student to pretend to be her witness.

She drank some wine and called Piet and told him everything. "Yeah," he said finally, "I like your friend's idea. Say you're sick. Feminine problems, so they won't pry too much. Maybe, like, cysts."

She flopped on her bed. "Sadly, I can't think of anything better."

"So why didn't you ring up Malcolm?"

"Maybe I did."

"No, I called him to see. Look, I was there when you pulled the card. Seven of hearts meant you were supposed to go all out. Job and man and your life back on track, yeah? So anyway, I set up a meeting for you guys."

"You're an ass, Piet."

"Sure." She heard him slurping something. His date had gone well, and he was staying with this woman downtown. "Look, Al, what's the moral of the whole albatross poem? Isn't it something about taking charge of your life? Like, 'I am the master of my fate and the captain of my soul,' right?"

"No, wrong poem. It's about loving animals. He looks at these water snakes and decides he loves them, and then he gets saved. So the moral is love all God's creatures. It's a bad poem, Piet. When you stop and think about it, it's a *really stupid poem*."

"Okay, so it's about love, though. There you go. Go love your man."

They met at a little café and bakery near campus, and Alex couldn't help feeling she was in a movie. She'd watched it a thousand times, how the former lovers meet for coffee—at a table by the window, so one person could watch the other leave, then sit there brokenhearted—and now here they were. Except they were back in a corner, at a table that wobbled, with someone's kids running around screaming in soccer uniforms. Malcolm maintained an expression of deep concern and leaned a little over the table. He looked tired. He hadn't shaved.

"I shouldn't have done that," Alex said.

"Which part?"

She managed to smile. "I'd say the entire past six months. Starting with the albatross."

"Have you been seeing someone?"

She couldn't believe he'd think that. And she was actually flattered. She said, "I would never do that to you."

His cup was frozen halfway to his mouth. "No—I was asking if you were seeing, like, you know. A psychologist. A therapist."

"Oh."

"You just haven't seemed like yourself."

"Honestly, Malcolm, I've just been drunk a lot lately. I was drunk when I said I couldn't marry you."

He nodded and considered this. "How do you feel now?"

"Now? I'm sober."

"That's not what I meant." He made a concerted effort to drink some coffee. He set the cup down and licked his lips. "What do you need from me?" God, the man was so sweet. And she wasn't the type to appreciate a kind heart while secretly wishing for the rough Harley man. This really was what she wanted.

If she'd learned anything from Eden Su, it was that sitting there mutely doesn't get you anywhere. Tossman was right—she was idle, a ship frozen in a sea of trouble. And that would never do.

So she said, "I need to know how you see me."

"I think you're great, and I love you, but I think it wouldn't hurt you to get some help."

"No, I'm actually—I actually need to know what you think I *look* like."

He was confused, and for a second she thought she'd have to explain the whole thing, all her vain neediness, but then he reached into his pants pocket for a ballpoint pen, white with a blue cap. He turned over his napkin and began to draw.

"What are you doing?" She leaned to see, but he moved it behind his coffee cup. Finally he held it out, in both hands. It was a stick figure: round head, curly hair in every direction, smiling mouth, happy eyes. Under it, he'd written ALEX.

She laughed. "That's me?" He put it down on the table and drew wavy lines emanating from her face and body. "What's that?"

"That's your amazingness."

He tilted his head and grinned at her, exactly like someone in a movie—the one the girl was supposed to end up with. And she thought, it wasn't a Rossetti, but it was good enough. And she thought, if he was dumb enough to take her back, she might be smart enough to marry him.

In future years, when she told that story, she left out the part about Malcolm. It became instead the story of why she left Cyril College, of how she and Malcolm ended up at State, of how sweet Tossman had been to her, that year before he killed himself. Of how even in assessing all her misprisions, she'd still missed something enormous. But where had the signs been? There had been no signs: just poor Tossman slumped on the steps of the music building at midnight, gun in his hand. And no one seemed to know why. And really, she'd barely known him. She'd only read half his books.

She would tell the story to younger colleagues, starting with the albatross, focusing on Eden Su, ending with Tossman, whom they knew about already. The point, the moral, was how easy it was to make assumptions, how deadly your mistakes could be. How in failing to recognize something, you could harm it or kill it or at least fail to save it. But she wondered, even as she told the story, if she wasn't still missing the point. If maybe it wasn't something, after all, about love—something she was too cold to understand.

The telling was an attempt, of course, at penance. It never did work; penance so rarely does.

A BIRD IN THE HOUSE
(THIRD LEGEND)

*I*n almost any culture, it's an omen: of a death, or a birth, or a journey. Sometimes a bird in the house is said to be the ghost of the recently departed. We aren't capable of seeing it rationally—especially as it falls in love with itself in our windows, as it flaps frantically past family portraits, as it kills itself against our walls.

When I was four months old, my father's parents saw each other for the last time. My grandmother would be dead within the year, crushed under a bus on a Budapest street. My grandfather would live on in Hawaii for two sunburnt and hazy decades. The summer of 1978 was a rare convergence for them—Chicago being a fairly precise midpoint, the birth of a baby being a neutralizing force.

The scene, as it's been relayed to me: my mother in our family room, holding me. My grandmother at the kitchen table with my sister, peeling apples. My father in the living room, playing piano. My grandfather on the stairs, a threadbare towel around his neck. (His blind left eye, doomed in infancy when his tubercular mother broke out of quarantine and kissed it, dripped so constantly that the towel became necessary late in life. He lived out his second half as a hatha yoga instructor, and at least when he stood on his head the tears fell into his white hair and not his mouth.)

And then: A sparrow flew out of the fireplace and past my screaming mother, sprinkling ash, flailing in loud circles. It found its way through the kitchen door, and my grandmother, still seated but reaching one hand straight up, grabbed its tail. The longest feathers stayed between her fingers as the bird flew on, raining small, perfect circles of blood on the kitchen tiles, on the flesh of the peeled apples, on the lid of the Cuisinart.

The Mozart stopped mid-phrase and the bird found the upstairs hallway, following some unhelpful instinct of altitude equaling safety. My grandfather tried to throw his towel over it. When this failed (depth perception not his strength), he rolled the towel and snapped it like a locker-room bully until the wall was smeared with ash and blood, and the sparrow, dazed, beat its wings into the floor and tried to claw a foothold. The old man wrapped the towel around it like a sack, and flung the whole thing out the window with such force that the bird had five full seconds to stretch its wounded wings before it needed to fly of its own accord.

My grandfather credited his luck. He always won at the track, as well. His secret was to bet on the white horse. The white horse was the only one his good eye could follow.

My grandmother, who knew more than a bit about omens, was somber the rest of the day.

When the two guests had returned to opposite ends of the world, there remained in the house only the detritus of their stay: the gifts my grandfather had brought; a brown patch scrubbed indelibly into the upstairs wall; in my sister's room, where a writing desk had been set up for my grandmother, the typewriter purchased for the visit and the curiously tangled ink ribbons she'd abandoned.

She always shuffled cards as she wrote, but when my mother cleaned she found only five, their margins softly obliterated. Of the Hanged Man, only the bottom half remained. Lost in the fog of whatever world she'd been creating, or in the present world (announcing its intentions so brazenly), or perhaps in some past and brutal one, my grandmother had chewed and swallowed almost the entire pack.

EXPOSITION

Would a glass of water be possible?

June the fourteenth. The ███████ theater on ███████████

The rumors we heard—on entering the theater—were thus: That Sophia Speri had refused several opportunities to leave the country, that she remained maniacally insistent on completing this final concert. That her husband had divorced and disavowed her, that he had fled. [Unintelligible.] I don't know, mind you, if this—it was what they said.

Yes.

We heard a man say, "Ah, if she'd been a clarinetist, she might have run through the hills with her instrument. But she's married to the beast with ivory keys. She'd sooner cut off her own arms than run to a refugee camp in ███████ with no pianos." We did not engage him in conversation. This was heard in passing.

Remember, please, that it was dark.

I believe that everyone in attendance understood the gravity of the situation. The invitations were secret, the hall was blackened. No one uttered her name. I made note of this.

———

I don't recall. There—the only further talk was of the music, the sheet music.

That her brother had smuggled it into the country.

This is only what the woman was saying, a woman's voice in the dark. That he had [unintelligible] the trick by reprinting each sheet of the piano score, along with mismatched lyrics to folk songs, confident that the border police could not pick out the tune. That the piece was thought unperformable by only two hands, a sort of composer's joke, you know, that it required at least three hands, with one pianist sitting on the other's lap.

I wish to add that this story cannot be true. Our border police, like all fine citizens, surely recognize our nation's traditional songs.

Yes, she did.

The information, the story that we overheard—and again please remember that we did not take part, ourselves, in the—the story went that she'd been unwilling to trust a duet partner and had worked her own nail beds bloody.

Three years. And that she had even stretched her hands on a contraption like the one Schumann invented. Have you heard of this? It destroyed his hands, Schumann's. But then I suppose Sophia Speri understood this to be the last concert of her career. Perhaps she understood the risk.

———

No, sir. I misspoke. Those were the speculations of others in the crowd. They weren't my—no.

Around sixty, though please recall that it was dark. The theater holds three hundred.

Among ourselves, only. The three of us.

No matches, no lights. It was a condition of entry.

She had memorized it, naturally.

I do not know.

Her footsteps. And then the sound of the bench, and of course the music beginning.

No one announced her.

We were—will you believe me if I say we were stuck to our seats? We knew that we ought to move, that to stay there any longer was foolishness itself.

Yes, sir. They had been clear and explicit. There was no confusion, either before or during the concert.

Here is where I'll stumble in my explanation. It was hypnotic. The music. The very reason it had been banned, I'm sure. It hypnotized, it entranced, it gave the listener visions of worlds beyond the borders of—

———

No, not our national borders. I mean the borders of the human heart.

If I might request more water . . .

I thank you for your patience.

I was saying, perhaps, that it prodded the heart with lust and ambition and false hope.

Around five minutes.

I cannot account for the discrepancy. I maintain, five minutes.

Like every star in the heavens had dropped a fine, taut string, and the stars had wrapped these strings around the earth. Like something our grandmothers used to sing.

Which is to say, it was wicked. To trick us, even us, in this way.

I understood it to be in F. I'm no musician, sir.

One of us moved.

I cannot say.

It might have been. Perhaps we all three moved as one.

[Unintelligible.]

Exactly as planned, exactly as ordered.

We surrounded the piano, and ███████████ removed the light from his hidden pocket.

We did not hesitate.

The audience—when the light appeared, yes, they saw her. They screamed, but I could not see which way they moved. I assumed most of them were leaving. Please recall that there was no light, except on Miss Speri.

She was beautiful.

I apologize, yes—I mean to say that she remained on the bench. That she continued playing.

Even as the barrel pressed a circle to her temple.

She did not drop a note.

An old joke for you, sirs, with a new punch line: What is black and white and red all over?

We remained, as instructed. On the stage.

 and ███████████

Let us presume there were sixty, minus us three. But even if we had fired at them—into the dark, as they ran—we had between us only eight more bullets.

May I humbly remind you that those were not our orders?

Even allowing that it was ten minutes, ten minutes of music. The entire piece, the whole concert, would have been thirty.

One-third.

Yes, sir.

A fair amount, I grant.

For our slowness, I apologize, as we have apologized before.

Please let me repeat that it was not ███████ for us to fire on the crowd.

Within thirty seconds. A minute at most.

Ourselves?

Again, it had not been ordered. I imagine we each felt, in that moment, that we could be of greater service to ███████ alive than dead.

Yes, even with the—please do understand, sirs, that I cannot recall a note of the music. It was complicated, not a child's ditty that lodges in the ear unbidden.

I could not. Not a note.

Had we been instructed to do so, we would not have hesitated to end our own lives on that very stage.

———

I believe so. Not to unhear music, but to forget it. Are they not the same?

The only way a lost tune, a truly lost tune, may return, is if one happens to hear it again. Surely you don't wish to suggest that our new President could permit such an oversight as to allow a second performance of the—

I apologize most meekly.

But this was precisely my point.

We wrapped her in the black cloth that was shaped to cover the piano.

In the wings of the stage.

It seemed fitting.

No, we did not.

In that moment? I was not trying to recall the music in that moment. I was committed to my duty.

I swear to you that it does not. You could chop us open from head to foot, you could pull our hearts from our chests, and you would not find the notes.

I trust to your wisdom, kind sirs. I beg you fervently. I ██████████ ███████████████. I pray.

CROSS

*T*here was garbage on the lawn, or maybe a construction sign, or (now that she was close enough to notice the flowers and ribbons) discarded decorations from a prom. But it was late August, not spring. And no, it wasn't prom garbage, but a small cross.

Celine had formed a cocoon of the summer's clothes around her cello case in the back of the little red Saab, and driven no faster than forty-five from Vermont to Albany and the rest of the way home. She was crawling so slowly on these cracked and narrow streets that she didn't need to brake to see the display. A white wooden cross, already weathered and tilting into more of an X than anything perpendicular. A sash across it: "Our Angel." Red artificial flowers, crumbling brown organic ones. Stuffed animals around the base. A red velvet ribbon, the kind intended for oversize Christmas gifts, tied around the top and already frayed and faded from weeks of rain and sun.

She coasted the ten feet to her driveway, then slowly pressed the gas as the car rumbled over the gravel: under the drooping trees, past the raised beds that had once been vegetable gardens, out of sight of the memorial.

Her first reactions were horror and empathy—cut with that strange exhilaration she'd learned not to feel guilty about when passing car wrecks on the highway. Later that fall, when she became fairly sure she was a terrible person, she would at least have this to hang on to: She did feel sorry. For those first few moments, she knew she was sorry.

———

After she turned on all the lights, after she stomped her hiking boots to scare away any mice, and let the taps run till the water turned clear, she turned on her computer and googled her street and "car accident," but there was nothing. She found a can of tomato soup in the cupboard, and while it heated on the stove she called the sheriff. "I'm wondering about an accident on Grove Road this summer," she said. "There was a fatality."

"Oh, right." The man might or might not have been the sheriff himself. "Yeah, teenage girl on the back of her boyfriend's motorcycle. Tried to avoid a truck, and they hit a tree pretty bad. Boyfriend's okay, woke up from a coma back in July. You know what, it was out in front of that oriental musician's house. That famous lady musician. She your neighbor?"

Celine hadn't even noticed the tree, but when she went back outside she saw the old white oak had some bark missing and a decent gouge three feet up. The tree was fine, though. It had, after all, won this particular battle.

She straightened the horizontal bar of the cross and nudged one of the small teddy bears with her boot. It was rain soaked, polyester stuffing erupting from the back. Birds and chipmunks, she presumed, had been hauling off the fluff to line their homes.

It started to rain again as she carried her bags into the house, and she dug the umbrella out from under the passenger seat to hold over the cello case. She sat in the living room and played the Kodály she'd been working on for Philadelphia, his Capriccio, then rested there, silent, and enjoyed the stillness of her house and the creak of the walls—such a change from the constant noise of Marlboro, where the young, excited stars and the seasoned virtuosos had made glorious rackets for seven long, hot weeks.

By the time the smoke alarm went off, the tomato soup had already burned to a solid mess.

———

Twelve days later, she still hadn't unpacked. That first day she'd considered herself too tired, too thrown by imagining the calamitous summer of emergency vehicles and witness statements she had so serendipitously avoided. And then classes started at the college, and rehearsals started in the city, and she was hardly ever home when it was light. Over the next week the clothes spread outward from the open suitcase, the hair dryer found its way back to the bathroom, and the sheet music migrated to the coffee table. She could find everything she needed, and she might never have unpacked at all were it not for Gregory and the two Mikes coming to stay.

She pushed the couch back for more rehearsal space and brought in extra chairs, and finally filed the old music away. She scraped the moldy gray cucumber out of the crisper drawer, checked the guest rooms, which only needed a sweeping and a change of pillowcases, and then at last sat cross-legged on her own bedroom floor to excavate the shirts and sandals and performance dresses of what seemed at least a year ago.

The smell of stale sweat grew stronger with each layer she lifted, but also the smell of Vermont, of grass, of the cigarettes she hadn't touched since she'd been home. There was the black dress, the one that wasn't long enough to work with a cello between her legs, but which she'd worn, with various disguising accessories, to everyone else's concerts. The back was dirty, she saw now, from leaning against buildings to smoke, and she wondered if it had been like that all summer. She hadn't found much time to do laundry up there. No one had, really. It was almost unthinkable now, back in the real world, that she'd worn this dress at least six times since it last saw detergent. And yet she didn't remember smelling funny, even in the last week when she'd worn it with a long pink scarf to the Mozart piano trios. That night, Gregory had found her during an intermission behind the auditorium and told her he felt old. "There's too much youth here," he said.

"They're good kids," Celine said. "They're not *that* much younger."

He said, "No, I misspoke. I meant my own youth." He'd been there, like Celine had, as a young star just out of the New England Conservatory. They'd missed each other by five years, so whatever heartbreak and triumph and sublimity and romance had filled his summers she couldn't know, but she assumed they must have run pretty much parallel to hers. Celine herself had fallen in love that first summer with Lev Moskowitz, the forty-year-old composer in residence, and they had spent the next thirteen years miserably married. She'd been worried, when she was asked to return to Marlboro to guide and collaborate with the younger musicians, that she'd spend the summer awash in self-pity. But instead she'd felt just the opposite: young again, and silly, and almost beautiful.

That Gregory had then kissed her—that she'd kissed him back and let his dense, abandoned stubble scrape her chin—seemed almost inevitable, just a by-product of all that youth and music and summer. They'd been rehearsing Bartók together that week, and it seemed to follow naturally that the interweaving of melodies should lead so directly to the interweaving of limbs. As it so often had, in the history of Marlboro. In the history of music, for that matter.

He had wedged his thigh between her legs, and she felt her feet leave the earth, felt the damp of the building soak through her dress. Gravity rearranged itself so that leaning back against the theater's slippery verticality was enough to keep from floating off into the night.

The next morning, she could still trace the red patches on her skin where Gregory's mouth and chin had scraped and bitten: down her neck, along her collarbones, down her sternum. And it was only then, the next morning, standing in her towel in front of the narrow closet mirror in the Marlboro dorm room, that she could process what had been so unusual, what left her so shaken and oxygen deprived. Every man who had kissed her good night in the past year of formal and tepid dating had done so with a tactical purpose: obtaining a second date, getting invited upstairs, letting her down easy. But Gregory and his fervid mouth had only demonstrated the simplest and most emphatic things: *clavicle*, they said, and *shoulder*, and *teeth* and *thirst*.

And then he had lowered her, slow and weightless, to the ground—where his hand against her cheek and then his heading to the theater, staring back over his shoulder, had not seemed in the least like a breaking off. Nor did it particularly seem like a story that was to be continued.

At lunch the next day there was no awkward avoidance, only a sly grin, which made it all right to rehearse peacefully with Mike and Mike that afternoon, to glide through the rest of the summer's rehearsals and meals and concerts with neither longing nor regret, just shaky wonder.

Outside, she heard a car drive up and stop. Gregory and the Mikes weren't due until the next morning, and she had a moment of dread imagining that Gregory might have decided to show up a day early. But the car wasn't in the driveway. It was out on the road near the oak tree, and when the doors opened two women worked their way out. A few leaves had already fallen from the trees, affording her a clearer view of the cross than she'd had before, and as the women began circling it, she could see their bodies and their pale hair. One was extremely thin, almost ill-looking, so that the other, though not obese, was nearly twice her weight. They wore jeans and unzipped fleeces, and the larger one seemed younger—mother and daughter, perhaps, and perhaps the mother and sister of the dead girl. Celine had pictured something very different before. She'd imagined the dead girl as petite, with dark skin and long, straight black hair. Exactly like her teenage self, she realized now, and wondered why she'd formed such a narcissistic picture. But no one like that could feasibly be related to these two women who were now walking partway up the driveway to peer at Celine's car, to stare suspiciously at the house. Celine ducked out of the window frame and only looked again a few minutes later when she heard music blasting from the little blue car. They had turned on the radio and opened all the doors, so that now they had a soundtrack of anemic rock for the redecorations they were attempting around the cross.

They didn't seem to be taking anything away, just adding. Celine grabbed her father's old birding binoculars out of her desk and watched the women jab individual plastic flowers into the ground around the cross's base. She inferred from the cardboard box still full of blue and white and pink that they intended to plant an entire plastic garden.

Over the next hour, as Celine went back and forth between unpacking and cleaning and staring out the window, the women, too, alternated their plastic horticulture with sitting on the hood of the blue car, smoking, laughing loud enough for Celine to hear.

At several points she considered pulling on her coat and walking out there, bringing the women mugs of hot cider, asking if there was anything she could do to help. But she never knew what to say in these situations, and she worried that her distaste for the new lawn decorations would show on her face. The way they kept looking at her car, kept pointing at her house and talking, she felt strangely judged. They already guessed her to feel superior, and they were right.

———

When the Mikes showed up the next morning—Mike Langley, the gay blond one, and Mike Cho, the young straight one who, in a fit of bravery, had slapped his arm around Celine that summer and called her his "half-breed half-Asian half sister"—she was in a frenzy of breakfast preparations. She had covered the kitchen table with pitchers of orange juice and milk and plates of fruit and toast, and over at the stove she was working on "eggs with stuff," which she was sure had a fancier name somewhere in the world. It occurred to her, as she hugged them both and showed them their rooms and ran back down to stir the browning vegetables and sausage, that filling the air with the smell of onions and peppers and mushrooms and meat might have been, in some way, an attempt at compensation for the hollow welcome of an empty and under-decorated house.

The Mikes sat at the table fidgeting and ate huge plates of eggs. Mike Langley was in his twenties, and this had been his third summer at Marlboro, but Mike Cho was only eighteen. She had suddenly wondered, in the midst of all the arrangements for this week, if she should perhaps be calling his parents. Langley had picked him up from Juilliard this morning and driven him west in his little Honda. Despite their enormous talent, both had been noticeably intimidated that summer by both Celine and Gregory, and she hoped this week would put them at ease.

She was displeased with how frequently she found herself checking the clock, how busy her hands wanted to be. "There's a used bookstore in town," she said, "and a coffee shop, if you want to drive in. I thought we could all go out to dinner tonight, or we can order pizza. And tomorrow's the day Julie comes, from Deutsche Grammophon."

"Oh, Jesus," Langley said. "Don't tell me."

"You can pretend she's my sister, and she's visiting from Canada. My blond sister, ha! But she's going to love you."

Julie was thrilled by the prospect of the quartet, especially since it involved Gregory, who was already on the label. But Celine hoped, from a sort of motherly perspective, that Julie would fall so in love with Mike and Mike that she'd develop independent relationships with them.

Gregory had, apparently, just let himself right in the front door, because there he stood, duffel bag in one hand, violin case in the other, his thinning hair still bleached from the summer, his face unshaven. He put his things on the floor and hugged everyone. Celine held her wooden spoon out awkwardly behind her back so she wouldn't get grease on his coat.

"Quite a display you have out front there."

"We were wondering!" Mike Cho said. But then he straightened his face, clearly worried he'd made a mistake. "Was it your dog?"

"A girl on a motorcycle." Celine went back to the stove and started cracking eggs into the new batch of vegetables and sausage. Too many eggs, probably, but she couldn't stop herself from cracking one more, and then one more. She told them the story, as she knew it, and about the recent additions. "I haven't been out yet this morning. How bad is it?"

Gregory considered while he poured a mug of coffee. "I'd say it's *sprawling*."

She turned from the stove, relieved to have found a topic of limitless conversation. "Okay, here's the issue, then. Pretend you're advice columnists, and I'm depending on you for a moral answer: What do I *do*? I can't take it down. I can't live with it forever. I can't move. I can't ask them to make it more tasteful. It's selfish, I know, but I'm not okay with a shrine on my lawn. Not forever."

"Could you plant a shrub in front of it?" Mike Langley asked.

"That's good! But maybe—no, it's too close to the street. There's only a couple feet of room. And in winter you'd be able to see right through anyway."

"You should complain to village hall," Gregory said. "They probably own the land by the road for putting in phone poles, right? They wouldn't want that on town property. Separation of church and state."

"This is a town that erects a life-sized Last Supper on the green for Easter."

"I want to see it again," Mike Cho said. "We're creative people. We should be able to come up with something."

When he stood, Mike Langley followed him, leaving Celine with a pan of eggs she was about to serve Gregory, and Gregory with an empty plate. She scraped the eggs onto the plate—a mountain, really—and handed him a fork. "You can carry this, right?"

"I thought I'd stay here and chat with you and enjoy my coffee." He looked straight at her and didn't blink, and she saw that it was a challenge, or at least an offer.

"It's so nice out!" she said. "And we'll be sitting all day. Let's get some exercise."

And so he followed them all out the door, eating his eggs.

It was worse than she'd imagined. The flowers were spread over at least twenty-five square feet, all the way out to the street and all the way back to the oak, but three times as long as that—a carpet of white and blue and pink. They had jammed the plastic stems so far into the earth that it was botanically bizarre—roses and tulips and carnations that blossomed only three inches above the ground. The stuffed menagerie had expanded, as well. A plush moose and what looked like an off-brand Cabbage Patch doll were now slumped near the base of the cross, like winos at a bus stop.

Mike Langley clasped his hands behind his neck. "I'm *offended*, aesthetically," he said. "This is possibly the ugliest thing I've ever seen."

Celine shook her head. "So tell me, then: Am I a bad person? I *do* feel sorry for them. But that doesn't mean they can have my lawn."

"You're a good person," Gregory said. He was circling the scene with his eggs. "They can't make a shrine on your property."

Mike Cho suddenly grew excited. "Could you mow the lawn and just chop them all down? And then it would just look like your lawn people did it."

"I don't think these are the kind of folks who would assume anyone had lawn people. Which I *don't*, except when I'm out of town. And it would ruin my mower."

They all found themselves straightening things, just as Celine had the day she'd first found it. "Are you even religious?" Mike Cho asked. "Are you, like, Christian, or . . . ?"

"Not since I was fifteen. I love sacred music, though. I love masses, and I love requiems. The Verdi *Requiem* might be my favorite thing in the world, even though I don't believe a word of the text. Is that weird?"

Mike Langley poked a fake tulip with the toe of his shoe and said, "I think *weird* has just been redefined."

Back in the house, Celine toasted more bread and refilled everyone's coffee and started another batch of eggs. "Look at you," Gregory said. "You're Snow White, feeding all the little men."

The Bartók went beautifully, as if a day hadn't passed since Marlboro. Of all the groupings that summer—cello with piano, cello with flute and harp, cello with clarinet and alto—this string quartet had been the one that instantly justified itself, that proved revelatory. Rehearsals had left her sweaty and exhausted and jubilant. It had been a long time since she'd felt that way about any collaboration, and it had been at least a year since she'd felt she was making any progress, musically. She knew the Mikes must still be wondering what on earth these two experienced, successful musicians could want with two young kids. They didn't understand yet what they were bringing to the equation themselves: fire, energy. And marketability, to be quite honest. It was an interesting concept, one that Julie from Deutsche Grammophon thought would sell nicely. "The music press will *love* it," she'd said. "Because it's about teaching, and it's about a meeting of the generations, and it's about Marlboro."

Gregory was a subtle leader, so subtle that Celine found herself not just listening to his first violin but watching him closely for any twitch of the mouth. When he looked back at her, just as when either of the Mikes caught her eye, it was with the unapologetic stare of collaborating musicians. There were musicians who never looked up from their hands or their instruments, but she'd seen quartets of straight men gaze at each other like they were making love.

They finished the Allegro and Prestissimo movements and stopped to talk about balance. "You have amazing acoustics," Gregory said. "We could record right here."

She looked around the room, at the high ceiling and bare walls, the bare floor, the couch and coffee table crammed into a corner, the empty and cavernous fireplace. "It comes from having no furniture," she said.

Mike Langley raised his viola bow tentatively in the air, asking permission to speak. The Mikes would both have to get bolder, be willing to argue with Celine and Gregory. "Should we come up with a name?" he asked. "Before your Deutsche Grammophon person gets here? Would that help?" No, it wouldn't, particularly, but Celine didn't want to shoot him down.

"I'm sure Marlboro Quartet is already taken," Mike Cho said.

Gregory laughed. "No one has dared for a very long time."

"The May-December String Quartet," Celine offered. "Because two of us are so damn old."

The Mikes both looked horrified, and confused about whether they should protest. "She doesn't mean that," Gregory said. "She's only forty. What she means is the two of you are so damn young." How Gregory knew her exact age, she had no idea. She wondered if he'd been googling her. "The Happenstance Quartet," he offered. "The House in the Middle of Nowhere Quartet. The Get Your Cross off My Lawn Quartet."

Langley raised his bow again, but this time it was in triumph, and Celine was thrilled with his confidence. "The Cross-Purposes Quartet." He didn't need to spell out the various meanings. It was perfect, just like the quartet itself.

And when they played the Allegro again, lo and behold, it had a more solid shape, a stronger arc. They knew who they were.

That night, the Cross-Purposes Quartet drank mulled wine in the chairs they'd pulled in front of Celine's fireplace. Gregory had gone knocking at half the front doors on the long, twisty road until he'd happened on an old man with a woodpile and a generous heart. The other three had watched, laughing, from the front porch as Gregory pushed an actual wheelbarrow back up the driveway.

Celine had left the room when Gregory opened the flue, afraid bats or mice would tumble out. She'd never had a fire in this house, but now that it was roaring along pleasantly, she imagined she might do it again sometime this winter. She might even invest in a real poker, rather than the barbecue fork Mike Cho was using to prod the logs.

"What if you moved it?" Mike Langley said, out of nowhere. "You could just transplant the whole thing one house down, in front of some other tree, and when they see it they'll assume their minds are playing tricks." He was joking, but she actually considered it for a second.

"I bet they've got an album full of photos with your house in the background," Gregory said. "That's something else—if the city does own that property, and you tear the shrine down, could these people sue? They'd have proof."

"Oh, God. Take that back." Celine found that she was looking at Gregory's shoulder, his Adam's apple, anywhere but his face. How strange, when it had been so comfortable to lock eyes during rehearsal. He wasn't terribly handsome, but he didn't need to be. He was a perfect example of what her grandmother had always said: After forty, you look how you deserve to. Here was Gregory, whose eyes were creased with laugh lines, whose arms were taut from music, whose habit of leaning forward into every conversation was a sort of invitation.

But Celine was absolutely not interested, and three years after the split from Lev she was fully and finally settled into her decision to be on her own. She had bought the house, and she had told her well-meaning friends that no, in fact, she did not want to be set up. It was a lot like naming the quartet. She'd decided who she was, and this was what allowed her to move forward.

The conversation had turned back to religion. "I'd call it half-assed Buddhism," Mike Cho was saying. "Like, pretending to be Buddhist in front of our grandparents. There was a lot of shoe removal. That's all I really registered: a lot of OCD shoe stuff."

Celine said, "Don't you think there's a connection? I went through obsessive-compulsive phases as a child, and they always went together with my religious phases. Touch everything three times, kneel and cross your chest, you know? That's what those women are doing out there. It's compulsive ritual."

"I imagine it has more to do with grief, Celine." Gregory was smiling, but she still took it as a judgment.

"You see, I *am* a bad person."

The night grew sillier and happier as the mulled wine turned to regular wine and then to coffee. Celine was persuaded to do her "cello blues" trick, with Gregory and Mike Langley trading verses ("Got a big white cross sitting on my lawn / Got a big white cross sitting on my lawn / Got the white trash blues / Lord I wish that cross was gone") and Mike Cho giggling like a sugared-up little girl. It occurred to her only then that she'd been serving alcohol to an eighteen-year-old. She poured him more coffee.

Despite the hilarity she was angry with herself, all night, for having let on how superior she felt to those two women. And perhaps, after all, she was only so disgusted with the women because she saw her younger self in them, in their pointless adding and adjusting. She remembered a period—she must have been ten—when every time she was alone in a room and sneezed or belched, she had to say "excuse me" to God one hundred times. If she lost count, she had to start over. One day when she was supposed to be practicing Bach, she sneezed but felt that she didn't have time to stop playing, so she kept going, whispering "excuse me" on the first and third beats of every measure. And if she hated the child she had been, the one who had tried to control a frightening world through the details, then wasn't it also natural that she should want to shake these adults by the shoulders, these grown women acting the same way?

She showed everyone where the towels were, and the linen closet, and the extra soaps, and she demonstrated the bathroom tap that had been hooked up backward, so that the hot water was to the right and cold to the left. She spent five minutes trying to get the window closed all the way in Mike Langley's room, even though he said he didn't care, and then she found herself opening and closing all the drawers in that room's tall old dresser, to make sure there was nothing inside. Gregory patted her shoulder and said, "How's that OCD coming?"

Mike Cho was hungover in the morning, slumped at the table with his forehead on a bag of frozen peas. Celine made him a grilled cheese sandwich and forced him to drink glass after glass of water. Julie was due at the house at noon.

She agreed to go for a run with Langley—and really, it was also an excuse to check what damage had been done to the cross by the early-morning thunderstorm—and Gregory promised he'd do his best to detoxify Cho in their absence. As Celine and Langley stretched together on the porch, she realized she hadn't run since Marlboro, when the combination of damp, cold air and lingering cigarette smoke had made each deep intake of breath at once vital and strangled, as if she were running with the flu.

The shrine looked approximately the same, except the stuffed figures were slumped farther over and the rain had left the flowers and the cross itself bright and glistening. It looked a little less like a grave and more like an Easter display. It had occurred to her, half-asleep during the storm, that the cross might be struck by lightning—that God, offended by the tackiness of the display, might vaporize the whole thing and let the poor girl rest tastefully in peace, let Celine have her lawn back, let the women move on with their grief. It was strange, the way her brain clung to the notion of God, twenty-five years after she'd last prayed or made sure to touch the Communion cup equally with both hands. Much like the way she still found herself budgeting money for hypothetical vacations when there was no one to vacation with, and when she'd never liked traveling with Lev in the first place.

She managed to keep pace with Langley, despite his alarmingly long legs. "So tell me about Vitrello," he said, meaning Gregory. "What's his deal?"

In the several steps it took her to catch enough breath to speak, Celine considered how she was meant to answer. "He likes you guys," she said. "I think he's committed to this."

Langley was laughing beside her. "That was my subtle way of asking if he's queer. I was trying to figure it out all summer. Sometimes I swear he's flirting. But wasn't he married once? Clue me in."

"He wasn't married," she said. "But he's straight. Sorry."

Langley, she realized, was barely jogging, just sort of loping along, the way you might pretend to run with a small child. "You know for sure?" he asked, and when he turned to hear her answer, she knew she'd already given it: Her cheeks were burning, and her hand had fluttered to her forehead. "*Really*," he said, and kept jogging with his head turned, as if she might tell him the whole story.

She didn't, of course, and she was horrified at herself for blushing, but at least the adrenaline carried her all the way to the end of the road.

By the time Julie showed up, Mike Cho had emptied his stomach several times and was weak but functional. Celine worried, as they started tuning, that he would fall asleep on his viola's chin rest. Langley, in contrast, never stopped moving his feet or rocking his body back and forth, and seemed in danger of chewing his own lips off. And then there was Gregory, staring her down.

Julie had shown up in a black pantsuit and heels, nearly falling when she tripped on the gravel drive. She was reclining barefoot now on the couch in the corner, drinking tea and waiting for the music.

Gregory started them far too slow, Mike Langley seemed to be playing a different piece than everyone else entirely, and Mike Cho was nearly catatonic. Celine herself was still bothered, really, by her own reaction to Langley's questions. She'd acted like an idiotic child, one who didn't understand that what happened at Marlboro did not translate into the real world. Well, maybe the music did—though what was this mess they were presenting to Julie, then?—but not the sex. It was like Vegas, in that regard. As it should be.

They were making a disaster of it, although really the first movement of Bartók's fourth quartet was dissonant enough to hide the rough edges to less trained ears, and Julie was more a businesswoman than a musician. They muddled their way through three awkward movements and arrived at the Allegreto Pizzicato: three minutes of entirely plucked strings, which when done well sounded playful and crisp and strangely elfin, and when done badly sounded like arguing birds. Langley's manic energy and Cho's nauseated languor didn't bode well, and when they all leaned over to put their bows on the floor, Cho stayed down a full five seconds.

Gregory and Celine started too loudly, but it gave Langley something to follow and it seemed to snap Cho awake. It was like leading students rather than colleagues, but it worked. And then the accented notes that require those insane Bartók pizzicati—where the player plucks the string so hard it slaps back against the fingerboard—somehow electrified the room, so that by the end of the movement they were back together, back in some caffeinated and blessed rehearsal space in Vermont, and Julie was sitting up on the couch.

When she was much younger, Celine would have taken all those fours to mean something: four instruments playing the fourth movement of the fourth quartet. One more four would have been better: four to the fourth power. The four points of the cross, then. Maybe that would count. But then, she wondered what she meant by *count*. Because who was doing the counting?

———

Julie loved it—had loved it from the beginning, in fact—and was anxious to talk about recording schedules and the Marlboro tour that fall and publicity and a website. Gregory, for some reason, was more anxious to talk about the cross, and he told Julie the story. "There's really no good answer," he said. "I was sitting up half the night thinking about it."

Celine was strangely flattered by this validation of her own obsession.

"You should get a lawyer," Langley said. He had turned his chair around to sit in it backward, like a twelve-year-old punk. He couldn't stop grinning at Julie.

"No! No, I can't have you involved in a lawsuit!" Julie had found the whole thing funny, up till now. "And not about *this*!"

Mike Cho excused himself then to lie down upstairs, and Celine followed with a glass of water. She put a garbage can next to his bed and closed the curtains against the sunlight. When she came back, Julie was offering her own solution. "You leave a note," she said, "where you offer to build something more permanent. You say you've noticed the rain damage, and you'd like to buy them a marble slab. Or a fountain, or something. One of those saints made of poured cement."

"Or a real garden!" Langley said. "Which would conveniently hide the marble slab."

It was a good solution, befitting Julie's polish and young professionalism. Those were qualities Celine knew she herself lacked. Or rather, she'd always lacked polish, but now, blushing at the sight of the first violinist, measuring the distance between their bodies, she had lost her last ounce of professionalism.

Julie left that evening, and the boys stayed three more days. Celine made sure to delay the Mikes until Gregory was ready to go, then said good-bye to all of them at once, standing on the porch without a coat and hugging herself against the cold. She kissed them all on the cheek, and maybe she did feel a little like Snow White, sending her dwarfs off into the mines. Only they were carrying curvy black cases instead of pickaxes. They'd see each other in November for the Marlboro tour, and then they'd start recording. "Take a flower on your way out!" she called. "As a souvenir!" The Mikes started toward Langley's car, but Gregory lingered behind, was even turning back to the porch, and so Celine went inside and quickly shut the door behind her.

She took Julie's advice, and the next day she wrote a note on her nice stationery, sealed it in a Ziploc, and stuck it to the cross with duct tape. She phrased it nicely, offering several different options for "a more permanent memorial."

Weeks passed, and she thought the women might not come back at all, but then there they were one morning, exactly a month after their last visit. It must have been the anniversary; the accident must have happened on July 10. So she could expect them again on November 10, and every tenth thereafter. She ran for her binoculars and watched from the guest room where Gregory had slept. She realized, kneeling on the bed for a better view, that she hadn't changed the sheets, hadn't even straightened the covers. It had been a long month, one of those months that last two years. It had been wet and cold and horrible, and Lev, she read in the *Times*, had gotten remarried. The bed felt strangely warm, as if Gregory had only just rolled out to grab some breakfast.

The women took a box from their trunk, then spent a long time walking around the cross before they finally peeled the Ziploc off and opened it. Celine couldn't see their faces as they read, but when they finished they stepped closer for a better view of her house. They stood staring up at the windows, hands above their eyes to block the sun. She didn't move, but she put the binoculars down. She actually did want them to know she was home, in case they felt like ringing her doorbell to discuss the offer.

There was something about their body language that she didn't like, something about the way they both stood with their weight to one side, one hip jutting out, that felt angry and unpleasant—as if she'd done exactly the wrong thing. The older woman said something, and they both laughed. Celine could tell even from up here that it was a bitter laugh, a sixth-graders-on-the-playground, sarcastic sort of laugh. The older one took the note and ripped it into pieces, and walked to Celine's car. She lifted the windshield wiper and stuck the shreds underneath it, like some perverse flier.

The women took little plastic pumpkins out of their box and spent the next half hour sticking them around the cross.

Celine decided she'd e-mail the rest of the quartet in the morning: "What do I do now? Does this give me the right to be mean?"

Over the past month, both Mikes had become more and more comfortable, at least via e-mail, with expressing their opinions. Mike Cho had been brave enough to shoot down Gregory's Haydn idea before Celine could veto it herself. Julie, meanwhile, was nagging them all to come into the city and have photos taken. Celine knew it was important, that Julie couldn't start any publicity without it, but she kept putting it off. She was busy, truly, and she was getting ready for Vienna, and there were student recitals. But mostly she didn't want to pose in a little row, staring seriously at her cello, turning red from her proximity to Gregory. She was like one of those apocryphal native people, worried the camera would steal her soul. Or at least, in this case, expose it.

That night Celine was playing Saint-Saëns in the living room, sitting on one of the same four chairs that had remained in a vacated semicircle for the past month, when the doorbell rang. She had wanted so badly to talk to the women before, but now it was dark, and she knew they were angry. They'd had enough time to go home and come back with Lord knows what. Weapons, or pictures of the dead girl. She held her bow in front of her like a saber and sat perfectly still in her chair. They rang the bell again, and then again, and then they started knocking, loud and fast. They'd have heard the cello through the door, and if the sheriff was willing to tell a perfect stranger on the phone about the "oriental lady musician," he'd surely told these women the same thing at some point in the paperwork process. He'd probably added "famous" and "rich," neither of which was really true in the grand scheme of things, but that was her reputation in town.

The knocking was odd and irregular, and she wondered if they had come back with the girl's drunken father. Or sent him alone. And she deserved their spite, she realized. How condescending must it seem, for the lady in the big house to offer to buy something nicer? *Excuse me, could I please make your grief a little more tasteful?*

It took her a good half a minute to realize the knocking wasn't irregular at all. It was the *William Tell* Overture, in perfect rhythm. She stood and walked slowly to the door, bow still perpendicular to her stomach. She called, "Lev?"

"No." The voice was familiar and vaguely hurt, and the knocking stopped. She opened the door and there was Gregory, his violin case and his duffel bag at his feet, as if he'd never gone anywhere at all.

He said, "I come to plead sanctuary. I saw your cross out front. This is a church, correct?"

And what could she do but laugh and invite him in? She made a pot of coffee, and he lit a fire with the wood left from September, and the whole time she didn't ask what he was doing there, and he didn't offer an explanation. She wanted to ask if he thought he was in a movie, that he could just show up at someone's door expecting love or sex or friendship, or whatever he was after. But there were worse kinds of movie.

They pulled the couch up to the fireplace, and she told him about the note that was still out there under her windshield wipers.

Gregory said, "And I showed up the same day? It's a sign."

Instead of asking what it was a sign *of*, Celine said, "I don't believe in signs." She was holding her cup in both hands, grateful to have a fire to look at.

"Sure you do." She didn't answer, and so he said, "You must, because you believe in music."

"But you came today on purpose. Did you figure it out, about the anniversaries?"

He put his coffee on the floor and finally unbuttoned his thin coat. "I came because I have another solution. I think you should leave this place."

"That's ridiculous."

"You don't seem happy here, and there's no good answer to the cross problem, and I want you to know you're welcome to stay with me in the city. Just for a while. A week. A month. Longer, if you want."

"I teach, you know. At the college."

"Which is closer to the city than to this house."

The warmth was getting too much for her, between the hot cup in her hands and the fire, and the blood roaring through her face.

"You've exiled yourself out here, and I don't know why. *Come live with me and be my love*, as they say."

"Who says that?"

"I do. I just did." He laughed, and she refused to look at him, she absolutely refused, but she could hear his fingers touching his beard. She could see his brown shoes, stretched toward the fire.

"Gregory, I'm an adult. I can't run away from my problems."

"But," he said, "wasn't that what you were doing when you bought this house?"

"So I should just run away again."

"Think of it as running *toward* something."

"What, I'm Cinderella, and you're going to sweep me away in a pumpkin?"

He leaned so far into her field of vision that she couldn't help but see him. "We've been over this. You're Snow White."

She said, "Listen. You're crazy, but I'm not insulted. I will forget, for the sake of the quartet, that you ever presumed to tell me what to do with my life. The old folks shouldn't quarrel in front of the children." She didn't add that she was terrified. That she was tired of running in *any* direction, away from things or toward them. That maybe the reason she'd bought this house, so big and solid and remote, was the hope that it would keep her pinned down in one spot for the rest of her life, where she wouldn't have to make decisions. That the cross bothered her so much because it was a wedge in her perfect isolation—an invasion.

She brought Gregory a bowl of butternut squash soup and a glass of wine. They tried some of Bach's two-part inventions, but they had no sheet music and they couldn't remember any through to the end. Celine kept trying to sing Gregory's part, to remind him, and they'd both end up laughing.

She said, "The bad news is, your sheets are dirty. The good news is, it's your own dirt."

He said, "See? Another sign." And he went up to bed without even trying to kiss her.

Celine stayed down to make sure the fire was fully dead. She straightened Gregory's shoes by the door so they lined up perfectly with her own, and she made sure all the doors were locked. She sat back on the couch, and at that very moment the last log tumbled forward against the grate, shooting up a shower of sparks.

If she still believed in signs, they would indeed be clear today: the dying fire, the scene of death on the lawn, the ripped-up note under her wipers. Time to move on. And here was Prince Charming on her doorstep with his fiddle. What other sign could she be waiting for? Except, perhaps, the one that would make her believe in signs again at all.

She walked up the stairs and brushed her teeth and looked out the bathroom window. There were no streetlights this far out in the country, and so no cross, no flowers. You'd never know anything was out there at all, beyond your own reflection on a glassy sheet of blackness. And what a reflection! She stared in bafflement at this bright-eyed stranger. There she was in the mirror, too, her pulse so fast and exuberant she could see it in her neck and temples. She scratched her cheek to see if it was sunburnt or just flushed.

Well, there were signs like crosses and runes and totems, and then there were the signs of the body. Those ones didn't play fair, didn't sit on your lawn and wait for interpretation. They hijacked you. Before her body could betray her any further, before it could carry her to Gregory's door, she grabbed the shampoo from the side of the tub and squeezed a good quarter cup of green slime right on top of her head. She said out loud, "You're not going anywhere like that."

But the shower didn't help, the ratty towel didn't help. She put her clothes back on.

The lamplight under Gregory's door. This stubborn and idiotic lust. Sometimes, after all, a thing wasn't an omen but the event itself, as solid and irrefutable as an oak in the path of your little motorcycle.

She walked into the guest room and sat on the edge of Gregory's bed. He closed his novel and tugged the sheet up to his armpits. He was bare-chested. "I bet your apartment doesn't even have room for a cello," she said. "You want to hear a cello every morning when you step out of the shower?"

"Yes. I want that very much."

"You're not going to take me out on a date first? And we might hate each other. Don't you think it could ruin the quartet? It could."

He held his hand out to her, palm up. It took her a moment to realize he wasn't offering any answers but that.

And she took the hand, and he pulled her into the bed and under the covers, and even in the lamplit darkness, even as the whole house dissolved around them into the gray, ecstatic haze of two a.m., she was wide awake.

His mouth on her shoulder was warm. The universe flipped in on itself. She found the deep and hollow place where his neck became his chest.

GOOD SAINT ANTHONY
COME AROUND

The story goes that Chapman, leaving a meeting in Seattle—this was the seventies, he was still designing posters—looked up toward a noise in the sky and got hit in the face with a fish. No one saw, no one pointed and said, "Christ, man, that's a fish!" but there it was, flailing on the cement. Up in the air, two cormorants still fought loudly. Chapman picked the thing up: a six-incher, cold and dense. He ran with it down the street, shouting at people in his way, dodging bikes. Around a corner and into a Vietnamese takeout place. "Cup of water!" he yelled. "Cup of water!" And when the woman didn't understand, he grabbed a cup from the trash and filled it at the soda machine and dropped the fish in headfirst. Later he'd carry it to the ferry docks in a borrowed bucket and dump it back in the bay. The fish wasn't doing well and would just be easy prey again, but what was he supposed to do, take it to a vet?

My point here isn't that Chapman would do anything to help you out, although that's true. My point is, he was the kind of guy stuff happened to. Some people live their whole lives according to the laws of probability. If there's a one in six thousand chance of getting hit by lightning, they won't. They won't win the lottery, either. Because someone like Chapman will. Someone whose stars made strange and intricate patterns at the moment of his birth.

Chapman met Francisco Ling the same way he met many great artists of the late eighties: He knocked on his door one day and

punched him. He'd had the idea over drinks with a friend. "I want
to punch Keith Haring in the face," he'd joked, and the friend had
said, "Do it." And somewhere along the way, the idea became serious, became the seed of a great photographic series: famous and
influential artists, right after Chapman hit them in the face. Chapman would ring the doorbell, wait for the artist, and punch him
square with his right hand, clicking the camera with his left in time
to catch the artist's shock, pain, blood. And if the artist fought back,
Chapman kept clicking. He'd explain what he was doing, and—if
you can believe it—most of the artists understood and forgave and
were even flattered. The series was called *anXiety of influence*, and
he would patiently explain its Oedipal undertones, its message of
forceful reinvention. *Aperture* ran an article and Chapman let them
publish his Haring photo (cowering, bewildered, bloody lip) and
the Rauschenberg one (mouth agape, shouting) before the series
was even complete. His reputation was made.

Was Chapman inspired by that fish hitting him ten years earlier?
Possibly. Which is to say, we all became aware of the fish incident
through the interviews surrounding his eventual solo show. Journalists would ask if he'd ever been surprised like that, if he'd ever
been hit in the face, and he'd tell the story.

By the time he got to Francisco Ling in May of 1988, the *Aperture*
article had run, there had been hot debate over Chapman's decision
not to hit women (chivalry, or a move to exclude them from the
canon?), and Francisco Ling, looking through his peephole, recognized the guy.

He called, "I'm sick. You're not hitting me today."

"Okay," Chapman said. "Can we stage something?"

So Ling opened his door onto the hallway of the Hotel Chelsea
and saw the man rocking on his heels. Chapman's beard and flannel
shirt did nothing to make him look straight—they were almost an

ironic gesture—and his eyes (the way Ling told the story) were wet and brown and strangely apologetic. Perhaps this was because, as soon as the door was open wide enough, he swung anyway and hit Ling in the nose.

Ling bent double, his mouth filling with blood. The camera clicked and clicked. Ling spat so he wouldn't drool, and then he said, "I have AIDS."

"I know."

"Check your hand. Check that you didn't cut your hand."

Ling would later credit Chapman with not checking his hand at all, with saying, "Let me get you some ice." Chapman would always maintain that he was just busy shooting the rest of the roll—sometimes the best shots came later—and thinking pragmatically that if he'd cut his hand, noticing sooner wasn't going to make much difference.

They wound up on the couch in any event, Ling holding a Ziploc of ice chips to the bridge of his nose, Chapman drinking orange juice from a small glass. They talked about the heavy rain, about Ling's new sculptures, about how he wanted, like Yves Klein, to patent his own color.

I told you Chapman was the kind of guy things happened to, and maybe what I mean in part is that he *let* things happen to him, let change wash over him. Because within a week, anyone who dropped by Ling's found Chapman now living there, too, moving his stuff from the East Village one cardboard box at a time. In seven days, Chapman and Ling had settled into a quiet companionship that seemed built on thirty years' intimacy.

Ling threw a party at the end of the month—or really the two of them did, as we discovered when we showed up, wine bottles in hand—the purpose of which was to announce their pairing to the world. It was nice for Ling, we conceded, even those of us who'd last seen Chapman when he hit us in the face, even those who still felt a pulsing in our cheekbones when it rained. Ling's nose was bruised, and when Chapman leaned in to kiss him, we winced.

Over canapés and cava, a few of us whispered that we didn't trust Chapman. Keep in mind that we didn't yet know about his years of struggle, his earnest and energetic paintings. We feared that his life was a gimmick, that he himself was a gimmick, and we feared he was using Ling to advance his own career. But look at the way they leaned on each other's shoulders! Look at the way Chapman brought Ling his pills and his carrot juice as the party died down, the way he insisted on the couch and blanket, the way he picked up Ling's cat and held it to his own chest.

We sent Juney Kespert in for reconnaissance. "Take him for lunch," we said. "Find out what his deal is. Find out what he wants." Juney was a photo-realist. It made us see her as rational, objective, though that certainly wasn't true.

You have to understand that Francisco Ling was someone we all adored with a ferocity that had nothing to do with his sculptures or even his suave Brazilian smile, but with his generosity. He was fifty, older than many of us, and to me, at least, he was New York itself. I'd come there from Indiana, a twenty-year-old boy with no more connections than meat on his bones, and although Francisco Ling wasn't the first person I met in the art world, he was the first who welcomed me. He asked me to show him my work, and I nervously did—a small portrait of my brother—and he closed his eyes and sighed as if deeply and finally satisfied. I discovered later that a lot of us had similar stories, but even then I didn't doubt his sincerity. The idea that someone might take advantage of Ling's kindness, of his vulnerability, panicked us.

And so Juney invited Chapman down to Veselka late that summer, and we waited for her pronouncement. She called us one by one. "He's a decent guy," she said. "There's not much to tell. He drinks too much, but who doesn't?"

I said, "A decent guy who punches sick men?"

"He has a good heart. He needs to be needed, I think. One of those. But tell me why that isn't perfect for Francisco right now."

That "right now" stuck with me, and I found myself thinking about it later that night in a cab, my eyebrow against the cold window. This would be the last boyfriend Francisco Ling would ever have. We didn't need Chapman to be perfect, or even faithful. We just needed him to stick it out till the end. We needed him not to leave Ling on his deathbed. Ling had gotten tested in 1985, as soon as he could, and had no idea when he'd been infected. Most of us resisted the test, at least for a year or two, but there he was practically knocking down the clinic door, wanting to know whatever they could tell him. There was no point; remember that there was no medicine yet, that no one was living more than a couple of years beyond diagnosis. I'd bought a suit just for funerals.

It wasn't long before Chapman felt like part of the landscape. We all wanted to visit Ling, but we were sick of sickness, sick of death. The East Village was a minefield of disasters that year, and when we trekked up to Chelsea it was more for Chapman's vivacity than for Ling's pallor and fatigue. We were tired, after all—some of us were dying ourselves—and Chapman had the energy to crack a joke. Unlike Ling, he could jump up to grab a book from the shelf, could explain with great vigor why you needed to take a second look at Käthe Kollwitz.

Ling had a solo show planned for the following spring at the Whitney, with the unspoken but universal understanding that it would be his last. The apartment was filled with the finished pieces, lumpy twisted things lacquered green and yellow, plus a series of quasi-phallic clay reliefs waiting for their final glaze. Missing were the monolithic forms on which Francisco Ling had made his name, abandoned along with his studio, with his ability to walk down the block. For a while he'd been using a shopping cart, leaning on the handle and wheeling it around the work. In the cart were trays with sponges, putty knives, spray bottles, towels, chisels, clamps. But now even that was too difficult, and a rolling stool became his seat. His tools lay on the floor in a dish rack. When I went there in October, Ling was on the couch with a cup of tea. The television blared campaign news, and he asked me to turn it off.

He said, "You remember Kip." I hadn't known this was what he called Chapman—at the party, it had still been Christophe—but I nodded. Chapman's beard had a way of making his eyes the only thing on his face. Just hair and then eyes, spectacular in the way they refracted light. "He never hit you, did he? Kip, did you ever hit him?"

"I didn't have that honor," I said.

"Well, he should have." It was a compliment.

At this point, Chapman brought me a glass of water and their whole bowl of Halloween candy ("I don't think we'll get any kids," he said, "so eat it all") and told me he'd found a fifty-dollar bill in a library book that morning. Just when they needed grocery money.

"Everything happens to Kip," Ling said. "He's a magnet for fortune."

I wondered if Ling was including himself in that magnetic field—and if so, whether he considered himself good or bad fortune for Chapman. Famous, but sick. Handsome once, but no longer. Living at the Chelsea, but dying there, too. Adored, but needy.

Artforum, in writing about the buildup to the Whitney show, called Chapman "Mr. Ling's amanuensis." A careful, glossy word— as if he were taking dictation for Ling's memoirs, rather than giving him sponge baths. It was a term I'd learned only recently, one that now, when I hear it, brings back New York 1988 in full Technicolor.

We were in a terrible state that year, all of us. The big art money was gone with the '87 crash. We were pinning our hopes, for Christ's sake, on Michael Dukakis. And yet there was urgency to everything. Each visit was maybe your last, each voice something to be memorized. It was worth ordering another glass of champagne. When I hear "amanuensis," I see Chapman's face, his young face, and I see Ling's hands, cragged and ruined, and I feel like jumping out of my chair to do things, to see people, before it's too late.

That day, I showed both of them the Polaroids of my new acrylics. Ling shook his head and told me I should go back to oils, that the oils loved me better. I'd have ignored him, but it turned out to be the last thing he ever said to me, and how can you ignore the last thing a great man says to you?

It's chilling, how you can spend years with someone and be left with only the smallest pile of scraps. That sentence was one of my scraps. And so eventually I went back to the oils, which did, indeed, love me better.

Here's what happened: In April, on the night of the Whitney opening, Chapman left Ling at home and headed over early. Ling trusted him to check the lighting, the positioning, to make sure the curator hadn't messed things up overnight. Ling was supposed to take a cab uptown at eight. He was still strong enough to walk out of the building, but he was going to call Juney if he felt too weak. Chapman had helped him dress, had combed what remained of his hair.

It didn't feel odd to arrive before Ling, to be greeted by Chapman, his beard soft against your cheek, a drink somehow already in your hand, as the sea of patrons and artists swallowed you up. The work was extraordinary—what had looked small and half-finished in the apartment suddenly luminous and monumental, each piece a triumph of fluidity—and we were awed, each practicing, privately, what we'd say to Ling, testing the words on each other first. "It's gentle," I remember saying. "It's like a détente, a melting." But the crowd never parted for Ling, the room never hushed. Instead Chapman breast-stroked his way through, sweaty and flushed, and grabbed Juney's arm. "You're sure he never called you?"

A few of us stayed behind and tried Ling's number, again and again, from the pay phones by the entrance, and a few close friends even remained in the gallery, circulating and keeping things upbeat, but at least ten of us sardined into cabs and rode back down to Twenty-third Street, slapping our faces to sober up and wondering if we remembered our CPR, wondering if we'd have the courage to put our mouths to Ling's.

My cab was the second to arrive at the Chelsea, and when we got up the stairs and through the door and to the living room, Chapman was on the phone with the police—not the paramedics—and we joined in ransacking what was, aside from the absence of Ling, a normal apartment. Wherever he'd gone, he'd taken his essentials: wallet, satchel, toothbrush. His painkillers, but not his AZT. Not the cat, who walked in circles, mewling. What he left behind was a page of shakily written instructions for Chapman: pieces willed to friends, unfinished works to be destroyed. At the bottom, he wrote—at a different slant, an afterthought—"I grant Christophe J. Chapman legal rights to my artistic and physical estate. Please consider this legally valid."

It was a warm night, and everything was wet when we set out to blanket the city. I wound up with Juney, who braided and unbraided her hair as we walked. She had me carry her shoes. She was never one to be afraid of broken glass. Juney taught me the prayer her Catholic grandmother had used when she couldn't find her passport or purse: *Good Saint Anthony come around, something's lost and can't be found!* We chanted it over and over, searching the sidewalks and stoops all the way to Gramercy Park and then beyond. I've been using it the rest of my life, and it hasn't brought me much luck ever, except the few times I've found my car keys when I certainly would have come across them anyway. I looked Saint Anthony up years later, expecting him to have found a child in the woods or food in a famine—but all he ever found was his lost psalm book. If that's enough to make you a saint—the reappearance of your book— what, then, were we, wandering in packs and alone, posting signs outside the hospitals and around NYU, not sleeping for three days? Saintly, maybe, if you're generous, but not saints. Sainthood requires divine intervention, or at least the type of luck that passes for it. But we called the Chelsea every two hours till our quarters were gone, and Ling never came home. We kept our eyes open around the city for months, and no one ever saw him.

A year later we held a memorial service of sorts, a gathering in what was now Chapman's apartment. The Chelsea had let him stay on, and he was doing well enough to afford the place. It was still full of Ling's art; Chapman would have to wait six more years for the issuance of a death certificate and so, despite the will, couldn't sell or donate a thing.

I should admit that there had been some attrition, beyond the kind we'd all grown to expect in those days. A few of Ling's friends, not having seen Chapman's tears and panic on that first night, his desperation and mourning on the subsequent ones, whispered foul play. Of course they did. Some held that Chapman had been a predator from the start. Others said he killed Ling out of mercy, that they had planned it all together.

The official theory was that Ling, madly in love for the first and last time in his life, wanted to spare Chapman—and the rest of us, for that matter—his slow and ugly death. That he'd checked himself in to one of the small and discreet hospices that had sprung up in that decade, the ones where everyone was dying of the same thing and anonymity was understood.

My own take was that Francisco Ling had been the one using Chapman the whole time. That the answer to his last days had shown up on his doorstep and punched him in the face: young, healthy, patient, useful. The kind of man who would run around Seattle with a dying fish. Easy on the eyes, good for running to the store, opening your AZT, clipping your nails.

A year is a long time, and we had already returned to our own lives, our own deaths. We had other sick men to tend to. That search through the city had been only one of many panicked nights, a dot on a long and vicious timeline. Everyone's soul was a slippery fish.

That night, we made toasts, we cried, we told stories that required us to imitate Ling's accent. The more we drank, the better we got at it. We left empty-handed, which was unusual. So many men had been disowned by their families, and left all their things—the books, the clothes, the wine—to their friends, that I had a small shelf devoted to artifacts. But six years later, Chapman would call us all up and ask if we wanted to have something. "The store is finally open," he'd say. I would take Ling's dish rack, the one that had held his tools.

If you sat down today and read about Chapman's life, his time with Ling would merit only brief mention, between the punching series and the Berlin work. It might be an explanatory footnote to his series of photos of Ling's abandoned things: the shopping cart, the stool, the detritus of three decades' fevered creation. He referenced Ling in his 1996 Liner Notes show—the set of thirty-six fake album covers, one of which featured a photo of a hollow-cheeked

Ling under the title *Kaposi's Sarcasm*, a complicated joke that many found inappropriate, in part because Ling never had a sarcoma.

But Chapman was a guy things happened to, and that's why the Ling episode would be buried. There was his car crash and his miraculous recovery; there was his show in Moscow, the first solo show by an American in the former USSR; there was his studio fire, his MacArthur grant, the time he made national news when Mayor Giuliani singled him out for what he considered an obscene installation at JFK. Through it all, he did what Ling used to—he mentored a generation of young artists, found them representation, kept them out of the soup kitchens. The ones who needed saving found their way to him. Or he found them. Or they just seemed to fall on him, out of the sky. He was one of those saints of lost things.

And meanwhile, there were the rest of us, or what was left of us. Things happened, but they were the predictable things. People got sick, and they died, and then buyers discovered their work. The smart buyers knew who was sick, bought early. I never got sick myself, and maybe this was the most remarkable thing that happened to me. It felt more like a blow from heaven, a singular and unearned benediction, than anything else in my life.

But here's the strangest thing that ever happened to Kip Chapman, stranger than the fish: In 2007, Francisco Ling died in São Paolo, Brazil.

Which is when we all—Chapman, everyone—found out he'd ever been *alive* in São Paolo, that he'd lived past the night of the Whitney show in April 1989.

There was a story in the *Times* Arts section, with photos of a studio full of unshown late work, and an interview with Ling's "life partner, the composer Félix Maria Silva" telling how Ling had returned to his native Brazil in '89, intending "to die in Portuguese."

But instead he'd gained a little weight, met Félix, got new drugs, got the cocktail when it came around, got the next thing and the next thing. Lived out the rest of his life in quiet seclusion. Died, finally, not of AIDS but of complications from those early years of AZT.

I sat at a table in a bakery, a human stone, staring at the photo of Ling and Silva that accompanied the second half of the article. I wanted to call Juney up, to tell her we'd found him at last. I wanted to say, *Your saint came through.* But Juney was nine years gone. An overdose. I wanted to say, *We should've looked a little south of Gramercy Park.* I wanted to say, *Juney, we need to redo the tallies.* Juney was the one who kept lists of the ones we'd lost. She was the one to know how many we buried each year, how old they were, how much they'd left unpainted. I wanted to say, *Juney, we found him. So why does it feel like we've lost something?* I sat there a very long time. The waitress knew me, and when she saw my face she said, "Oh, honey." She brought me a scone.

Chapman, I heard, was devastated and inarticulate—both vindicated and humiliated. According to his sister, he didn't eat for a week. Certainly he'd known about the more malicious theories, and here was proof of his innocence. But he refused all interviews on the matter. He'd moved down to Evans, Virginia, a few years earlier, to a converted barn, and was undergoing treatment for pancreatic cancer, a sickness he blamed on alcohol even as he continued to drink. No one was much surprised that he didn't attend Ling's retrospective.

I did go. I wouldn't necessarily have placed the work as Ling's— difficult, angular shapes, hardware and nails, a roughness and anger I found completely unfamiliar. The room was full of faces I'd never seen. What was I expecting? Juney Kespert and the other ghosts of twenty years past? I suppose I did. I expected Hugh Steers and Patrick Angus and Luis Frangella. I expected Peter Hujar. I expected, somehow, Chapman and Ling, arm in arm, a mere twenty years late to the party. In the middle of the room, I mouthed Juney's prayer. Not an actual prayer, just an homage, maybe. Because I didn't believe anything would happen. I couldn't raise the dead, I couldn't bring back our innocence, I couldn't even believe—as Chapman could—that something remarkable was always around the corner. My only magic was in survival.

The rumor started that Chapman was working on a portrait of Ling. The two of us only communicated by occasional e-mail at that point—but we shared a dealer, the young and optimistic Beatrice, and she was the one to whisper to me in awe. "It's eleven feet by thirteen," she said. "And it's not a photo."

"He's painting again?"

She leaned in. "With his *fist*."

Beatrice was good to me. I'd spent the past two decades painting heaps of clothes, medicine cabinets, chairs. They sold, but I didn't love them. If they were about my life, it was obliquely—the chairs and clothes being, after all, empty.

When the portrait arrived in New York six months later, I walked up to the gallery just to see it. Bea left me alone with the thing. She locked the front door.

I was more overwhelmed than I'd been by any piece of art since I was a very young man. Primary colors plus green, a sloppy stippling done, yes, with the fist. It was clear he hadn't really punched it, because there was no splattering, no puckering. He must have pressed the backs of his fingers patiently to the canvas a thousand times. Even so, a sick man shouldn't have tackled a piece that large. I knew, and the dealer knew, and I believe everyone who cared about it knew, that this was his last work. How could you continue, after something like this? What would be left to give?

It was Expressionist, if you had to categorize it. Maybe a bit derivative of Chuck Close, but only in scope—not in execution.

And if you stood across the room, it was Ling.

Not Ling as we'd all known him, but Ling as he'd appeared in the *Times* photo. Smiling, better than he'd looked in '88 despite the white hair, despite the jowls. What had it meant for Chapman to put his fist to Ling's face again? I'd never be able to ask. Was he absolving him, or executing him? Or had these always, to Chapman, been the same thing?

There's one more story about Chapman, the one we told at his funeral. After his funeral, rather, at the Thoroughfare Diner in Evans, Virginia. Imagine the New York art world—three hundred of us, at least, dealers, painters, photographers, critics, former students—descending on the bed-and-breakfasts, the truck stops, the knickknack stores of a town that hadn't seen a gay man, as far as they knew, since that one kid took off for San Francisco in the nineties. Chapman had blended in fine, beard to his chest by that point, rusty red pickup.

We took turns telling it, adding up the different details he'd given each of us: how toward the end, in the shower of his barn studio's bathroom, Chapman slipped and fell. He hit his head and he twisted his ankle. Dizzy, unable to bend his neck, foot useless, he lay a long time on the bottom of the tub, feeling the water pelt his knees. He was weak from the cancer, weaker still from the chemo—and the wall of the tub was a porcelain cliff, insurmountable. He might pull up with his left hand to sit, but then what? Cross his injured right leg over and step out with it, lose his balance again on the wet floor? The metal safety rail was inches above the reach of his fingers. He knew he was going to die there.

He told people, later, about looking out the open bathroom

door—how the only thing he could see was the giant portrait of Ling across the studio, half-finished. Ling's eye, Ling's ear, Ling's hairline. He told everyone that Ling had saved him. I believe something different. I believe he summoned his strength one last time so he could save Ling. So he could resurrect him, finish him, send him home to New York. What I'm saying is: If you have a fish in your hand, it's easier to run.

The solution came sudden and clear as a miracle: Hand over shoulder, blind, he stopped the drain with the rubber plug and switched the control from shower to faucet. He waited twenty minutes as the tub filled around him, as water poured over the side. It bore him up, Noah on the flood, until he could finally grasp the metal bar. He pushed against it, sailed himself to the lip of the tub, to the waterfall that ended on the tile floor and the submerged bath mat. It wasn't graceful, he told us later, but we suspected it was more than that. It was grace itself. He floated over the edge, dropped into the puddle below, and—blessed, exhausted, fingers pruned—rolled to safety.

*T*he most alarming photograph in my possession: my sixth birthday, eight children gathered at a picnic table, staring at a bomb. In the background, my grandfather's hands rest on his bald head; my father stares at the sky. Above and behind them, unnoticed by anyone but the camera, my sister is flying.

Five minutes later, my mother would exchange the camera for a tray of chocolate cupcakes. Erin Tazio would throw the bomb up into the tree house, and as we sucked the crumbs off our crimped wrappers, we waited for the little hut to fly apart in fiery shards.

Ten minutes later, the sky would crack open with thunder as we all ran screaming for the house. My sister, underneath the neighbor's trampoline, at first did not understand the sound of slicing rain.

Exactly six years before the picture was taken, I came out purple, the umbilical cord wound three times around my neck—as if some tribunal *in utero* had found me guilty for the crimes of a past life. My pardon came from the doctor's quick fingers.

Two years and eight months later, my grandfather would call to joke about the time difference. "Happy New Year! I'm calling from the old year! Tell me, what is the future like?" We were as delighted by the joke as by the elaborate obstacle courses he set up in the basement the few times he came to Chicago—mazes and prizes and puzzles and traps.

Twenty years later, looking at the photo and forgetting the thunderstorm looming overhead, I would wonder if it was the suggestion of a bomb that made my father turn his face to the sky, where the bombs of his childhood had screamed. He squints, hands on hips, as if awaiting a message.

Less than one year later, I would take my first photograph, a color Polaroid of my grandfather balancing on his head in his Honolulu apartment. He was bare chested, his legs lotus folded in the air. He would stay like that for twenty minutes.

Another photograph, fifty years older: that same grandfather in strikingly Napoleonic parliamentary uniform, inscrutable and highly decorated, a wry smirk my daughter will inherit. He was also (in one of the all-time great conflicts of interest) the editor of Budapest's daily newspaper. Sometime in 1941, following the suicide of the beleaguered and betrayed Hungarian president, Pál Teleki, and following the gains of the fascist Arrow Cross Party and the manipulations of the Germans, he denounced the encroaching forces at a meeting that the Gestapo officer Veesenmayer had called for Hungarian journalists. He was already running an anti-German radio station from the Buda Hills. It would broadcast until March 19, 1944, the day he was arrested.

Six years and seventeen hours before the photo of the bomb, I began to push my way out. My mother could not get up to change the channel on the hospital-room TV, nor could the Jewish woman in the next bed, and so for an hour, including the time it took for the short nurse to find a taller nurse who could reach the buttons, their labors were presided over by the final episode of the NBC miniseries *Holocaust,* starring Meryl Streep. The next day, the twentieth, I was born. It was the eighty-ninth anniversary of Hitler's birth. Whether NBC planned the broadcast accordingly is unclear.

Twelve and a half years after the picture was taken, when my sister was in her thirty-ninth hour of labor, I would light a votive for her in Ely Cathedral because, although I didn't believe in anything like that, she did. I would remember the picture, how her twelve-year-old body flew through the air, her black hair straight out behind.

Forty years earlier, held in a Budapest jail cell, my grandfather learned hatha yoga from a shot-down RAF pilot named Nigel who had grown up in India during the Raj. They closed their eyes and, as the bombs rained light through the small, unreachable windows, tried to levitate.

Ten minutes before the picture, the air had grown so thick with humidity that my grandfather, his lungs worn and clogged, had to elevate his arms to get enough oxygen.

Four hundred and forty-three years before the photo was taken, Suleiman seized the city of Buda without firing a single shot. There are those who would pinpoint this moment as the beginning of the end of Hungarian autonomy—a trajectory that continued through entanglement in a pointless world war, a 1920 treaty that carved off 70 percent of the country's land, and obeisance to increasingly dangerous German demands. But many would argue that the moment the country crossed from mere capitulation into actual complicity, the moment Hungary's moral Rubicon was crossed, was with the writing and passing of its own Jewish laws in 1938, 1939, and 1941.

Two minutes before the photo was taken, I had unwrapped Kyle Davidoff's present, a black plastic ball with a thick white string protruding, cartoon-style. "It's a *real bomb*," he said. "*Not* a toy. It'll blow up in about, like, two minutes." So we put it on the table and waited.

Twenty-five years later, a man in the audience will raise his hand and ask why all my stories are about guilt. I will say, "I hadn't realized they were."

Less than a second earlier, my sister had bounced up, impossibly high, from the neighbor's trampoline, one backyard and a steep hill behind ours. Her arms stretched east, and her feet pointed west. She would belly-flop, but in the picture, it looks for all the world like she's flying and won't ever come down.

Seven years after the photograph, another call from Hawaii, my grandfather attempting his old joke: "Which happened first for you?" he almost shouted into the phone. "The sunrise or the sunset? It is very important that I know!" He sounded strangled.

Forty-five years before the photo, the Second Jewish Law, significantly harsher than the first, was introduced to the Hungarian legislative assembly. The law was penned, revised, introduced, and argued for by the man born Makkai János in Transylvania in 1905, the man who died John D. Makkay in Waianae, Hawaii, in 1994. There were several practical motivations, if one can use the word, having to do with intense German pressure, with the promise of regaining lands lost in the Treaty of Trianon, with the country's overcrowding by a wave of Jewish refugees from Germany and Romania. But then there are also his words, entered in the public record: "Jews, wherever they are present, regularly bring forth anti-Semitism out of themselves." Long after the bloodstains of the ensuing years have faded, those words are indelible.

Six years, forty-two weeks, and five days before the photo, I settled suspended in the amniotic pool. I would spend an extra half month there, breathing liquid and floating.

I have been assured, for what it's worth, that he felt remorse. What that remorse entailed, how deeply it was felt, and whether his anti-Nazi stance represented any change of heart regarding the Jews or was simply a further expression of racial superiority, this time against the usurping Germans, I am unable to work out. And even if I could, the question would remain: Is chronology character?

In two seconds, my sister would hit the trampoline screaming. My father's head would turn at the sound.

In the grips of dementia, he would call again. 1993. Little left to his eroding mind but quotation. "The time is out of joint. Oh, hateful— The time is out of joint. And how goes the rest? The time is out of joint. What country, friends, is this?"

In 1940, after his first visit to the nation that would one day be his home, my grandfather wrote that the anti-Semitic movement could never truly gain hold in America because of the percentage of citizens who held foreign birth certificates, and whose ethnicity could therefore not be confirmed. It was a land of anonymity.

Ten years after the picture was taken, my grandfather died in a Honolulu hospital, following six years lost in a sea of Alzheimer's that erased the recent past, obliterated the entire notion of future, but left intact the events of half a century ago. Toward the end, he refused food. His beard grew to his knees.

Between 1941 and 1944, over half a million Hungarian Jews died at the hands of their countrymen and the Germans. Many, before the deportations even started, died from a thousand less infamous killers—those diseases particular to the hungry and cold and poor, to those with no way to earn a living.

Sixty-five years before the photo, twenty-three years before the prison cell, twenty years before the penning of the law, János followed a beautiful girl up a tree and toward the little wooden platform there. They climbed forever, weightless, into the sunlight. She was his cousin, with a wit that put his to shame. She would be his first wife, the mother of his only child. I cling to her life like a raft.

What will strike me most, twenty-seven years later, staring at this thing, is its profound and static silence. Rectangles of photographic paper are always silent, but this one particularly so. Eight children still and focused, mouths closed in tight lines. My father and grandfather looking up, reaching up, into the muting humidity. My sister stretched along the horizon, my mother presumably silent behind the lens.

———

After the war, in the Buda Hills, a group of escaped Nazi prisoners put their one Russian speaker at the front of the line. When they were stopped at the pass, he explained in flawless Russian that he was a Soviet soldier transporting these German prisoners. The real Russians asked him to count back from one hundred. His foreign tongue, so capable counting forward, was tripped up in reverse. The men were executed.

A week later, I would find the bomb in the tree house. It would live in the corner with the pine needles another two years, till the sun bleached it silver. When I was feeling brave, I'd nudge it with the toe of my sneaker. I was never entirely convinced that it wouldn't, one day, explode.

THE MUSEUM OF THE
DEARLY DEPARTED

$\mathcal{T}$here had been a leak.

Deep in the basement and then through the walls and floors of the building, gas had poured, scentless, at two a.m. After the fire trucks and news trucks and gawkers had dispersed, after one body had been sirened away and eleven more secreted out under sheets, the building sat empty for a week. The only survivor died in the hospital, never having woken. All twelve of them, that meant, died in their sleep. There had been no calls to 911, no bodies sprawled halfway to the door—just the mailman's cry for help the next morning after three poisonous minutes at the lobby mailboxes. Despite the earnest reporters' enunciation of "deadliest" and "perfect storm," the public was not as horrified as it pretended. "That's really the way to go," people murmured to their TVs.

On the eighth day, the hottest of July, the old Hungarian couple returned from Cleveland and stood staring at the yellow tape, suitcases by their sides, taxi waiting to be paid. They hadn't heard.

In seven law offices across Chicago, seven apartments passed to the survivors of the deceased. One of those beneficiaries, Melanie Honing, was a wiry little woman who had in fact never met the occupant of apartment D. Hers was a deeply awkward conversation with the lawyer. Early in their meeting she picked his stapler off his desk and held it in her lap, opening and closing the top. He didn't stop her. Apartment D had been co-owned by Vanessa Dil-

lard, who'd lived there the past twelve years, and Michael Salvatore, the man who'd been found in her bed beside her. He was the
beneficiary of her will, as well as the disaster's sole survivor, for all
of an hour. Whether there'd truly been hope of resuscitation or if
the paramedics had just fixated on their one chance to avoid total
failure, they defibrillated him all the way to the hospital. Because
of that later time of death, the apartment and its contents had
passed to Michael. Michael Salvatore's will in turn left everything
to Melanie, the woman he was to have married nine weeks after
the leak.

"I know this is sensitive," the lawyer said. He was a sweet, serious man, but in that moment Melanie imagined ripping the white
mustache off his face. "You aren't required to claim anything of Ms.
Dillard's. Her family in Wisconsin has made notes of the personal
effects they'd like, although you understand you aren't legally obli-
gated. Her will was quite basic." He picked at the edge of a folder.
"As Mr. Salvatore's executor you can get in there pretty quickly. As
soon as six weeks. I imagine you'll want closure." Her uncle, the one
who'd done up their wills as an early wedding present when he'd
passed through Chicago that spring, had volunteered to be here
with her, to "speak lawyer" with this other attorney. But Melanie
had wanted whatever privacy she could still manage.

"She was his ex-wife," Melanie said. "You figured that much out."

"And you were his fiancée. I can't imagine how—"

"But he'd told me she was dead."

The lawyer let out a descending whistle, blinked hard.

"I even looked her up online once, the dead wife, and all I found
in the city was this living woman, this film producer. I figured it was
a different person." She refused the Kleenex he held out. "He told
me she died in a car crash in 2003. And I didn't know his friends, not
the old ones. I mean, they sent Christmas cards. But now I realize I

never met anyone who'd known him more than ten years. The thing is, why would I have counted? We only dated eleven months."

The lawyer scratched his chin, pen in hand, leaving a streak of blue down his cheek. He said, "We take most everything at face value. Otherwise how could we get by?"

Melanie had promised her sisters they could help. But she couldn't stand the thought of their pity, their mercifully hiding things from her—and so one morning two months after the leak, a week before what had been her wedding date (Melanie had thrown out her calendar, with all its circled reminders for salon appointments, bridal luncheons), she drove down from Highland Park alone. Noble Square was a postage-stamp neighborhood just west of the Kennedy, one she'd never set foot in. One she'd never even heard of. As she entered the building, a young man with shoulder-length hair rushed out past her, nodding. On the ground floor someone was cooking bacon and blasting the TV. She found apartment D on the second story, and the key—miraculously, it seemed—fit the lock.

She stood on Vanessa Dillard's welcome mat and stared through the open door. She saw brown plants on the windowsill, and felt a dull anxiety that there might also be a dead cat somewhere. She didn't see one, but she saw a blue couch and sunlight and dishes still on the counter. A print of an O'Keeffe painting, the one of white jimsonweed.

Melanie waited for some dramatic feeling to wash over her. But she hadn't registered much emotion that summer, unless numb was an emotion. Grief would be an embarrassing surrender, considering the new facts. Rage was inappropriate, given Michael's death. The two reactions had stalemated each other. She was an abandoned chessboard.

She walked in.

Here is all she'd learned in the time since the leak: It was true that Michael and Vanessa were married from 1998 to 2003, as he'd told her. It was true they'd met in college. She produced educational films. She was survived by a mother, a brother, a niece.

Here is what Melanie learned in her ten-minute search of the apartment: Vanessa had no pictures of Michael on display. She had beautiful shoes. She was asthmatic. She read crime novels. Her bra size (one still hung on the shower rod) was 34B. She liked James Taylor and white wine and Japanese art. She chose photos of herself with her head turned, smiling. Her hair was wavy and chestnut and long.

The sheet lay bunched at the foot of the bed, but this might have been the work of the EMTs. Melanie suddenly wanted to sit, and although there couldn't have been gas still in the apartment—not with people living here again and a new furnace and updated ventilation—she imagined she could smell it, and that she was passing out or maybe dying. She took her key and sat out in the hall, head between her knees.

She clung to a possibility her friends had offered: What if Michael had come over just that once, to tell Vanessa he was getting married? And then when the leak started he felt so tired that he lay on the bed. (In this scenario, her friends helpfully surmised, he still co-owned the place only to take care of her, the woman he'd once loved.) But why, then, had he been there at two a.m. on a weeknight? Why had he told Melanie this woman was dead? Why hadn't Vanessa changed her will? Michael's personal effects, handed over at the hospital, weren't clues: a T-shirt, boxer briefs, running shorts. What he slept in, but also what he exercised in. She'd been given no shoes.

The man she'd seen before—the one with the long hair—came

up the stairs, moving like a sleepy and comfortable animal. He started up the second flight, then saw her and turned back. "Do you need help?" he asked. "You want me to go in there for you?" He seemed recently practiced in his grief counseling.

He sat beside her and told her his name was Jed, that he was a grad student at the School of the Art Institute, that his grandparents had left him their apartment. "I threw away their sheets." As if the fact would make her feel better. Oddly, it did. "I'm using their furniture, but I couldn't keep those."

She said, "Could you just stand here? Stand in the doorway and wait for me."

He did, and Melanie went back to the bedroom and around to the far side of the bed. She knelt on the floor and looked underneath. Michael's shoes. His khaki pants, belt still in the loops. His blue striped shirt. His bag.

Jed, in the hallway, heard what sounded like a scream held underwater for years that had finally, violently, bubbled to the top.

When Melanie returned two days later, she walked up to the third floor to thank Jed for the Kleenex and to return the umbrella he'd loaned her when she started home in the rain. He invited her in, and she was glad for the delay in getting back down to the empty cardboard box she'd left outside apartment D. Jed was a lovely distraction. At thirty-eight Melanie figured she had a good fifteen years on him, though, and she shook herself of the notion that his grin was a flattering one. He divided a beer between two glasses painted with oranges.

He said, "How goes the aftermath?"

"I like that word."

Jed gestured around the apartment, by way of a tour. He'd pushed most of his grandparents' furniture against the north wall to make a studio space by the southern windows. "I don't mind it," he said. "It's a little boring, compared to yours." She'd told him, between sobs the other day, the basics of the story. "I did find an old bottle of antidepressants. That's the only surprise up in here."

They sat on a red velveteen couch with wooden armrests too ornate to rest their glasses on. Jed had gathered his hair with an elastic, a look Melanie hadn't seen much lately. Her own college boyfriends all had long hair, and maybe this was why she felt so instantly comfortable with Jed. That and the way you could tell just by looking that his blood pressure was low, that he slept well at night.

Melanie said, "You don't mind living this far from school? From your friends?"

"I'll be honest with you. There was a, uh, ill-timed *tryst*, let's call it, with my roommate's sister. It was a good time to move." He laughed and shrugged.

It was momentarily beyond Melanie's comprehension, how silliness between young single people could necessitate a move across town. Had she once cared about things like that?

He said, "How much hunting are you going to do in there?" He waited, squinting his eyes and widening the hole in the knee of his jeans with one finger. He was pure empathy, and she almost couldn't stand it. She might cry again, or run out the door.

Instead she said, "The problem is I don't know what I'm digging for. I mean, I don't know what physical objects I'll find, but beyond that—I don't know if I'll find peace, or just more disturbance."

"Like what if they had a kid."

"They didn't."

"Right. Sorry, right." He looked lost. "Have you tried talking to the Hungarian couple downstairs? The guy doesn't speak English, but his wife does, and they've been in the building forever."

She said, "The ones they interviewed in the *Trib*. The ones who didn't know."

"László and Zsuzsi. It's like Zsa Zsa, but different vowels. She was an opera singer. Holocaust survivor, too."

"Yeah. The article said that, about the Holocaust. Can you imagine? I just—it's hard to explain, but I think I need to compartmentalize. Whatever was wrong with my fiancé, that was one thing he clearly did very well."

"Compartmentalize?"

"I'm just here to sort objects."

"Listen," he said, "speaking of which. I'll take anything you don't want. I'm doing a project." The grin was back, and he led her past the kitchen to what had once been his grandfather's study. Jed lifted the flap of a cardboard box and pulled out a handful of LPs, their jackets sun worn and softened. "These are from Brooke, on the ground floor. She lost her aunt. She kept the collectible ones, but this crap"—a mangled Burl Ives—"is more valuable to me." He showed her a manual Smith Corona, a bag of old shoes, a stack of *TV Guides*, and a chess set, from the inheritors of apartments C, F, G, and H. "I'm sure your person's family wants her stuff. But if there's anything extra, or anything you can't deal with. I'm crazy about this project."

She swallowed the urge to point out that Vanessa Dillard was not "her person." She said, "What will it be?"

"It'll be . . . part of my thesis show. Other than that . . ." He threw up his hands. She realized, when she smiled, how unaccustomed to it her muscles had grown.

Melanie now had three piles to make: the things on the family's list, intriguing items for Jed, and the artifacts she intended to examine in greater detail when she had the stomach. The Evidence, she felt like calling this last collection. She had no intention of keeping Vanessa's possessions, and she planned to send a letter (along with the package containing the jewelry, the family photos, the pewter turtle from the bookshelf) saying that although it would take a while to get her affairs in order, she would soon hand over the apartment's entire contents. She hoped they'd understand.

Her sisters kept telling her she was right to sell and profit from the apartment itself. After all, the caterer, the band, the woman from the reception hall—they'd been apologetic but firm that no, the deposits could not be returned. Then there was the dress and Michael's engraved ring. And Melanie had missed, so far, twenty days of work, only a fraction of which her boss forgave. ("But don't you count yourself lucky?" he'd asked. "To be rid of the bastard?") She considered the apartment her settlement in the civil suit she hadn't needed to file.

A cracked seashell went into the box for Jed. A sheer black thong, too: What mother would want her daughter's thong? For the family, a silver bracelet left on the coffee table. An asthma inhaler for Jed. For her own box of evidence: Vanessa's dead cell phone. Three slim photo albums. She dropped them in by the corners as if they'd been dipped in poison.

Deep in the desk was a phone bill from 2012, with certain charges circled in green—the remnant of some battle with Verizon. Melanie rested her water glass (Vanessa's water glass) on the counter and scanned the page. Between those circled charges, many calls to Michael's cell and office. Eleven thirty at night. Three in a row on a Saturday afternoon. This was a year before she'd met Michael herself, before he stole her from her date at a rooftop party and took her for Korean barbecue and midnight bowling, before he put his hand on her wrist and told her his wife was dead.

What the hell. She said it aloud, to the walls and dead plants. She put her forehead on the carpet and screamed the same thing. *What. The. Hell.* Spoiled by movies, she wanted a video montage to fill her in. She wanted to find a diary with every sordid detail. She wanted the moral permission to call Vanessa's mother and brother and friends. "Just the past twenty years," she'd say. "Just give me the past two decades, more or less."

On the other hand, there was very little of Michael in the apartment. The bottle of scotch could have been his, but who was to say? There was more than one toothbrush in the bathroom, but she had no DNA swabs. On the floor of Vanessa's closet, behind a row of purses, was an XL T-shirt from the investment firm where Michael worked. She put it aside for Jed.

Then she sat on Vanessa's couch, Evidence box in her lap. Like a train passenger with luggage on her knees. There were footsteps in the hall, and she flinched. But of course they passed. Who would have been looking for her? Part of her was still waiting for a second bunch of reporters to show up—the tabloids, perhaps—but a wave of tact had apparently washed over the city, as if kindness had leaked out with the gas.

Melanie almost wished there *were* some intrepid reporter snooping around, interviewing Michael's cousins, asking what kind of lunatic could pull off so flagrant a lie. Her mother had offered to hire a PI, but really—what would one even find? That the man was a sociopath. Maybe that he and Vanessa had planned to run off with Melanie's money. None of it would be useful. All of it would be humiliating. So here she was instead: gumshoe, archivist, bereaved.

She should have waited—for more distance, for a shot of whiskey—but sitting right there she opened the top photo album. Baby pictures from the early seventies. A sweet girl, growing, losing teeth, a Laura Ashley phase. The album ended with a shot of Vanessa and her brother at a picnic table, shooting sarcastic glares at the camera. Melanie pulled out the next album to see what havoc adolescence had wreaked, and was greeted instead with a wedding portrait: Vanessa and Michael, nose-to-nose. The same Michael but slimmer, a goatee, smiling so broadly that lines spread from his eyes where one day there would be permanent creases. Vanessa's dress was simple, off the shoulder, still chic sixteen years after the fact. Melanie shoved the box from her lap and scooted down to the carpet to flip through the other pages. Michael's late parents she'd seen before in his own photos. There they were, dancing. His sister, with whom he'd always said he had a falling out, would be that concave brunette posing wanly between Michael and his mother. But beyond that, she didn't recognize a soul. Not the raucous men in tuxedos, arms around Michael, hands mussing his hair. Not the old woman kissing his cheek. Twenty faces around the cutting of the cake. She knew no one.

The last picture hurt her physically: Michael down on one knee, Vanessa's hand in his, his mouth goofily open in what must have been song. Bridesmaids clapping and laughing. Vanessa's eyes rolled back in embarrassment or ecstasy or both. Michael had never looked at Melanie with such silly abandon. She'd always found him hollow in a pleasant way, like a Greek urn. It was a silence and melancholy she'd attributed to his losing a wife.

Melanie resisted tearing the plastic sheeting from the photo and tearing the photo itself to shreds. Instead she rose and emptied Jed's box into a library tote bag. In the box she put a tiny iPod. A pair of blue Cole Haan pumps, size seven and unscuffed. (She was glad they wouldn't fit her, glad there was no temptation to keep them rather than sell. She could get fifty dollars for those, at least. A decent dinner out.) A full bottle of Chanel. A Cross pen. A green cut-glass vase. An armload of DVDs. She remembered some book she'd read as a child in which a girl had to wander the palace of the gnome king picking out the objects her friends had been transformed into. Here: an Hermès scarf.

She walked the box down the stairs and out the front door, and when she was halfway to her car someone called from the window. "Sad lady! Come inside to sit!" A woman's voice with an accent. Melanie tried to see through the screen. "I make for you a sandwich."

She unlocked her car and set the box on the passenger seat.

"I have for you some orange juice!"

Melanie was exhausted. Jed had said they should meet. And the compartmentalizing wasn't going so well anyway. Plus, could you really say no to a holocaust survivor?

So she turned and went back in.

Zsuzsi looked younger than Melanie expected—the *Trib* had put her at ninety-four—but she was soft and round, which always hid the wrinkles. "Our young artist tells me about you. Come, come, come, come, come." She was asking Melanie to follow her, to sit on the cracked blue vinyl of a kitchen chair. Melanie found herself eating a cheese and lettuce sandwich and being introduced to László, who passed the doorway on his tennis-ball-footed walker and nodded briefly. "He spoke once little bit, but after his stroke he knows just Hungarian. He remembers English only for songs he has known many years. He sings still all the Christmas carols. He sings the old commercials. I talked to Chicago *Tribune* by myself!"

The kitchen, cluttered with Post-its and magnets and pot holders and herbs, smelled like decades of cooking.

Melanie said, "You've been in the building a long time."

"In Chicago it is sixty-six years. When I was young like you I sing for twenty years in the chorus at the Lyric Opera! But here in this building it is only fifteen years."

"That's still a long time."

Zsuzsi laughed. "For you, yes."

She said, "Did you know Vanessa Dillard, the woman who lived right above you?"

Zsuzsi broke a wide smile, the kind that should have infuriated Melanie but actually, against her will, made her feel warmer toward Vanessa. "She is lovely person. So beautiful! Frankly, I do not see why she should be in scandals." She pronounced it "frenkly"— a softer version of the word. "She has parties always for her film workers. After the film is finished, up they come to her apartment and she gives wine."

Assuming the present tense was a language issue rather than a senility one, Melanie pressed on. "There was a man named Michael. He came here."

Zsuzsi shook her head, and for a moment Melanie thought she might say that no, he didn't. "He stands outside in the street six, seven times and shouts like Marlon Brando. And the rest of the time is fight, fight, fight." She pointed to the ceiling. "Or thump, thump, like rabbits."

Melanie was careful to breathe. This was truly for the best, she told herself. More anger meant less mourning, at least of the traditional variety. "This man," she said, "he was balding? Dark hair, a bit of a stomach. Michael."

Zsuzsi swept the crumbs onto Melanie's empty plate and walked them to the garbage. "No good for her, I tell her lot of times. But what man is not bad news?" She leaned hard on Melanie's shoulder. Or maybe she was attempting to comfort her. "Frenkly, you are lucky you do not run off with him. People judge."

"Oh. No! You're not understanding."

"In Europe, no one cares about this. The President of France, he has mistresses. But Bill Clinton has his little affair and they try to *kkkhhh*!" She put her hand to her neck like someone getting hanged. "In Hungary once there was a famous affair, a princess and a Gypsy. And do you know what we do? We name after the Gypsy a wonderful sponge cake. Rigó Jancsi. This is all we care! Does it make a good dessert. But you, you are young and pretty. You can find still a man who is free. Some women have babies now, forty, forty-five year old."

"We weren't having an affair. It wasn't—" Melanie's breath caught and she thought she might start screaming, so she stopped herself from talking at all. She wanted to get away from the kitchen. From the whole building, in fact. She thanked Zsuzsi for her hospitality. When she got back outside, her car was unlocked, as she'd left it. The box was gone from the passenger seat.

She intended to stay away a few weeks, returning equipped to handle things. Maybe with a sister in tow. But Saturday was the day of the wedding—the absence of the wedding, rather—and all morning friends called to say things like "I'm thinking of you," then wait for her to say something back. Flowers arrived from her father. At one o'clock, a confused soul from the limo company called, confirming that no limo was needed. The next time her phone rang, she threw it across the room, picked up her purse, and took the Metra to the city, then a cab to Noble Square.

When she arrived, a dazed couple was trailing a real estate agent down the front steps. Melanie wanted to stop them, to say, "You know they all died in there," but surely they'd already heard. It would account for the wife's pallor.

She arranged Vanessa's liquor bottles on the counter and sloshed some of the unopened cranberry juice from the pantry, with vodka, over ice cubes that Vanessa herself must have poured into the plastic trays. Or Michael. By the time she began circling the apartment with the Evidence box, she was on her second drink. She'd been gentle before, eyeing a shelf and plucking out only the most compelling things. Now, the word of the day was *ransack*. Papers, high school yearbooks, shopping lists, the contents of the medicine cabinet. No antidepressants here, but birth control pills—the last taken on a Thursday, probably with the glass of water that still sat crusting on the bathroom sink. They'd died on a Friday morning. Here, in the very back of the bedside table drawer, was the elusive charger for Vanessa's phone. Melanie fished the phone from the box and plugged it into the wall.

It was four thirty—the time when someone should have been finishing her hair, when one of her sisters should have been slipping her an early glass of champagne. Only she wasn't allowed to envy that girl, that phantom self, the one about to marry an impostor.

She sat on Vanessa's toilet, staring at the nail polishes clustered on the shelf like a little rainbow army. She slid her feet from her shoes and looked at her toes, dry and callused. In the alternate universe, she'd have spent all yesterday at the spa. And because her only other choice was to break down and cry over something so ridiculous, she plucked a bottle from the shelf—petal pink—and figuring that Vanessa owed her this, that sweet Vanessa might have *insisted* had she known, she took the bottle to the living room floor, along with one more drink, and made her feet pretty.

As she finished, Vanessa's phone gave a short buzz. Melanie jumped, tipping over the polish, and a pink puddle oozed across the cream carpet. She stepped around it. Fifteen messages had arrived from the cellular cloud. None were Michael, and the first was Walgreens. The second was from the morning after the leak: "Evelyn K.," the screen announced. A woman with a crisp British accent. She said, "Well, yes, let's talk, Ness, but you know what I'm going to say. I'm going to tell you he's a narcissist, and he thinks you're his mother. That carousel just goes round and round again. I will most definitely be using the word *wanker*."

Melanie had the brief instinct to jot down the message, as if Vanessa would step through the door soon and pay her for house-sitting. Instead she deleted it. She'd be passing the phone to the parents, who doubtless didn't need confirmation that Michael was a wanker.

The message had verified something she'd felt in her bones: Vanessa couldn't have known about Melanie, about the wedding. If she had, surely she'd have confided in this friend, or what was the point of asking advice? And if the friend knew, stronger epithets would have been employed.

The phone lay in her hand like a grenade. The other messages were all from the two days following the leak, six of them from "Mom." They'd be panicked and wrenching, and Melanie understood that listening would be something she could never undo, a far deeper violation than going through the photographs.

And more dangerously: Somewhere in that phone, if she touched the right button, would be old texts from Michael. They'd be adoring or angry or sexual or mundane. They'd be cryptic. They wouldn't be about *her*, but about whatever this tenuous, unkillable thing was they had between them. It would be like watching them kiss.

She mustered enough clarity—it might have been the most mature moment of her life—to see that this would be the worst thing she could do to herself. There were other places she could be. There were other ways to hide from the ghost of her wedding. She needed to leave, and not come back alone.

She picked up the tote bag of items for Jed and decided it was full enough: T-shirt, thong, inhaler, seashell, an Animal Control magnet, a very old pack of cigarettes. She carried her shoes—her toenails weren't dry—and knocked on his door till he opened it, wild-eyed and happy. She put on her silly movie star voice. "This is good-bye, old friend!"

He blinked, and Melanie wondered what she looked like. Not good, presumably. He said, "Then you have to see the project!" Before she could make an excuse, he swept her back to the study, where there stood what looked like a huge dollhouse, or a bookshelf with a roof. Two cubbies wide, four rows tall, of freshly sawed plywood. In each compartment, a display. "I'm calling it *Dearly Departed*. Or possibly *Aftermath*. The outside will look like our building. I'm thinking of this photo-realist idea where I cover everything with paint that looks just like the thing itself, but—you know, it's paint."

As he pawed through the tote bag, Melanie explored the structure. On the third story, in the space corresponding to this one, a Golden Oldies record jacket perfectly filled the back wall. In front of it sat the infamous bottle of antidepressants and a cheap plastic apple. Next door, in what would have been apartment F: a Joe Cocker album behind three plastic film canisters. The fourth floor was full, too. A crucifix necklace in front of Louis Armstrong, a phalanx of chessmen in front of Glenn Gould solos. But Vanessa's apartment was empty. "I wanted you to pick the music," Jed said. "Check it out, I have opera arias for the Hungarian lady." He pointed to the ground floor, where the back wall was indeed filled with Maria Callas's face. "I want it to be like the music they're hearing in heaven. Because I'm doing this whole thing with echoes. Right?" Melanie stooped to poke at the small leather satchel in apartment A, the calligraphy pens and ink bottles in C. "Do you think I should leave the Hungarians' floor empty, though? Is that too literal? I mean, they're not dead, but visually there won't be balance. My adviser would hate that. Should I ask them for something?"

Melanie flipped through the stack of remaining records and

found an Etta James one from 1973. *Only a Fool*. She pushed it carefully to the back wall. "I think Vanessa would have liked her, too."

Out of all the things in the bag, Jed had settled on the stale cigarettes. He dumped them on the small floor in front of Etta. "These'll
be cool. I can get some height, once I glue it all. Oh, and look. The
typewriter won't fit, so I want to set it out for people to type their
thoughts. Like this." He pushed the Smith Corona, and the TV table
it sat on, in front of the house. He waited for her reaction.

In a previous life, she'd have kissed him right then. She'd have
led him to the bed. She wondered, though, not for the first time, if
she'd ever really want someone again. What was the point, when
you could never know him even a little bit?

There was a piece of yellow paper in the roller, so Melanie walked
around and started typing. The keys were loud and deep. *It's beautiful*, she wrote. *Let's go get something from Zsuzsi*.

It wasn't that she couldn't bring herself to leave. But she found
herself somehow invested in Jed's project now, and its completion
might feel like closure. She'd never answer her million questions or
sort through all Vanessa's things, but she could see the last room of
the little museum filled. She slipped her shoes back on.

When they knocked at apartment B it was László who answered.
He waved them toward the kitchen table, turtling behind with his
walker. Zsuzsi wore a bathrobe over a nightgown, and she stopped
washing dishes to sit with them, rubbing lotion into her palms. Jed
explained the project—"a memorial to the ones we lost," he called
it—and asked if there was any small object she'd like to contribute.
Melanie was taken aback by how vigorously Zsuzsi nodded, by how
quickly her eyes filled. She grabbed Jed's forearm. "This I have been
waiting," she said. She disappeared into another room while Jed
and Melanie looked at each other bewildered and László eased
himself into a kitchen chair.

She came back cupping something between her palms, and waited for Jed to extend his own. It was a stuffed gray mouse, worn moleskin stretched over a lumpy plaster body.

László let out a monosyllabic shout, angry rather than startled, then mumbled to Zsuzsi in Hungarian. She shot back, repeating something firmly until he was calm. She brought him a glass of water, and he reclined to stare at the ceiling, his head too heavy for his long, thin neck. Melanie wanted nothing more than to leave—she should have known this was a mistake—and she was surprised that Jed seemed so planted in his chair, waiting out the storm as if it were a real one from which he was responsible for sheltering the little mouse.

"This comes from my sister. She also is murdered by the gas, but many many years."

Zsuzsi pronounced "gas" like "guess," and Melanie fixated on this just as she'd fixated all week on Vanessa's possessions instead of Michael's death. *They were killed by the guess.*

"László, he is okay. I tell you a whole story. Because you know that the gas comes back for a reason. Yes? And here you are this beautiful couple full of life. Do you see what it means to have your life in front of you?"

Jed said, "We do," and he put his free hand solidly on Melanie's knee. It was half a gesture of restraint, and half a display for Zsuzsi: Yes, we are a couple if you say we are, and we will stay a couple till you've finished your story.

László was fuming but quiet, drinking his water now like a shamed child, and Zsuzsi leaned close to Jed. "All my life I think, the gas will come back. And here we are almost to the grave until it does."

Jed said, "But you got out safely. That was so long ago." There was that empathy again, beaming from him like a light. Melanie wondered if this was how every day was for him, near-strangers confessing seventy-year-old secrets just because of those clear eyes, that forward hunch.

"In 1944, in October, I am standing in the line at the train station. They have in the lines families, and a line for the old men, and a line for the women with no rings, so here is me and here is my sister Kata who is seventeen, and I am twenty-four. Back when I am eighteen I am singing soprano at the state opera in Budapest, and I am called the ingenue. Many flowers, many men. But then 1939 I am no longer a star. I can sing at the Jewish music hall only. Five years pass, and I am in the line, and everywhere is crying and pushing, and László, he recognizes me. I have never seen him. He is only nineteen years old. Do you understand?"

Melanie shook her head, and was glad when Jed did too. "No."

"He is a music lover. Every week he goes to the concert hall or the opera, and he remembers me from five years. I have at this time hair to my waist, all black. And he says to the other men, 'We make a mistake. This woman is not a Jew, this woman is with me.' So he takes me from the line, and the last time I see my sister is she is getting on the train."

Zsuzsi put her face into her hands, almost an embarrassed gesture, and once Melanie reassured herself that Zsuzsi wasn't crying, just bracing herself and collecting her breath, she tried to process the story. Jed had taken his hand off her knee and now it hovered over his own lap, as if he might need to catch something in a moment. László just sipped his water.

"Many years later, our old neighbor sends me this." She meant the mouse. "It is my sister's but she gave to the neighbor boy when he was crying. And they send it then back to me."

Melanie was the one to talk. She worried that Jed, in all his patience, wouldn't ask the question. And one more unanswered question would explode her. "Are you saying your husband was there in the . . . he was in the capacity of a soldier?"

Zsuzsi lifted her head. "He already loved me, from the opera. He knows my name, and he tells all the men this is his girlfriend. He does not save me just to save someone. He saves me because Cupid has hit." She tapped her own rib cage. "He is musician too. At school he was studying the piano. Even now he plays. Frenkly, this is one blessing: The stroke takes from him the language of English, but leaves the language of piano." She hit her palm on the table with conviction, as if this were the salient point of the story. "We spend three weeks together, and then he sends me to his cousin in Holland, and then I am on a boat to Norway, and he meets me in Toronto after the war and we are married." She was talking again to Jed, and Melanie considered that she might need to readjust the look of horror on her own face. She settled for covering her mouth and nose with both hands. "He was Arrow Cross. Do you know what is Arrow Cross?" They both shook their heads. "I will put this way: They take it upon themselves. Without the Germans there yet, they take it upon themselves. But when the Germans come, Arrow Cross is still helping. This is when we meet."

"And you *stayed* with him?" Melanie said. She couldn't help it. "This is the same person? *Him?*" She refrained from gesturing, so that László could remain in the dark. He was contemplating his empty glass.

"I fell in love. Maybe it makes no sense."

"Not really," Melanie said, but only under her breath.

Zsuzsi said, "But I had no children with him. Is like the two of you. You are a beautiful couple, and you should not care what are the rules of married and not married and who is widow. You know: Not everyone survives."

Melanie wasn't following anymore. Was she the widow? Was Vanessa?

"And now you see: The gas comes back for us. We are gone in Cleveland and the gas comes back, and instead it finds other people. It finds your beautiful friend." Zsuzsi began sobbing into her hands, and Jed found the right moment to touch her shoulder. Melanie, near panic herself, looked across at the old man, at the absent way he observed his crying wife. She wondered what Zsuzsi had told him to calm him down—if she'd lied to him about the mouse, or even about Jed and Melanie. Told him they were doctors, psychologists. She studied his face: his caved-in mouth, his long, unruly eyebrows. His blue eyes milky with cataracts.

Zsuzsi looked up at Melanie. "You forgive yourself now for moving on. It is good your affair has ended, yes? Those two go together to their grave, and you are here and finding love. But I know from the first time I see you that you worry you make this happen, that your sins made come the gas. And I tell you this story because you need to know it was not from you. It was from me."

Melanie opened her mouth to say, "No, I never had an affair, I had an engagement and a betrayal and a collapsing of my universe, no, you're very confused," but Jed shot her a look—a gentle glare, a blaze of green—and it was like an emergency transfusion of clarity. *This story is not about you*, the look said. *Shut up.*

"You cannot help that you fall in love with that man," Zsuzsi said.

"No. No, I couldn't. We don't choose, right?"

Zsuzsi nodded vigorously. "Who is ever to choose?"

László started coughing, a thick cough that rattled his whole body, his hands braced against the table, and Jed jumped up to get him more water. He put the glass in front of him, but the cough continued with such intensity that he couldn't stop to drink. Zsuzsi rose and stood behind him, lifting the glass to his mouth, and he breathed some water in, then dribbled it out into his white stubble. Eventually, the coughs spread out and stopped. He said something to Zsuzsi and waved her away.

Jed said, "It's late." And it was. It was dark outside. (The band would have been starting to play right now. Melanie had almost forgotten.) The mouse was still nestled in Jed's palm. He said, "Are you sure you want me to take this? I'll show you the memorial when it's done." But László was coughing again, and Zsuzsi was back at his side. Jed and Melanie slipped out of the kitchen, out of the apartment, up to the second floor hall, where Vanessa Dillard's door was still ajar from what Melanie had thought would be her quick farewell trip to Jed's.

He was saying, "I can't paint over the mouse. I couldn't do it. But that'll be cool, right? It can be the only unpainted thing, like it's the rawest and it stands out."

Melanie nodded and said, "I think I'm stopping here. I need to get off this ride now."

"I mean, *wow*. It's called Stockholm syndrome, right? Do you think she's really loved him all this time?"

"I can't imagine."

"I mean, talk about *compartmentalizing*. Ha! Okay, so does that mean he was a Nazi? Is that the same thing? I mean it sounds, like, as bad or worse than Nazi."

"I don't know."

"Oh, God. Oh. Why are you crying? Hey."

She wiped at her nose and tried to unscramble her brain. "It was true down there, that look you gave me. What Zsuzsi said had nothing to do with me. We think we're part of the story, but we're just the tangents. It's the same thing I've been—you know? In there."

Jed looked horrified. "I don't understand, but I know that's not true!"

Melanie leaned against the wall and wondered how she could possibly still have tears left when she was so very dehydrated. "I'll put it this way. You look into that dollhouse. Okay, that wasn't fair, not a dollhouse. The museum, the memorial. You look into it from outside, and you have a few little relics, and you try to put a narrative around them, decipher them, but really you're never going to know. Are you satisfied with that? Standing on the outside looking in?" He was quiet, and she worried she'd offended him. It was easy to forget how young he was. She said, "I'm sorry. I mean, maybe that's the role of the artist."

Jed's voice was as kind as any nurse's, any teacher's: "I think it's the role of the survivor."

"Oh." It was the point of his whole project, and she'd missed it completely. "Oh."

Why was she always five steps behind?

He smiled, and she knew then that he would have slept with her, if she'd wanted. He would have taken her up to his apartment and made her feel young and unbetrayed again for one night. Of course he would have. It wasn't so complicated. But he was still holding that little mouse, fragile and gray, and she didn't want him to put it down for her or anyone. She wanted it to go straight to the waiting little room, in front of Maria Callas and home, at last, to the land of forgotten and remembered and misconstrued objects—after seventy years, at last. And she wanted to go home and sleep for a week.

Outside, there was a cascade of sirens—someone else's emergency—and then they passed.

She said, "Good night, good night, good night," and Jed started up his last flight of stairs, the mouse cupped in his hands, until she could see only his feet, then nothing.

It was, by design, her final image of the building. She sealed it there, like a movie director watching the dailies and selecting from among hundreds what would be the film's closing shot: here, at the perfect angle, a beautiful man from below, fragile relic in his rough hands. Mouse equaling survival, et cetera. Sirens in the night. Fade to black.

She locked Vanessa's door, leaving the Evidence box inside. Her sisters would be glad to handle the apartment's sale, the transfer of personal effects, the donation of furniture to the women's shelter.

It wasn't quite true, she knew, that there was nothing for her in Zsuzsi's story. The woman had managed—not just eventually, but right there on the spot in 1944—to forgive the most heinous acts of her lifetime, all for the sake of love. Or at least self-preservation. And here was Melanie, who knew that the rest of her life would be defined by the degree to which she could forgive Michael. This was the role of the survivor as well: the passing of judgment, the issuing of pardons. But she didn't even think she *ought* to forgive Michael. She could only note, with slight astonishment, that at some point in the recent past she had managed to forgive Vanessa Dillard completely. Wasn't that a triumph of sorts?

She walked down the stairs, trying to be exactly like someone in a film, an actress with a mark to hit, a single motivation, a paycheck on the other side of the front door.

She almost made it.

From inside apartment B, piano chords vibrated, delicate but insistent, and above them hovered a cracked soprano. A ravaged voice, a Stradivarius left in the rain.

It was down by the Sally Gardens my love and I did meet
She crossed the Sally Gardens on little snow-white feet.

Was this what they did, then, every night? This couple that should not have been a couple, this inexplicable by-product of the twentieth century's worst moment? They gazed at each other and sang Irish love songs? Melanie pictured snifters of brandy. László's clouded eyes, emanating a love that couldn't really have been any different than any other human love in history, could it? There were seven billion love stories on the planet, but when you cracked them open, if you ever cracked them open, didn't they all have the same unoriginal love at their core? She wanted to ask. She wanted to demand an explanation.

But the door was closed, and so she could not see and she could not ask. She walked down the steps and onto the street, and the song continued.

She bade me take love easy, as the leaves grow on the tree
But I was young and foolish and with her did not agree.

Both of them were singing now. Dear God, what was that? What was she meant to do with *that*? Both of them were singing.

ACKNOWLEDGMENTS

Appearances, as always, are deceiving. This book, appearing a year after my last novel, is in fact the product of thirteen years' labor; the oldest words in here were written in June 2002. To look at my own table of contents is to see those thirteen years—and the people who carried me through them—in glorious Hollywood-style montage. (My first snail-mail rejection letters, the monolithic Dell I used to write on, Harkness tables full of sharp workshoppers, kind editors, two babies who aren't babies anymore, mountains of drafts, utter despair and brave students and artists' colonies and friends who toast survival.) My entire career—my entire adulthood—has happened in this collection.

Infinite thanks to Kathryn Court and Lindsey Schwoeri, my brilliant and patient editors; Holly Watson, Angela Messina, and Carolyn Coleburn; Emily Hartley; Lynn Buckley; Veronica Windholz; and all the scouts and book reps and other footsoldiers. If I could afford to, I'd send flowers every day to Nicole Aragi, the best agent who ever agented, and Duvall Osteen, the best assistant who ever assisted.

Almost all of these stories had their first homes in literary journals. It was 2003 when David Hamilton of *The Iowa Review* sent me my first acceptance letter, but the fact that he wrote it in purple fountain pen helps my feeling that this happened centuries ago. A decade later, Harry Stecopoulos, now at the *Iowa* helm, published "The Museum of the Dearly Departed" and edited it with a sharp eye. R. T. Smith at *Shenandoah* not only published "The Worst You Ever Feel" but gave me a job back in college and an introduction to the literary journal landscape. Rob Spillman edited "Peter Torrelli" for *Tin House* under extraordinary circumstances, for which he deserves some kind of plaque. Boundless thanks as well to Emily Stokes and the very patient fact-checker Jacob Gross at *Harper's*; Stephen Donadio and Carolyn Kuebler at *New England Review*; Ladette Randolph and guest editor Tony Hoagland at *Ploughshares*; Phong Ngyuen at *Pleiades*; Sascha Feinstein at *Brilliant Corners*; Garrett Doherty and Anthony Varallo at *Crazyhorse*; Jonathan Freedman at *Michigan Quarterly Review*; and Jordan Bass at *McSweeney's*.

One night in March 2008, while my first baby slept in a basket on the floor (at a time when I couldn't imagine ever being able to prioritize writing again), Heidi Pitlor of *The Best American Short Stories* sent me the single best e-mail of my life. Neither this collection nor my career would look the same without her support then and over the following years.

Salman Rushdie, Alice Munro, Richard Russo, Geraldine Brooks, Dave Eggers, and Kevin Brockmeier kindly chose stories included in this collection for anthologies. I'm still geeking out about this.

These stories have benefited from innumerable readers and volunteer editors over the years. Notable among them: Rachel DeWoskin, Gina Frangello, Dika Lam, Emily Gray Tedrowe, and Zoe Zolbrod gave me invaluable edits on "The Miracle Years of Little Fork" and "Good Saint Anthony Come Around" as well as writerly friendship as this book came together. A lifetime ago, David Huddle encouraged early drafts of "Suspension," "Acolyte," and "The Worst You Ever Feel." He also made me, in a thousand ways, a better writer. Julie Snyder, Ben Calhoun, and Sarah Koenig at *This*

American Life put a dent in my bucket list by letting me read "The November Story" on air—but more important, Julie Snyder's edits helped improved the story tremendously. Years ago, before this book looked anything like it does now, someone got me a well-intentioned but premature introduction at Chronicle Books. They wisely turned down what was an inchoate collection, but an editor there named Brianna Smith took the time to write me back and suggest that the stories might eventually coalesce around some of the themes she'd noticed—notably, music or war. *Oh.*

Some further debts: The violinist Kathleen Thomson kindly read both "The Worst You Ever Feel" and "Cross" for musical accuracy; remaining mistakes are mine. A childhood friend, Elizabeth Pulbratek Randisi, went and grew up into an estate planning lawyer and gamely helped me figure out the inheritance details in "The Museum of the Dearly Departed." Any lingering plausibility issues are no reflection of her excellent legal skill. Alex Ross's 2009 *New Yorker* article "The Music Mountain" launched my obsession with the Marlboro Music School and Festival, and allowed me to imagine the place that would hover in the background of "Cross." At a dinner one night, Brian Bouldrey told me a story about the composer István Márta; I went back to my hotel room and wrote "The Singing Women."

This book would not exist yet if it weren't for the Corporation of Yaddo, the Ragdale Foundation, the Ucross Foundation, and the National Endowment for the Arts.

I was blessed to be born into a strange and artistic family, one that I'm still struggling, in many ways, to understand. But I was handed more stories than I could ever decipher or use, and—more important—I was instilled from the beginning with the understanding that the arts were, while perhaps not the best way to make a living, the best way to make a life.

Jon Freeman is now married to a busy writer but used to be married to someone with delusions of being a writer. I'm not sure whether my neuroses were greater now or then, but he's put up with all of them and edited the hell out of every story here. This book is for him.

Rebecca Makkai's novel
The Hundred-Year House
is also available from Penguin.

Read on for the first two chapters of . . .

"A gleeful tale of ghosts,
vengeance, and family secrets."
—*People*, "The Best New Books"

THE

HUNDRED-YEAR

HOUSE

a novel

Author of *The Borrower* and *Music for Wartime*

REBECCA MAKKAI

I

For a ghost story, the tale of Violet Saville Devohr was vague and underwhelming. She had lived, she was unhappy, and she died by her own hand somewhere in that vast house. If the house hadn't been a mansion, if the death hadn't been a suicide, if Violet Devohr's dark, refined beauty hadn't smoldered down from that massive oil portrait, it wouldn't have been a ghost story at all. Beauty and wealth, it seems, get you as far in the afterlife as they do here on earth. We can't all afford to be ghosts.

In April, as they repainted the kitchen of the coach house, Zee told Doug more than she ever had about her years in the big house: how she'd spent her entire, ignorant youth there without feeling haunted in the slightest—until one summer, home from boarding school, when her mother had looked up from her shopping list to say, "You're pale. You're not depressed, are you? There's no reason to succumb to that. You know your great-grandmother killed herself in this house. I understand she was quite self-absorbed." After that, Zee would listen all night long, like the heroine of one of the gothic novels she loved, to the house creaking on its foundation, to the knocking she'd once been assured was tree branches hitting the windows.

Doug said, "I can't imagine you superstitious."

"People change."

They were painting pale blue over the chipped yellow. They'd pulled the appliances from the wall, covered the floor in plastic.

There was a defunct light switch, and there was a place near the refrigerator where the wall had been patched with a big square board years earlier. Both were thick with previous layers of paint, so Doug just painted right on top.

He said, "You realize we're making the room smaller. Every layer just shrinks the room." His hair was splattered with blue.

It was one of the moments when Zee remembered to be happy: looking at him, considering what she had. A job and a house and a broad-shouldered man. A glass of white wine in her left hand.

It was a borrowed house, but that was fine. When Zee and Doug first moved back to town two years ago, they'd found a cramped and mildewed apartment above a gourmet deli. On three separate occasions, Zee had received a mild electric shock when she plugged in her hair dryer. And then her mother offered them the coach house last summer and Zee surprised herself by accepting.

She'd only agreed to return home because she was well beyond her irrational phase. She could measure her adulthood against the child she'd been when she lived here last. As Zee peeled the tape from the window above the sink and looked out at the lights of the big house, she could picture her mother and Bruce in there drinking rum in front of the news, and Sofia grabbing the recycling on her way out, and that horrible dog sprawled on his back. Fifteen years earlier, she'd have looked at those windows and imagined Violet Devohr jostling the curtains with a century of pent-up energy. When the oaks leaned toward the house and plastered their wet leaves to the windows, Zee used to imagine that it wasn't the rain or wind but Violet, in there still, sucking everything toward her, caught forever in her final, desperate circuit of the hallways.

They finished painting at two in the morning, and they sat in the middle of the floor and ate pizza. Doug said, "Does it feel more like it's ours now?" And Zee said, "Yes."

At a department meeting later that same week, Zee reluctantly agreed to take the helm of a popular fall seminar. English 372 (The Spirit in the House: Ghosts in the British and American Traditions) consisted of ghost stories both oral and literary. It wasn't Zee's kind of course—she preferred to examine power structures and class struggles and imperialism, not things that go bump in the night—but she wasn't in a position to say no. Doug would laugh when she told him.

On the bright side, it was the course she wished she could have taken herself, once upon a time. Because if there was a way to kill a ghost story, this was it. What the stake did to the heart of the vampire, literary analysis could surely accomplish for the legend of Violet Devohr.

2

Doug worked in secret whenever Zee left the house.

The folders on his desk were still optimistically full of xeroxed articles on the poet Edwin Parfitt. And he *was* still writing a book on Parfitt, in that its bones continued to exist, on forty printed pages and two separate diskettes. The wallpaper on his computer (Zee had set it up) was the famous photo of Parfitt kissing Edna St. Vincent Millay on the cheek.

But what Doug was actually sitting down to write, after a respectful silence for the death of both his career and the last shred of his manhood, was book number 118 in the *Friends for Life* series, *Melissa Calls the Shots*. He hid the document on his hard drive in a file called "Systems Operating Folder 30." This book, unlike the Parfitt monograph, even had an actual editor, a woman named Frieda who called once a week to check his progress.

Doug's stopover in the land of preteen literature was only the latest in a wretched chain of events—lack of money, paralysis on the monograph, failure to find employment, surreal indignity of moving into the coach house on Zee's mother's estate—but it would be the last. He would get this done and get paid, and then, because he'd be on a roll, he'd get other things done. He would publish the Parfitt book, he'd land a tenure-track post, and somehow along the way his hair would grow thicker.

He'd found Frieda through his friend Leland, a luckless poet who wrote wilderness adventures at the same press for "two grand a pop." Leland talked like that, and he drank whiskey because Faulkner had. "They give you the entire plot," he said, "and you just stick to the style. Really there *is* no style. It's refreshing." Leland claimed they took a week each, and Doug was enchanted with the idea of shooting out a fully formed book like some kind of owl pellet. He hadn't written fiction since grad school, when he'd published a few experimental stories (talking trees, towns overcome with love) that now mortified him, even if Zee still adored them. But these publication credentials, plus Leland's endorsement, landed him the gig. He knew nothing about wilderness adventure, but the press was suddenly short a writer for their middle-grade girls' series—and desperate enough to hire a man. And so. Here he was.

The money would be nice. The coach house was free, but not the food, the car payments, the chiropractor. And that last wasn't optional: If Dr. Morsi didn't fix Doug's back twice a week, he'd be unable to sit and work on anything at all. Frieda sent him four other books from the series, plus a green binder labeled "THE FFL BIBLE" with fact sheets on each character. "Melissa *hates* dark chocolate!" came several bullet points above "Melissa's grandfather, Boppy, died of cancer in #103."

"The first chapter," Frieda told him on the phone, "introduces the conflict, which is the Populars on the team, will Melissa ever be goalie, *et cetera*." He'd never met Frieda, but imagined she wore pastel blazers. "The second chapter is where you recap the founding of the club. Our return readers skip it, so you can plagiarize chunks from other volumes. The rest will be clear from the outline. Everything's wrapped up at the end, but there's that thread you leave hanging, 'What's wrong with Candy,' which is where 119 picks up; 119 is being written already, so—as we tell all our writers—it's important you don't make uninvited changes to the world of the series." Doug took comfort in the fact that this was clearly a memorized speech, part of the formula.

He dumped the books at the thrift store, hid the "Bible" pages among some old tax forms, then went to the library every day for a week to skim the series.

And meanwhile, the little house was strangling him, tightening its screws and hinges. There was an infestation of ladybugs that spring, a plague straight out of Exodus. Not even real ladybugs but imposter Japanese beetles with dull copper shells, ugly black underwings jutting out below. Twice a day, Doug would suck them off the window screens with the vacuum attachment, listening as each hit the inner bag with a satisfying *thwack*. The living ones smelled like singed hair—whether from landing too close to lightbulbs or from some vile secretion, no one was sure. Sometimes Doug would take a sip of water and it would taste burnt, and he would know a bug had been in that glass, swimming for its life and winning.

There was a morning in May—notable only for Zee storming around in full academic regalia, late for commencement—when Doug, still in bed, nearly blurted it all out. Wasn't it a tenet of a good marriage that you kept no secrets beyond the gastrointestinal? Hundreds of movies and one drunken stranger in a bar had told him as much. And so he almost spilled it, casual-like, as she tossed shoes from the closet. "Hey," he might have said, "I have this project on the side." But he knew the look Zee would give: concern just stopping her dark eyes from rolling to the ceiling. A long silence before she kissed his forehead. He didn't blame her. She'd married the guy with the fellowship and bright future and trail of heartbroken exes, not this schlub who needed sympathy and prodding. When she dumped her entire purse out on the bed and refilled it with just her keys and wallet, he took it as a convenient sign: *Shut the hell up, Doug.* He might have that tattooed on his arm one day.

Zee's mother, Gracie, would sometimes include the two of them in her parties, where she'd steer Doug around by the elbow: "My son-in-law Douglas Herriot, who's a fantastic *poet,* and you know, I think it's *wonderful*. They're in the coach house till he's all done writing. It's my own little NEA grant!" Doug would mutter that he wasn't a poet at all, that he was a "freelance PhD" writing *about* a poet, but no one seemed to hear.

The monograph was an attempt to turn his anemic doctoral dissertation on Edwin Parfitt into something publishable. Parfitt was coming back into style, to the extent that dead, marginal modernists can, and if Doug finished this thing soon he could get in on the first wave of what he planned, in job interviews, to call "the Parfitt renaissance." The dissertation had been straight analysis, and Doug wanted to incorporate some archival research, to be the first to assemble a timeline of the poet's turbulent life. In her less patient moments, Zee accused him of trying to write a biography—academically uncouth and unhelpful career-wise—but Doug didn't see what harm it would do to set some context. And the man's life story was intriguing: Eddie Parfitt (Doug couldn't help but use his nickname, mentally—after nine years of research he felt he knew the guy) was wealthy, ironic, gay, and unhappy, a prodigy who struggled to fulfill his own early promise. He committed suicide at thirty-seven after his lover died in the Second World War. Parfitt had left few personal records, though. Nor had he flitted about the Algonquin Round Table and cracked wise for posterity. Entire periods—the publication gap between 1929 and late 1930, for instance, after which his work became astonishingly flat—lacked any documentation whatsoever.

Not that it mattered now.

Each morning, as Doug switched off his soul and settled in to write (*"Twelve-year-old Melissa Hopper didn't take 'no' for an answer,"* the thing began), he imagined little Parfitt stuffed in the bottom desk drawer on those diskettes, biding his time between the staplers, choking with thirst. The ladybugs hurled their bodies against his desk lamp, and it sounded like knocking—like the ghost of Parfitt, frantically pounding against the wood.

———

In the brief window between commencement and the start of Zee's summer teaching, Gracie invited them to the big house for brunch. They ate on the back terrace overlooking the grounds—the paths, the fountain, the fish ponds. It was like the garden behind a museum, a place where art students might take picnic lunches. Bruce, Gracie's second husband, had conveniently excused himself to make his tee time when Gracie announced that she had invited Bruce's son and daughter-in-law to move into the coach house too.

"It's really a two-family house," she said, "and what was done, way back, was to keep the gardener's family there as well as the driver's, and they all shared the kitchen. Can you believe, so many servants? I couldn't manage."

Zee didn't put the butter dish down. "Mom, I've met Case *twice*. We're strangers." Bruce's children had always lived in Texas.

"Yes," Gracie said, "and it's a shame. Didn't you dance with him at our wedding, Zilla? You'd have been in college, the both of you. He's quite athletic."

"No."

"Well he's out of work. He lost five million dollars and they fired him. Miriam's a wonderful artist, but it doesn't support them, you know how *that* is, so they need the space as much as you."

Doug managed to nod, and hoped Zee wouldn't hold it against him.

"So they'll both hang around the house all day," Zee said.

"Well yes, but it shouldn't bother you, as you'll be at work. It only concerns Douglas. He could even write about them!" Gracie rubbed the coral lipstick off her mug and smoothed her hair—still blonde, still perfect. "And something will open up at the college for Douglas, I'm sure of it. Are you asking for him?"

"Really," Doug said, "I don't mind. I can get used to anything."

———

That afternoon, Doug watched his wife from the window above his desk. She stood on the lawn between the big house and the coach house. Anyone else might have paced. For Zee, stillness was the surest sign of stress. She stared at the coach house as if she might burn it down. As if it might burn *her* down.

She wouldn't let herself pitch a fit. At some point she and Gracie had come to the tacit agreement that no actual money or property would pass between them. It was the apotheosis of that old-money creed that money should never be discussed: In this family, it couldn't even be *used*. Doug had doubts whether Zee would even accept her eventual inheritance, or just give it directly to some charity Gracie wouldn't approve of. She was a Marxist literary scholar—this was how she actually introduced herself at wine and cheese receptions, leaving Doug to explain to the confused physics professor or music department secretary that this was more a theoretical distinction than a political one—and having money would not help her credibility. But she had accepted the house.

And now this.

The Texans were just *there* one Tuesday in June when Doug returned from the gym. He picked a box off the U-Haul lip and carried it up to the kitchen, which sat between the two second-floor apartments. Doug loved the feel of an upstairs kitchen, of looking out over the driveway as he flipped pancakes.

A woman with curly brown hair stood on the counter in cutoffs and a tank top, arranging plates in a high cupboard. He put the box down softly, worried that if he startled her, she'd fall. He waited, watching, which seemed somehow inappropriate, and he was about to clear his throat when she turned.

"Oh!" she said. "You're—Hey!" He offered a hand, but she shook it first, then realized what it was for and held on tight as she hopped to the floor. She was a bit younger than Doug and Zee, maybe twenty-eight. And tiny. She came to his armpit. "Miriam, obviously. I hope we're not in your way. I had to scoot some glasses over."

"Doug Herriot," he said, and wondered at his own formality. "I can clear out the lower cupboards. You'll never reach that."

"I'm not so tall, am I! But Case is. We'll be fine." She opened the box on the table, saw it contained clothes, and closed it again. "This is a hell of a place."

He looked out the window and laughed. "Yeah, it's not subtle."

"Oh, I meant *this* place!" She tapped the open cabinet door. "This is quarter sawn oak!"

Doug had no idea what she meant, but he nodded. He wasn't surprised that the kitchen should be well built; the same architect had designed both houses, and presumably the same carpenters and brick layers had constructed them. The stone wall that bordered the estate also formed the eastern wall of the coach house, or at least its ground floor. The second story rose above that, making the structure look from the road like a child's playhouse perched atop the wall. Really it was quite large. The ground floor had at first been open garage space, with two arched entrances for cars. Gracie and her first husband, Zee's father, had the arches filled in with glass panels, and stuck a sunporch on the back. Why they bothered was unclear, except that in the post-chauffeur sixties they'd wanted an attached garage on the big house and felt they ought to transform the old one into something useful and rentable.

The estate had belonged to Gracie's family all along—the Devohrs, though Gracie never used her maiden name. The Devohrs sat firmly in the second tier of the great families of the last century, not with the Rockefellers and Vanderbilts of the world but certainly shoulder-to-shoulder with the Astors, the Fricks, and were lesser known in these parts only by virtue of their Canadian roots. Toronto was hardly Tuxedo Park. Of those families, though,

only the Devohrs were so continually subject to scandal and tragedy and rumor. An unkind tabloid paper of the 1920s had run a
headline about the "Devohrcing Devohrs," and the name had
stuck. So had the behavior that prompted it.

Before that infamy, back in 1900, Augustus Devohr (unfo-
cused son of the self-made patriarch), wanting to oversee his
grain investments more closely, had built this castle near Lake
Michigan, thirty miles straight north of Chicago. By 1906, after
his wife killed herself in the house—the suicide that had so bothered an adolescent Zee—he wanted nothing more to do with the
Midwest or its crops. In either a fit of charity or a deft tax dodge,
Augustus allowed the home to be used for many years as an artists' colony. Writers and painters and musicians would stay, ex-
penses paid, for one to six months. And—a knife in Doug's
heart—Edwin Parfitt himself had visited the colony, had worked
and lived right behind one of those windows, though Doug would
never know which one. It was the real reason Doug had even
agreed to move into the coach house: as if the proximity would,
through some magical osmosis, help his research.

Miriam climbed back on the counter, her small legs folding
and then unfolding like a nimble insect's. She redid her ponytail.
She wasn't exactly attractive, Doug decided (he'd been deliberat-
ing, against his will), but she had an interesting face with a jutting chin, eyes bright like a little dog's. And as soon as he thought
it, he recognized it. It was the beginning of a thousand love stories. ("She wasn't beautiful, but she had an interesting face, the
kind artists asked to paint.") And uninvited, the next thought
bore down: He was supposed to fall in love. It wasn't true, and it
wouldn't happen, but there it was, and it stuck. Anyone watching
him in a movie would *expect* him to fall in love, would wait patiently through the whole bag of popcorn. He tried to push the
thought away before she turned again, before she saw it on his
face. He excused himself and left the room.